*W*hat the critics are saying...

ℬ

Review Quotes for Harker's Journey

5 Blue Ribbons "...dark, dangerous and truly tempting with a strong heroine and a mysterious hero...For gothic and vampire fans, HARKER'S JOURNEY is definitely a keeper." ~ *Romance Junkies*

5 Hearts "All I can say is WOW!...filled with powerful emotion and exquisitely hot sex." ~ *The Romance Studio*

4 ½ Stars "...a spectacularly sexy and emotional story that any lover of the vampire genre will absolutely love!" ~ *eCataRomance Reviews*

4 Coffee Cups "This book is a keeper." ~ *Coffee Time Romance*

4 Angels "This is the first book in Ms. Walters's Dalakis Passion series and it is a great start with what promises to be some very erotic and intriguing storytelling." ~ *Fallen Angel Reviews*

Review Quotes for Lucian's Delight

5 Angels and a Recommended Read "…a touching and suspenseful, erotic paranormal…a story worth reading over and over again and has made a true fan out of me." ~ *Fallen Angel Reviews*

4 Hearts "Buy this book today and experience the magic that is the Dalakis brothers." ~ *The Romance Studio*

4 ½ Hearts "This truly is a unique series in itself and the way Ms. Walters creates and crafts her stories are pure gems!!! She literally is a masterful storyteller that will keep the reader guessing page after page." ~ *Love Romances*

4 Stars "…a talented author who never fails to capture my imagination. I recommend this second book in the Dalakis Passion series to anyone who enjoys tales of vampires and other things that go bump in the night…most definitely a keeper!" ~ *JERR*

"An edge of your seat romantic thriller…If you like the Carpathians, you'll love the Dalakis vampires." ~ *Romance Reviews Today*

"…I highly recommend finding every book in this series. For if you don't, believe me you are bound to miss out on some very wondrous journeys of the heart and soul." ~ *ParaNormal Romance Reviews*

N.J. WALTERS

DALAKIS PASSION

Dalakis EMBRACE

ELLORA'S CAVE
ROMANTICA PUBLISHING

An Ellora's Cave Romantica Publication

www.ellorascave.com

Dalakis Embrace

ISBN 9781419954924
ALL RIGHTS RESERVED.
Harker's Journey Copyright © N.J. WALTERS 2005
Lucian's Delight Copyright © N.J. Walters 2005

Edited by Pamela Cohen
Cover art by Syneca

Trade paperback Publication January 2007

Content Advisory:

S – ENSUOUS
E – ROTIC
X - TREME

Ellora's Cave Publishing offers three levels of Romantica™ reading entertainment: S (S-ensuous), E (E-rotic), and X (X-treme).

The following material contains graphic sexual content meant for mature readers. This story has been rated E-rotic.

S-*ensuous* love scenes are explicit and leave nothing to the imagination.

E-*rotic* love scenes are explicit, leave nothing to the imagination, and are high in volume per the overall word count. E-rated titles might contain material that some readers find objectionable — in other words, almost anything goes, sexually. E-rated titles are the most graphic titles we carry in terms of both sexual language and descriptiveness in these works of literature.

X-*treme* titles differ from E-rated titles only in plot premise and storyline execution. Stories designated with the letter X tend to contain difficult or controversial subject matter not for the faint of heart.

Also by N.J. Walters

ß

About the Author

~

N.J. Walters worked at a bookstore for several years and one day had the idea that she would like to quit her job, sell everything she owned, leave her hometown, and write romance novels in a place where no one knew her. And she did. Two years later, she went back to the bookstore and her hometown and settled in for another seven years.

Although she was still fairly young, that was when the mid-life crisis set in. Happily married to the love of her life, with his encouragement (more like, "For God's sake, quit the job and just write!") she gave notice at her job on a Friday morning. On Sunday afternoon, she received a tentative acceptance for her first erotic romance novel, Annabelle Lee, and life would never be the same.

N.J. has always been a voracious reader of romance novels, and now she spends her days writing novels of her own. Vampires, dragons, time-travelers, seductive handymen, and next-door neighbors with smoldering good looks—all vie for her attention. And she doesn't mind a bit. It's a tough life, but someone's got to live it.

N.J. welcomes comments from readers. You can find her website and email address on her author bio page at www.ellorascave.com.

Contents

HARKER'S JOURNEY

Dedication

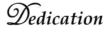

Thank you to my loving husband
whose support and encouragement has never wavered and
without whom I would never have had the courage to
begin, much less finish, any book.

Chapter One

ഹ

"This can't be happening," Johanna Harker muttered to herself as she limped off the gravel path to lean against a tree. Scowling at the road, she eyed the heel of her expensive Italian leather pump, a casualty of her forced trek.

Her rental car from the airport had broken down just as she'd coasted into the sleepy little village. With no time to get a replacement or have it repaired, she'd been forced to look for an alternative source of transportation. After asking around at both the gas station and the inn where she was staying, she found only one man who would hire out his vehicle for the arduous trip to Dalakis Castle later that same day. No amount of money could entice anyone else to drive her. The old man, with his stooped shoulders and snow-white handlebar mustache, had shown up late, and then when the castle was finally within sight, he had refused to take her past the point where the pavement ended and the dirt road began.

Nothing she had said changed his mind. After wasting twenty minutes she didn't have, alternately arguing and cajoling, she climbed out of the passenger seat and stared in dismay as the driver sped away, leaving her and her briefcase standing at the bottom of a long, dusty road.

With nothing left for her to do, she'd begun walking towards her destination. At least she hoped it was her destination. The old man hadn't spoken much English, but he'd nodded emphatically when she'd pointed, on her roughly sketched map, to the name of the place she was going. So far, all she had accomplished was destroying her shoe.

Cursing the driver of the battered old truck, she gave into the inevitable, propped her back against the tree trunk, and balanced herself carefully as she pulled off her unharmed shoe. Closing her eyes, she bent the heel ruthlessly backward until it popped off, then she shoved the shoe back onto her foot.

With her back still against the tree, she surveyed her surroundings. Thick woods that made her slightly uncomfortable, city girl that she was, surrounded the dirt road. Squinting, she could barely see more than a few yards into the dense undergrowth, but she could easily imagine all kinds of wild creatures. She could hear several different birds calling and singing to one another and the air was filled with the scents of the wildflowers that grew on either side of the road. Their vibrant colors of red, yellow, and purple looked even brighter against the dark green of the forest. It felt strange to be so alone.

She took a moment to loop the strap of her briefcase over one arm and around her neck before pushing away from the tree. Pocketing the damaged heel, she dusted off her beige linen jacket and limped back onto the road. "Cow path is more like it." Her voice startled a bird from the bushes, and it flew right in front of her. Johanna jumped back and stumbled on the uneven rocks, falling on her behind.

She lay in the road for a moment and surveyed her condition. It occurred to her that she could just stay there until someone drove by and found her. But no, with her luck she'd be lying there until she turned to dust. Besides, she had business to attend to. After all, that was why she was limping up this godforsaken path.

Rolling carefully to her knees, she slowly levered herself off the ground. Her nylons were shredded, her skirt was dirty, and her jacket had a rip. All in all, a day that had started out so well was quickly going downhill. Gathering her strength, Johanna continued trudging towards the castle in the distance, longing for her jeans and hiking boots that were back at the quaint little inn where she was staying.

It was her own fault for wanting to look professional. As a representative of the Baxter Corporation in Chicago, which was financing this trip, she'd wanted to look cool and composed for her meeting with their largest client, Mr. Dalakis.

It was an odd quirk of Mr. Dalakis that he insisted a company representative personally come to his home before he would sign anything. The company hierarchy humored the man simply because he was so bloody rich. How rich, they didn't even know, as he dealt with many other companies besides theirs.

As the newest member of the investment firm, she was the only one who could be spared from the office for an extended period of time. Therefore, she had been given explicit instructions by her bosses and saddled with the dreaded job of flying halfway around the world so their client could sign some papers. In truth, she'd prayed for weeks that she would be given the assignment. When it had been handed to her, she had nodded coolly and accepted the folder with the paperwork and her itinerary. The trip would last a week, at Mr. Dalakis' request, and whoever was dispatched would cool their heels in the local hotel until he sent word that he would see them.

Johanna had been thrilled when she'd found the note waiting upon her arrival, requesting her immediate presence. That meant she could get the business part of the trip finished and move on to the pleasure.

Stopping for a moment, she took in the sheer magnificence of the mountains rising in the distance. She was really here. Her aches and problems were momentarily forgotten as the reality of the situation set in. Turning slowly in a circle, she drank in the sights and sounds. The mountains, the flowers, the birds, and even the dark, scary forest enthralled her. After ten years of dreaming, she, Johanna Harker, was in Transylvania, land of the vampire.

Her briefcase bumped against her hip as she started walking again, more eager than ever to finish with business so that she could immerse herself in the experience. She'd already signed up for a walking tour around the town, and there was a university expert giving a tour of Dracula's castle that she definitely wanted to be a part of. Given the expense of the trip, this would probably be the only opportunity she'd have to visit, so she wanted to see and do everything.

Her friends had thought her weird, but Johanna had always been fascinated with vampires. It had begun the day before her eighteenth birthday when a friend had given her the classic novel by Bram Stoker for a present, making fun of the fact she had the same last name as one of the characters.

"Maybe you're a bloodsucking vampire," her friend had teased. "I mean, didn't one of the main characters have the last name Harker like you? Maybe you're a relative?" Johanna had devoured the book from start to finish, captivated by the powerful, alluring figure of Dracula.

Then the dreams had begun. Not the nightmares that her mother had predicted, but long, hot encounters with a man who, at the end of the dream, always turned out to be a vampire. She'd been having the dreams every night of the full moon for almost twelve years now. The night of her eighteenth birthday had been the beginning and she remembered that dream as vividly as the night it occurred...

Tucked upstairs in the far corner of her parent's home in an older suburb of Chicago, her childhood bedroom was shrouded in darkness, lit only by the glow of the full moon that poured through the open window. The sheer white curtains fluttered in the breeze as she rolled over in bed and gazed out at the night. One moment she was alone, and the next, he was there, standing in the shadows at the end of the bed. She was not afraid of his presence, but rather, she had been waiting for him.

He advanced towards her, his movements fluid and graceful. She gasped as a beam of moonlight illuminated his features. Striking and dangerous were the two words that popped into her head. Dressed entirely in black, his great height and massive shoulders almost immediately blocked out most of the light. As if sensing her need to see him better, he turned slightly so she could make out his features.

Long dark hair was swept back from his face, falling in a curtain of silk around his shoulders. His forehead was prominent, and his cheekbones were high. Quirked in a half smile, his lips were thin, yet surprisingly sensual. For a moment, his eyes seemed to glow an eerie red before fading to dark once again. As much as she strained, she could not make out their color.

"Green." His deep, slightly accented voice answered her unasked question.

She felt his voice, for it seemed to vibrate deep inside her, causing her to yearn for something. What that craving was, she wasn't sure, but she longed to hear him speak again.

"Sit, please." Scooting over to the center of the bed, she patted the white duvet next to her.

A satisfied smile crossed his face as he sank to the mattress. He said nothing and sat as still as a stone. *Predator.* The word flashed in her head and a deep fear rose within her as her heart began to pound in her chest.

His dark laughter filled the air, and one of his large hands covered her fluttering heart. The heat from his palm seared her chest. She wanted to move, but she was paralyzed by fear. His green-eyed gaze captured hers and she could not tear away from their terrible beauty. For a moment she thought she was dead, and lamented the fact that there were so many things left in life that she wanted to do.

As the thought flashed through her mind, his face took on such a look of pain and sorrow that she would have done anything he'd asked of her if it would alleviate his torment. She'd never seen such a look of anguish, and for a brief moment she experienced the deep suffering of his very soul.

"You are the one." His voice was laced with surprise and what sounded like hope. He sat back and pulled his hand away, holding it fisted in his lap. Johanna felt the loss keenly. It was almost as if he had taken her heart with him.

"The one what?" she whispered.

"You are my heart and my soul. The beautiful spirit that I have sought through the dark days of my existence. I will protect you with my entire being for as long as you shall live and beyond, if you someday choose to join me." Spoken like a vow, the words brought tears to her eyes. The deep emotion in his voice left her shaken and unsure.

Slowly, as if not to frighten her, he trailed a finger down her cheek, tenderly wiping away a tear. "I did not mean to frighten you, little one. You will forgive me, yes?"

She loved the way he spoke, sounding both old-fashioned and foreign. It gave him an air of charm and sophistication. Johanna raised one of her hands to her face and trapped his hand with hers. Guiding it to her lips, she kissed the palm of his hand. "Yes, I will forgive you."

He hissed when her mouth made contact, but did not pull away. "You are playing with fire, my love. But who am I to discourage you?" Pulling his hand away from hers, he placed both his palms on the pillow on either side of her face. Slowly, he lowered himself over her until his lips were almost touching hers. "One last chance."

Chapter Two

ߐ

Instead of answering him, Johanna raised her lips to his and kissed him. It was a slow, unhurried caress as she nibbled at his mouth, reveling in its softness and texture. She outlined the shape of his lips with her tongue, enjoying the taste of them. Even his lips tasted exotic and spicy.

Her entire body was tingling now, and was filled with a restless energy that was centered between her thighs. She was so enthralled with the new sensations coursing through her body that it took her a moment to realize he wasn't responding to her. Feeling embarrassed, she lowered her head back to the pillow and turned her head away from him, unwilling to see the look of pity, or worse, scorn in his eyes.

"Look at me." The dark command vibrated throughout the room. Johanna immediately complied. "If I take you now, you will always be mine." The tone and the words he spoke seemed to reach inside her and touch her very core.

Swallowing hard, she searched her heart and her mind and came up with one answer. *Yes*. The minute she thought it, he tore the covers back from the bed and she was left lying there in only a sheer white nightgown. The fabric clung to her curves, outlining her breasts and hips, and the shadow of her pubic hair was visible through the thin covering.

His hands traced the delicate lace collar of the garment before gripping it with both hands and tearing it straight down the middle. Pushing the edges of the torn cloth wide, he exposed her entire body to him. She felt slightly self-conscious at the smallness of her breasts and her long, skinny legs, but his eyes burned hotly as they studied her.

"Mine," he uttered.

Taking his time, his hands traced a slow path down her neck. The pulse at the base fluttered wildly and he bent forward and licked it. His tongue was hot and his teeth were sharp as he nipped her, leaving her feeling branded by him.

Standing, he tore off his own clothes and left them scattered by the bed. She'd thought him magnificent fully clothed, but naked he looked like a barbarian king. His black hair swept across his impossibly wide shoulders and back. Massive arms hung beside a heavily muscled chest that tapered down to his waist.

But it was his groin that caught her attention. His cock was thick, long and fully aroused. As she watched, it seemed to grow even larger. His burning gaze held her captive as he climbed into bed and lowered himself next to her.

She floated in a sensual haze as his heated gaze swept her body from head to toe, leaving no part of her untouched. Framing her face with his hands, his thumbs brushed her cheeks as he lowered his head, tracing her lips with his tongue.

Yearning for a deeper contact, she opened her mouth and stroked his tongue with hers. He laughed at her playfulness, before his tongue plunged between her lips. There was no part of her mouth and tongue left unexplored. Johanna was lightheaded, hardly able to breathe, as he continued to kiss her with abandon. Clutching at his shoulders for support, she was afraid she was going to faint. Her nails dug into his skin, leaving small crescent shapes on his back, as she struggled against his overpowering embrace.

Pulling away from her mouth, he left a trail of hot kisses along her jaw before his tongue swirled around the outside of her ear. He muttered words that she didn't understand, but the tone was universal — seduction.

She gasped for breath, her chest heaving with exertion as he continued to arouse her. His tongue plunged into her ear and flicked along the inside whorls before he nipped playfully at her earlobe. Sharp teeth tugged at the small gold stud in her ear and she moaned as a restless heat filled her body.

He laved her neck with his tongue, lingering over the small bite mark he'd placed there, before continuing downward to her aching breasts. Her dusky rose nipples were hard nubs of desire, and her back arched towards him in a wordless offering. Taking it as his due, he cupped both breasts in his hands and rolled her nipples between his thumb and forefinger. His head was bent in concentration, and the ends of his hair trailed across her sensitive skin, making her shiver with desire.

Johanna was on fire. She could feel the wetness and a throbbing emptiness between her legs. Her legs moved restlessly against the sheets as he lowered his head and lapped at her breasts. The rough texture of his tongue made her cry out with pleasure. Plumping her breasts together, he tugged a nipple into his mouth and sucked hard for a moment before gliding to the other side and pleasuring the other in the same manner. The fever inside her grew with each stroke of his tongue.

Reaching out her hands, she touched him wherever she could reach him. His neck and back were thick with muscle, and she could feel them tighten as her fingers stroked his flesh. She desperately wanted to run her hands over his wide chest with its small male nipples and a dusting of dark hair that started in the middle of his chest and ran all the way to his groin where it was thicker.

Leaving her breasts wet and aching, he kissed a path down her stomach, nibbling at her waist and hipbones as he went. Using his wide shoulders, he wedged her legs wide-open and draped one of her legs over his shoulder so that she was totally exposed to him. She couldn't close her legs even if she wanted to, which she didn't. Instead, she opened herself even wider to him, holding nothing back.

Bending forward, he breathed deeply, inhaling the scent of her arousal. Her hips rose towards him as she finally found her voice. "Please," she whispered. She wanted for him to taste her, to take her. Her blood was pumping thickly through her body as a great need, unlike anything she'd ever experienced, rose within her.

Taking his time, he traced the moist folds of her sex with his fingers before bringing them back to his mouth and tasting her essence. "This is mine. From this moment forward, you shall have no other." His eyes pierced the darkness and she could feel the barely contained anger swirling around him.

"Only you," she promised, hoping to calm the violence she sensed swirling within him.

"It is my nature to take." He moved closer to her waiting heat. "What is mine, I hold." His warm breath feathered over her clitoris, making her burn with desire.

Promise or threat, she didn't know and didn't care, for at that moment, he licked at the sensitive folds of flesh even as he inserted one long finger inside her waiting body. His teeth closed gently over her clitoris and held it captive as he flicked his tongue back and forth over it. Throwing her head back on the pillow, waves of pleasure washed over her body.

Instead of satisfying her, it only served to make her hotter. An unfamiliar wildness grew within her as he continued to pleasure her. Power and desire surged through her blood. Passion consumed her.

Pulling her foot back over his shoulder, she placed it on his chest and pushed until he released her. As she scrambled away from him, he growled at her, like some beast deprived of its intended mate. In reply, she hissed and launched herself at him.

She thrust her tongue into his mouth and began moving it in a parody of sexual intercourse. To help relieve the ache in her breasts she rubbed them up and down the hard planes of his chest, moaning when the dark, crisp hair rasped her nipples. Her hands reached between his legs and she wrapped them around his throbbing cock and began to pump her hands up and down.

In a frenzy of heat and desire, he answered her.

Holding her head captive in one large hand, he began to plunder her mouth. Almost savagely, he pushed her legs apart and shoved several fingers deep within her vagina and began to work them up and down. Johanna pumped her hips in time to his fingers even as her hands continued to do the same to his cock.

With barely restrained violence, he pushed her hands away from his body and tore the remains of her nightgown off her. "On your hands and knees, so I can take you from behind." His dark command filled her with fear and longing, but not for a moment did she consider disobeying him.

The need to have him inside her was too great to deny as she rolled to her hands and knees and thrust her bottom towards him.

"Spread your legs wider."

She immediately obeyed him, pushing her legs open until they could go no further. He knelt behind her with his knees spread inside her open thighs, making sure she couldn't close her legs. His chest covered her back as his hands came to rest on the mattress beside hers. His body caged hers completely.

Flexing his hips, his cock forged its way deep inside her. Johanna bit her lip as a combination of pleasure and pain shot through her. His cock was large and hungry and her pussy was small and untried. He paused for a moment when he reached the fragile barrier of her virginity, and whispered what sounded like a prayer, before piercing through the veil. Johanna cried out at the sharp pain, but it almost immediately began to dissipate, replaced by a deep feeling of satisfaction.

It was unlike anything she could ever have imagined. Her breasts hung heavy in front of her, nipples hard nubs that ached for his touch. She could feel the hot juices of her arousal, mixed with her virgin's blood, coating his cock. The air was heavy with desire and anticipation.

When he was seated to the hilt, he bit the back of her neck, holding her totally immobile. She felt totally dominated by him, and she reveled in it. The flames inside her burned even higher as she felt his teeth pierce the delicate skin on the back of her neck. He sucked long and hard, and she could actually feel the blood inside her body rushing to him. Her body reacted violently and she came hard and fast. Her inner muscles clasped his cock in a hard vise, but he did not move. She shuddered as wave after wave of pleasure washed over her. Johanna wanted to slump forward onto the bed, but he did not relinquish his grip on her neck and she was suspended there as he continued to drink from her.

Her vision blurred, and just when she was afraid she might faint, he retracted his teeth. His tongue bathed her neck, easing the sting. "Better than the finest wine," he whispered in her ear. At least she thought he whispered. All she knew was that she had heard his voice in her head.

Pulling back slightly, he wrapped one arm around her waist, anchoring her as he began to thrust heavily inside her. Unbelievably, she was immediately aroused again, and she began to push her bottom back to meet his pounding thrusts. His other arm moved down between her spread legs and began to tease her clitoris with light feathery touches followed by firmer strokes.

Her whole body was vibrating around his and she heard a purring noise coming out of her mouth. She was totally out of control as he plunged his cock in and out of her body.

Her heart was hammering in her chest as the flames of their passion threatened to consume her like a living beast. Her breasts swayed as she was pushed forward by the force of his thrusts. They felt heavy, and the motion was incredibly stimulating to her senses.

She could feel herself coming again and surrendered to it. As the flood of sensation filled her, she heard his low moan and then she could feel him come inside her. His cock pulsed deep inside her as his hot semen filled her. This time, she fell forward and collapsed in a heap on the bed.

He swore under his breath, but she was in no shape to respond. Then she felt herself being turned gently in the bed. His strong arms came around her and she was wrapped tight in his comforting embrace. Johanna would have gladly stayed there for eternity.

"I may hold you to that." His voice echoed through her mind. She smiled at that whimsical thought.

The way he held her made her feel special and treasured. His lips were soft on hers as he kissed her, lingering for a moment before sighing and gathering her tighter in his embrace. "I apologize. In my eagerness, I took too much. There is no excuse."

She lounged comfortably in his arms as his words washed over her. "I will give you some of my blood, but only a little. Enough so that I may always find you, but not enough to change you."

He raised his wrist to his mouth and punctured the skin with his sharp white teeth. When the blood was flowing, he held it to her mouth. "Drink," he commanded.

Her will deserted her, as she felt compelled to do as he asked. When his blood hit her tongue, it sent a wave of longing through her. It was hot, delicious, him. Long before she was ready, he was easing her away from his wrist. His eyes never left hers as he ran his tongue over the puncture wounds, healing them instantly.

"You will have the time you need to live your life. I cannot guarantee how much time I can grant you." Easing his arms from around her, he tucked her gently under the covers. "Sometime soon, you will have to choose your fate." In the blink of an eye, he was fully clothed and was once again the dark stranger standing at her bedside. "From this moment onward, every night the moon is full, you will be mine. I will have something of you for myself."

Johanna nodded as she began to drift off to sleep, already counting off the days until the next full moon. Satisfied masculine laughter filled her brain, and she sighed with pleasure as she fell asleep.

The next morning, she felt slightly hung over. She awoke tucked in her bed, and her first thought was that she had partied too hard the night before. When the coolness of the sheet touched her skin, she realized she was naked. Sitting up quickly, she clasped the covers to her chin and glanced around the room. Nobody.

The door was locked, but the window was still open a crack. The curtains billowed in the breeze, and she shivered as a cold gust of wind skittered across her shoulders. Her nightgown was lying on the foot of her bed, ripped to shreds.

It was then she noticed the soreness between her legs and the aching of her leg muscles. Slowly she peeled back the covers and saw a slight smear of blood on the inside of her thighs. The faint smell of sex drifted on the air.

"That was one heck of a dream." Her voice shook as she spoke aloud in the empty room. Her hand shook as she wrapped the sheet around her naked body. Gingerly, she slid off the bed and made her way to the window. She peered outside the window, looking for signs that the man in her dreams had really been here with her. A cold gust made her shiver and she quickly pulled the window shut and set the latch tight. An echo of male laughter rang in her head.

Something had happened. Johanna just wasn't quite sure exactly what. All the physical evidence screamed that last night's erotic adventure had been more than a dream. It had been all too real.

Goose bumps covered her skin as she peered out the window at the rising sun, desperately trying to mentally organize her scattered thoughts. She grasped the edges of the sheet tighter to her breast, trying to warm her chilled flesh.

Logic escaped her, but real-man or dream-man, he was part of her life now. Johanna somehow knew that to be an irrefutable fact, just as she knew the moon would rise this evening. She predicted that she hadn't seen the last of him.

Chapter Three

∞

Her prediction had proven correct, and over the years, he appeared to her faithfully on the night of the full moon. Johanna no longer questioned if her dreams were real. She accepted him as part of her life, wanting, no, needing to share her life with him.

As she'd grown older and moved away from home, their trysts had gotten longer and had varied. The sex ran the entire gamut from playful to passionate, slow and easy to hard and fast, and everything in between. Afterwards, he would gather her in his arms and they would talk about their lives.

Johanna shared all her hopes and dreams with her phantom lover. When she'd shyly asked his name during one dream, he had given her a wicked smile and replied, "Call me Cris." Over the past twelve years, there was no subject they hadn't covered.

He knew about her estrangement from her family, who thought her weird and slightly crazy. She sometimes talked to herself and knew things she shouldn't know, and this frightened her mother and father. Like the time she knew her father had been in a minor car accident before he'd called home to tell them. There was also the fact that she could always find misplaced items just by thinking about where they were.

She'd never told anybody about her dreams or how, at times of stress or great conflict in her life, she would hear Cris' calm, soothing voice urging her to a certain path. After the voice had been right several times, she'd always trusted it. In fact, one night it had saved her very life...

Johanna broke off her meandering thoughts as she stopped and surveyed her surroundings. The castle was getting closer and not a moment too soon. The afternoon sun was lowering in the sky and she didn't want to be on the road by herself after dark. She glanced around, slightly nervous all of a sudden. The woods were dark with shadows, and the locals had warned her that wolves still roamed freely deep within them. She could only hope that either Mr. Dalakis would be kind enough to drive her home or that he could arrange transportation back to her hotel. At this point, she'd take horse and wagon. Anything that didn't include having to walk.

Picking up her pace, she continued to limp along, her thoughts drifting back to the night she had almost died…

It was during her college days. She'd left the library late one night and had been hurrying back to her small apartment. She'd been lost in thought, thinking about her research project when the voice had shouted at her. "*Run.*" She hadn't hesitated, but run as if her life depended on it.

The pounding of footsteps behind her pushed her even harder. She didn't look back, but followed the directions in her head as he told her which way to turn and where to go. The glare of lights and the screech of brakes slamming didn't slow her down. A loud thump filled the night air, and she knew a passing car had hit whoever had been chasing her.

She kept running until she reached her apartment. Three times she dropped her keys on the floor before she was steady enough to jam it into the keyhole and turn it. Once inside, she slammed the door shut, locked it, and collapsed on the floor as tears poured down her cheeks.

Deep soothing tones broke through her terror and eased her shattered senses. At his urging, she had taken a long hot bath and tucked herself in bed. She drifted off to sleep to the sound of him singing. She didn't understand the words, but somehow she knew it was a lullaby from his childhood. "*I promised you I would protect you,*" he reminded her. Curling her arm around her pillow, she had slept.

She woke once in the middle of the night and could feel his arms wrapped around her. His large body was practically covering hers in a protective embrace. Heat radiated from him and Johanna snuggled closer.

One of his hands flattened against her stomach before slowly inching its way up to her breasts. Lazily, he circled one breast and then another, kneading the supple skin with his fingers before placing his palm over one of her distended nipples. She'd been cold when she'd first awoken, but now she was burning with desire.

She could feel his hot breath on her neck as his lips nibbled the sensitive skin of her nape. Moaning, she tilted her head forward, giving him better access to her throat. His low, sexy laugh made goose bumps rise on her flesh, and she shivered. His sharp teeth closed around the lobe of her ear and he tugged gently on it before tracing the whorls of her ear with his tongue.

Johanna could feel his cock prodding at her behind, so she pushed her bottom back against it and was rewarded when he groaned and tugged her even closer to him. "You are pure temptation," he growled in her ear.

She felt like a temptress. Wild and wanton. After the close escape tonight, she wanted to reaffirm that she was alive. Her blood was pumping through her veins, thick with desire. "I want you." Her voice was little more than a seductive whisper.

His hands left her suddenly and she felt bereft without them. Then just as quickly, they were back on her waist, turning her so that she was flat on her back in the bed with him looming over her, large and dangerous. His eyes were hard, edged with a need that only she could fulfill. Johanna arched her back, thrusting her breasts towards him, and was rewarded when the heat in his eyes grew hotter and his nostrils flared with desire.

His mouth took hers in a searing kiss that set fire to her entire body. Her breasts ached and she could feel the moisture pooling between her thighs. Clutching his shoulders, she tried to bring him closer to her. But he was in control now and touched her nowhere but her mouth. His tongue dueled with hers as he plundered her mouth.

Johanna rubbed her hands across the hard planes of his chest, wanting to stroke him everywhere. His hard muscles flexed beneath her fingers and his entire body turned to stone when she brushed his nipples with the tips of her fingers.

Cris sat back between her spread thighs and cupped her breasts, pinching the tips lightly between his thumb and forefinger. Need built inside her, deep, hard and hot. Her legs moved restlessly on the sheets as she hooked them over his hips, trying to draw him closer.

As if sensing her need for more, Cris slid his hands down the curves of her sides, caressing her hips before coming to rest on her inner thighs. Thrusting her legs wide apart, he lowered his head to her pussy, nuzzling the damp, slick folds before licking the heated flesh. Johanna clutched the back of his head, pulling him closer to her.

"More!" she cried as she tugged on his hair.

Cris swirled his tongue around her clit before flicking it softly. At the same time, he pushed two of his fingers deep inside her empty sex. Her inner muscles clamped down on his fingers as he moved them in and out in a steady motion. Sensations of pure fire filled her as her body strained for release.

She was close, so close to coming, when Cris pulled back again and sat between her legs. He was like a pagan conqueror, darkly beautiful and exciting, as his eyes devoured her. "Take what you want." His voice was thick with need and touched her deep inside. A wildness overtook her. A compulsion to claim him as hers.

Coming up on her hands and knees, she crawled towards him. He had challenged her and she would take what she wanted. What she needed. His chest glistened in the moonlight that shone through the window and she was reminded again just how massive and strong her dream lover was. Muscles bulged in his thighs, chest, and shoulders as he sat there. The only movement was the twitching of his cock as she moved closer.

Placing her hands on his rock-hard thighs, she moved them slowly towards his groin. He didn't move, but she could sense the tenseness in his body. His cock thrust out in front of him, proud and straining for her touch. She licked her lips as she stared at him, wanting to taste his masculine flavor. Liquid flowed from her pussy and she could feel it slip down her inner thighs. She was so hot for him.

Wrapping her hand around his length, she pumped it up and down, loving the feel of him against her skin. It was hard and soft at the same time, steel covered in velvet. And she had to taste it. Bending her head, she licked a pearl of liquid off the tip. He groaned and his hands came up to grip her head, holding her in place.

Johanna smiled. As *if* she'd stop now. She'd only just begun to explore. Swirling her tongue around the bulbous head, she lapped at it, loving the way he tasted. Closing her lips over the top, she sucked hard, moaning with delight as even more liquid seeped from the tip.

Taking as much of him into her mouth as she could, she pumped her hand in a steady rhythm as she moved them both up and down his cock. Cris used his grip on her head to guide her to the motion that he wanted. Johanna could feel him straining against her, and slipped her other hand down, cupping the sac hanging between his legs. As she massaged his balls, she could feel them tighten against his body.

With every stroke, she took him deeper. Using her tongue, she traced the dark blue vein that ran the length of his cock, enjoying his groan of pleasure. His fingers tightened their grip on her hair until it was almost painful, making her feel powerful and wanton.

Plunging her mouth down over him, she sucked his erection deeper into her moist depths until she could feel him touching the back of her throat, purring with pleasure as she did so. The vibration surrounded his swollen cock, causing it to twitch within her mouth.

His hips jerked towards her, thrusting his length as hard and deep as she could take him. She stroked the spot just below his testicles with her fingers as she continued to suck hard on him. Her entire body was thrumming with desire and his arousal was feeding her own into frenzy.

The next time she reached the tip, he popped his cock out of her mouth. In one motion, he yanked her up and impaled her on his length. Her pussy clenched around him as he pushed her down on top of him, her arousal coating his cock and easing the way.

With his hands cupping her bottom, he thrust her up and down his cock. His fingers dug into the flesh of her ass, squeezing and massaging it. Johanna threw back her head, wrapped her hands around his neck and rode him.

Her whole body was vibrating now and she knew she was close. When her orgasm exploded within her, she heard him growl and then she felt his mouth on her throat. His teeth pierced the skin and she could feel him feeding off her blood as her body milked his cock to completion.

She felt the moment he came deep within her still-pulsing flesh. His orgasm caused spasms deep within her once again. Her body trembled as pleasure continued to course through her veins until he finally pulled his fangs from her neck and ran his tongue over the small wound to heal it. Johanna slumped against Cris, totally exhausted and replete.

He held her in his arms for a long time with his cock still buried deep. She rested against his chest, feeling totally safe and cherished. Finally, he sighed and lifted her off of his lap and tucked her under the covers.

"Don't leave me yet," she pleaded when he tugged the sheets over her.

"I'll always be with you," he promised as he wrapped her in his strong embrace. Contented, Johanna drifted off into a deep, healing sleep.

When she awoke the next morning, she was alone in her bed. The local news was focused on the capture of a man who was wanted for the rape and assault of several college girls. The police had apprehended him the night before when he'd been struck by a car. Witnesses reported seeing a girl fleeing from the man. Johanna had known she was in trouble the night before, but it was at that moment she really understood what Cris had saved her from.

Focusing her attention back to the present, she realized that while she'd been daydreaming, she'd finally reached the end of the dirt road. Approaching the tall, forbidding castle, Johanna only hoped that her phantom lover was with her now. His voice had been strangely silent since she'd landed in Transylvania, and tonight was the full moon. She felt a little lost and bereft without it, as if a part of her was missing, and she couldn't begin to imagine a night of the full moon without him.

Chapter Four

ജ

The courtyard in front of her was deserted as she hurried across the cobblestone path. The sun was setting behind the mountains and she could hear an animal howling in the distance. She told herself that it was probably just a dog, but she wasn't about to take any chances.

Halting in front of a large wooden door that was easily seven feet high, Johanna unhooked the briefcase strap from around her neck and shoulder. Dropping the briefcase, she straightened her clothing the best she could. Her pantyhose were torn from her fall and looked terrible. Hesitating for a moment, she looked around to make sure she was alone before slipping off her shoes, bending over and peeling the hose down her legs. Crumpling them up, she stuffed them in her jacket pocket. Slipping what remained of her beautiful Italian leather shoes back on her feet, she took one final swipe at her skirt to rid it of as much dust as possible.

Satisfied that she'd done all that she could, she took a deep breath and slowly released it. Picking up her bag, she got a good grip on it before she raised the large brass knocker in the middle of the door and let it fall. She waited and waited and waited.

Deciding they probably hadn't heard her, she banged on the door with her fist. Five minutes later, she was still banging, but now she was yelling as well. "Anyone home?"

The sun had just set completely as the clicking of a set of locks being turned got her attention. "It's about time," she muttered.

The huge door opened slowly, creaking as it went. Squinting slightly, Johanna could make out the stone walls and an old wooden bench just inside the entryway, but she still didn't see anyone.

Enough was enough. She walked over the threshold, reciting her favorite lines from Stoker's book. "'Enter freely and of your own will! Come freely. Go safely, and leave something of the happiness you bring!'"

She thought she was alone until a voice came out of the darkness. "Surely it's not as bad as that. This is not Dracula's castle, but Dalakis Castle. We are much more civilized here."

Feeling the heat creeping up her cheeks, Johanna decided that her only option was to brazen it out. Tilting her chin up, she summoned her most professional voice. "Johanna Harker from the Baxter Corporation to see Mr. Dalakis."

Inwardly, she was thankful that it was only the butler, or whatever his title was, who had heard her. Hopefully, she'd have her papers signed and be out of here before Mr. Dalakis heard about her little opening speech.

"It is a pleasure to meet you. I am Cristofor Dalakis." A tall, dark shadow moved from behind the door and started towards her.

Johanna wished the floor would open up and swallow her whole. Shifting her briefcase to her left hand, she stuck out her right one. "I'm sorry, Mr. Dalakis…" she began, but he interrupted her.

"Call me Cris." The rich tone of his voice sent her senses reeling before his words registered in her brain. Her head snapped up and she watched in horror as the man from her dreams coalesced in the light of the full moon flooding the entrance.

Her briefcase fell from her nerveless finger, hitting the floor with a thud. Shaking her head, she tried to deny the evidence in front of her. It had to be a trick of the light. Her head was spinning as she watched him getting closer and closer to her. Blinking, she tried to clear her fading vision, but it was no use.

He was real. It was her last thought before she felt darkness overtake her.

Cris moved quickly to catch her before she hit the stone floor, grateful for his preternatural speed. He winced at the thought of her beautiful body being bruised, or worse, seriously hurt. And it would have been his fault. In his eagerness to have her here, he had taken her off guard and frightened her. Lifting her easily in his arms, he stopped long enough to snag her briefcase off the floor before carrying her down the long stone corridor and into the study.

A deep contentment filled him as he held her in his arms. Nothing would have pleased him more than to keep her locked in his embrace all night long. But that was not possible. He knew she would be frightened if she awoke that way, so he laid her on a long, plush velvet sofa that sat in front of a roaring fire, and placed her leather bag next to her. It took all the considerable willpower he possessed, but he forced himself to release her.

Waving his hand in the air, various candles around the room sprang to life. She didn't stir, so he took his time and examined her thoroughly. He threaded his fingers through her short brown hair. It was soft and silky and slid easily through his fingers in a cascade of chocolate, coffee, and a touch of auburn. Even though her eyes were closed, he knew they were a golden brown. Her slightly pointed nose and high cheekbones gave her an inquisitive air. Her complexion was flawless to him, even though he knew she despised the few freckles that scattered across her nose. They were hidden from view under a carefully applied layer of makeup, but he knew they were there. Her lips were parted slightly as she breathed easily. Unable to resist, he bent over her still form and kissed her soft, waiting lips.

Johanna moaned and turned towards him, returning his kiss for a moment before her eyes fluttered open. Stepping away from her, he retreated to the shadows by the fireplace and watched her awaken. Like a little owl, she blinked several times, trying to get her bearings.

Pulling herself upright, she ran a shaky hand through her hair and looked around the room. Her eyes came to rest on him and she took a deep breath. "What happened?"

"You fainted." Johanna shivered slightly and ran her hands up and down her arms as if to warm herself even though a roaring fire heated the room.

"I don't remember what happened." She frowned as she looked towards him. "I've never fainted before in my life. I'm really not sure what happened, but I do apologize."

"You owe me no apology. It is I who owe you one." Slowly, he left the shadows and walked towards her. "I'm afraid I startled you."

She stared at him as he approached, her look a combination of disbelief and amazement, as she took an unsteady breath to calm herself. "This is impossible." Her voice was little more than a strained whisper.

Cris hunkered down in front of her and her hand rose to touch him. It shook so badly that he wrapped his own hand around hers and held it to his cheek.

"You're real." Her fingers lovingly traced the features of his face. As he watched, he could see all her memories tumbling over themselves. She pulled her hand away and scrambled backward towards the corner of the sofa.

"You're my dream man, but that's impossible." Johanna wrapped her arms around her chest as if trying to ground herself in a world gone mad. "I don't understand how this is possible. You're Mr. Dalakis, but you're also Cris. My Cris."

"Yes. Surely you knew by now that you weren't dreaming all those years."

"Well, yes, but this is different. You've only ever come to me in dreams. I came to Transylvania on a business trip and to fulfill my dream of seeing this country. I never expected you to actually appear in my *real* life." Johanna frowned at him, shaking her head in denial. "Who are you, really?"

"I am Cristofor Dalakis and it is I who have brought you here." He saw the exact moment that she began to see all the possible implications of the situation. Her dreams and reality had collided and there were many truths she now had to face.

Her face was pale, but calm as she straightened her shoulders and met his gaze. Clutching her hands in her lap, she held them so tightly that her knuckles turned white. "What are you?"

"I am the same man who has come to you all these years." Standing, he began to pace the room, trying to give her some space, and at the same time find the words to make her understand. "I am of the family Dalakis. We have always been different."

"Different!" she exclaimed. "You've been in my dreams for years." She swallowed hard and her face paled even further before a blush began to creep up her cheeks. "We've had mind-numbing, heart-pounding, raw sex over and over in my dreams." Her voice lowered until it was barely a whisper. "Was it real?"

"Don't lie to yourself. You knew it was." He refused to soften the blow. "All of it was real. You are mine and I am yours. As it has always been." Coming to a stop at the end of the sofa, he loomed menacingly over her. "Ask the question you really want answered."

Scrambling off the sofa, she stood her ground and glared at him. "In my dreams, you're not human. But vampires don't really exist."

"Are you sure?" he taunted her.

Johanna took one step backward. "Are you a vampire?"

"You know I am." As he was finished speaking, Johanna started to bolt, but he reached out and grabbed her wrist, whirling her around to face him.

Her fear of him made him unreasonably angry. "Why do you run from me? I have had years to hurt you if that was my intention." His voice was soft, but she heard the underlying anger and flinched.

He released her and she backed slowly towards the door. "I'm not sure I'm ready for this." Her hand went to protectively to her neck. "It's not that you tricked me, but maybe I've deluded myself into believing that you were just a harmless fantasy."

Cris stalked towards her, not stopping until her back was pressed hard against the door. He loomed over her much smaller frame and ignored the hand she held out to ward him off. "You are fascinated by the idea and the lure of the vampire, but not the reality even though I have never harmed you." Wrapping one hand around her neck, he tilted her chin up as he slowly lowered his lips to hers. "Although at the moment, I am reconsidering my options."

Her eyes widened as he held her immobile with his gaze, and she did not fight him as his lips brushed hers. His tongue swept inside her mouth to claim what was already his.

For a moment, she did not move at all, but within seconds, he could feel her whole body softening towards him as her body remembered all the pleasure they had shared. Closing his eyes, he savored the taste of her and moaned when her tongue tentatively touched his.

While he explored her mouth, his fingers slowly undid the buttons of her jacket. Pushing the lapels back, he placed his hands on her waist, enjoying the way she arched her back and pushed her chest towards him.

Her nipples were hard little buds stabbing against his chest, driving him mad with desire for her. Unable to resist her allure, he swept his hands upward until they were covering her breasts. The lush mounds filled his hands perfectly, as he caressed them through the silk of her blouse.

As he nipped a path down her neck, he opened her blouse one button at a time. He could feel the heat of her skin on the backs of his fingers, and a rush of pleasure filled him. Expertly, he flicked the front clasp of her bra open and pushed the lacy cups out of his way until she was totally exposed to him.

Bending, he captured one of her nipples between his teeth. He rolled the tasty morsel around in his mouth, teasing it with his tongue, her hot flesh tempting him to take a bite.

Growling, he gripped her waist tighter as he feasted on her breasts. He could smell her arousal now and he inhaled deeply, allowing her fragrance to fill his nostrils. Her warm, musky scent enthralled him.

His cock was hard and throbbing, and every instinct he possessed was urging him to rip off the rest of her clothes and take her now. She was his. Pulling back from her luscious breasts, he grabbed her hips and ground her soft feminine mound against his cock. He could feel her heat through the layers of their clothing and knew that she wanted him.

Her tight skirt kept him from pushing her legs wide open, so he reached down and yanked it upward. Thrusting his hand between her legs, he fingered her pussy through her panties. She was so wet. So ready for him.

Sliding his fingers under the edge, he pushed the material away. He closed his eyes and savored the feel of her soft, downy pubic hair. Sifting his fingers through it, he slipped them between her legs, stoking the moist flesh of her sex. Not stopping, he dipped two of his fingers into her pussy. Johanna moaned and pushed her hips towards him. His cock strained against the front of his pants, wanting to be buried in her hot depths. Cris pushed his fingers deep inside her cunt, enjoying the way her inner muscles squeezed them. Using his thumb, he flicked at her clit. Johanna responded immediately, circling her hips and driving his fingers deeper.

Anticipation grew in him as he envisioned taking her here in his study with her back against the wall. He'd strip her clothing from her a piece at a time and pound into her hot, wet flesh until she was begging him for release. Cris felt his whole body tighten in anticipation.

Everything was perfect. Until she spoke.

"What are you doing to me?" The accusation in her voice as she turned her head away from him nearly shattered him.

It took every ounce of discipline he had to pull his hands from her aroused body. He brought his fingers to her mouth and stroked them against her lips, knowing she could taste her own juices. There was no denying that she wanted him.

"I am doing nothing to you. If anything, it is you who are tormenting me." The air in the room was electric now, his anger and lust a living thing waiting to explode.

He clasped her face in his hands, forcing her to face him. "For years, I have had to be content with stolen moments with you." His grip on her tightened and for a moment the temptation to just fuck her against the door taunted him. He could still smell her arousal on his fingers.

Clamping down hard on his primordial lust, he took a step away from her, but kept her pinned to the door with his fierce glare. "You have tormented me every night in my dreams." He stalked away from her, afraid that if he didn't, he might shake her.

Like some wary animal, she never took her eyes off of him as she shoved her skirt down, pulled her blouse closed and crossed her arms protectively over her chest. That she felt the need to hide herself from him enraged Cris. "I have waited endlessly for you to come to me and now that you finally have you are full of accusations and fear."

He forced himself to take a deep breath and center himself. A feeling of defeat swept over him. If she truly did not want him, he could not, would not, make her stay. He had to let her go quickly, for if he did not, the beast inside him would claim her regardless of what she wanted. Then she would hate him forever, and he would rather face the killing midday sun than face her hatred.

Determined, he strode past her, ignoring the fearful look in her eyes as he grew closer. Grabbing the briefcase from the floor by the sofa, he stalked to his desk. Opening it, he pulled out the folder with his name on it, withdrew the papers, scanned them, and signed them. Stuffing them back into her case, he returned to her and hooked the bag back over her shoulder.

He stared at her for one long moment, imprinting her image on his soul, knowing he would not see her again. Keeping his hands fisted at his sides to prevent himself from grabbing her and locking her away in a tower, he felt what was left of his soul begin to shrivel. He knew his eyes were glowing red now as the familiar longing to possess her raced through his blood. The full moon was rising. He could feel it, and longed for the nights gone by that they had spent together in its welcoming glow.

Gathering all his strength, he turned on her and smiled cruelly, flashing his elongated teeth. Gripping the door handles behind her, he flung the doors wide open. "Go," he commanded her.

She hesitated for a moment and he felt his resolve falter. "Go." His shout echoed down the empty stone corridor.

This time she didn't hesitate. This time she ran as fast as she could on her broken shoes and didn't look back. He closed his eyes and felt the pain move inside him as, with her, she also took his heart.

Chapter Five

🔊

Johanna tore through the front door as if the hounds of hell were after her. A cold gust of wind rushed over her as she raced through the utter blackness of the night. Dark, ominous clouds now obscured the moon, which had been so bright moments ago. She didn't look back as she skidded and slipped along the gravel path, her heart pounding and breathing labored.

Her body still ached with unfulfilled passion as she ran. She could hardly believe what had just happened to her. Vampire. For all her fascination, reading, and encounters with Cris in her dreams, the logical side of her brain had always told her that it was impossible. Vampires didn't exist, except maybe in dreams.

The hidden, wilder side of her nature, the part that craved the visits of her dream lover, had always believed in the possibility. But believing that it might be true and coming face-to-face with the fact were two different things. In the firelight, she could still see his fangs gleaming bright and his eyes glowing an eerie red.

Johanna had always kept the untamed part of herself tucked away, confined to the dark of the night. Most people knew her as sensible and career minded. No one knew the real her.

No one but Cris.

The night air around her seemed to still for a moment. Then the unnatural silence was filled with a roar of utter anguish. Deep in her soul, she knew it was him. Her legs slowed their frantic pace until she finally came to a complete stop in the middle of the road.

Opening her mind to him, she was suddenly filled with such despair that her legs crumpled beneath her, and she fell to

43

her knees. Pain. There was nothing but pain, longing and suffering. Wrapping her arms around her stomach, she rocked back and forth in the dirt, keening softly.

For the first time, she truly understood the suffering he had endured by choosing to wait for her. Everything was suddenly becoming crystal clear. He had given her time to forge her own path in life. Time to grow and experience life before offering her a choice. It was due to his patience that she'd had the opportunity to grow into the intelligent, independent woman that she was. Even now, he thought only of her and released her at the peril of his very soul.

Tears tracked down her cheeks as she was forced to face her own fears and selfishness. He had given her so much over the years and she had turned her back and run from him, treating him like some monster, when confronted with the reality of him.

Johanna was ashamed of herself. It was time to stop acting like some overwrought heroine from a Victorian novel, and be the strong, mature woman that she really was. This was the man she'd known and trusted for years, the man who, years earlier, had saved her life, the man she'd secretly loved for twelve years. But instead of embracing him and accepting him, she had feared him, scorned him, and run from him like a frightened child.

Another roar filled the darkened sky and suddenly she was back on her feet, running once again. Only this time, it was back towards the castle. Back to him.

A flash of something caught the corner of her eye, and she looked towards the woods. Something was running in there, keeping pace with her. She tried to run faster, but her lungs were burning and her stomach cramping from exertion.

The shadowy figure leapt onto the road in front of her, and the dark shape of a wolf took form. It was large and muscular, it's silver-gray coat shining in the moonlight as it blocked her path. Skidding to a halt, she froze as the animal bared its long, sharp teeth and growled. Eyes glowing, it stood in the center of the road staring at her.

Johanna whirled around, looking for an avenue of escape, but she came face-to-face with another large silver-gray wolf blocking the road behind her. This one looked slightly bigger than the other and had a silver patch on its chest. It too stared at her, but instead of growling, it was silent and still, but watchful.

They were both beautiful in a deadly way, with their powerful bodies, and intelligent eyes. Slowly, they began to circle her, readying themselves for attack. In that moment, Johanna knew that she was going to die.

Gripping her leather briefcase with both hands, she turned in a circle with them, watching their every step. She waited for them to make their move, prepared to swing the briefcase when they attacked. It wasn't much of a weapon, but it was all she had, and she wouldn't go down without a fight.

Mentally, she opened her mind and called to Cris, screaming that she was sorry for how she had reacted to him and that she would have returned to him if she'd only had the chance. She didn't want to die without trying to tell him how much he meant to her.

The first wolf sprang suddenly and Johanna swung the bag hard, hitting it in the head. With a yelp, it landed on all fours a few feet away from her, and scrambled to regain its composure. The large wolf canted its head and looked almost quizzical, as if it couldn't believe that she'd actually hit it. Tilting back its head, it howled. The sound was long and soulful and made her unbearably sad.

It howled once again before swinging its gaze back to her. "Great," she muttered as she braced herself for the next attack. "All that did was piss you off even more."

Her fingers tightened on the bag and she found herself praying as she waited for the wolves to spring. The larger of the two launched itself towards her, but never reached her. A blur flashed in front of her, and then the wolf was flying through the air and crashing into the bushes.

Another wolf had joined them. This one was just as big as the other two, but heavier and more muscled. Its silver coat was thick and Johanna was filled with the desire to run her fingers through it just to see if it was as soft as it looked.

Now she knew she was losing it. She had bigger concerns that what the wolf's fur felt like. Staying alive was at the top of that list. While two of the wolves were distracted, she started to edge towards the woods. She didn't think that wolves could climb trees, so if she could just get close enough, she might be able to take refuge in one of the large trees that filled the forest.

The third wolf planted itself between her and the possible safety of the woods. Its tongue lolled out of its mouth and if Johanna hadn't known better, she would have sworn it was laughing at her. A growl startled her from behind and she swung around, swinging the bag as she turned. The momentum turned her in a complete circle and she struggled to maintain her balance.

All three wolves were sitting in front of her, watching her every move. The stronger of the three, the one who had stopped the attack, padded over to her and sat directly in front of her. Johanna was afraid to move, not wanting to incite them to any more violence.

The wolf stuck out its head and nudged her hand. Her heart pounding, Johanna opened her hand, placed it on the wolf's head and then slid it down over its massive neck. The beast groaned and moved closer.

Sinking to her knees in the middle of the road, Johanna plunged her fingers through the thick silver coat. The muscles flexed beneath her fingers as she stroked its back and sides. Now that she was closer, she could see that its eyes were a familiar green and shining with intelligence.

"I'm not sure I'm ready for this." The other two beasts growled when she spoke and her wolf whirled around and growled at the other two. Before her very eyes, the beast began to change. His limbs lengthened outward and his hair began to recede into his body. The muzzle retracted and a familiar face took shape. In less than a minute, Cris stood before her, totally naked and still very aroused. His eyes were still feral as he growled at the other two wolves.

Cris was planted in front of her like a dark, avenging angel. With his arms spread wide, he spoke to the wolves in a harsh tone. As she watched in amazement, both animals hung their heads and whined. At his signal, they sat and waited. Johanna held her breath when he finally turned his dark gaze towards her.

"Did you mean it?"

Johanna was reeling from what she'd just witnessed, but she immediately knew what he meant. "Yes. I was coming back to you." She could feel conflicting emotions rolling off him in waves.

"I cannot release you again. I will not." He hadn't moved, but she could feel his threatening presence growing larger.

Johanna knew there was no choice to make. Slowly, she got to her feet, walked towards him and took him by the hand. "Take me..." She glanced at his huge erection and felt her nipples tighten in anticipation. "Home."

He squeezed her hand for a moment before leading her over to the waiting wolves, which were sitting and waiting patiently with their tongues hanging out. Her natural instinct was to run from them, but she trusted Cris and allowed him to hold out her hand towards them.

"Mine," he uttered in a low, but authoritative tone. Both animals sniffed her fingers before licking them in a friendly gesture. They were acting more like oversized dogs than ferocious wolves, and Johanna patted one on the head, unable to resist its thick, lush fur. "They will protect you with their lives, and they will inform all the other wolves in the forest to do the same."

"Why would they do that?" She was still slightly dazed by the fact she hadn't been torn apart by the wild creatures. "It goes against all their natural instincts."

"They do not want to face my wrath if you come to harm." There was humor and affection in his voice now as he gave both wolves one last stroke and sent them on their way.

Johanna fell silent at his reply, awed by his power to command the wild beasts. Both animals paused at the edge of the woods and gave them one final look before disappearing into the forest. It was almost as if they were saying goodbye, which was a foolish thing for her to think.

"You will see them again." Cris turned towards her as he spoke, the wolves forgotten as he focused all his attention on her.

She nodded absently, still trying to absorb all that she'd seen. There was no doubt that Cris was standing in front of her with no clothes on. He looked totally relaxed and comfortable with the fact that he was standing in the middle of the road, buck-naked.

"Aren't you chilly?" She realized how absurd her question was, but she'd never learn all she needed to know if she didn't ask.

"No. I'm quite warm." He placed his hands on her shoulders and allowed his body to brush against hers. "In fact, I'm quite hot."

"You were really a wolf?" It seemed obvious, but she was compelled to ask.

Cris buried his face in her hair and nuzzled it. "Yes. I can shape-shift when I choose."

"But doesn't it hurt when your body changes that drastically?" She hated the thought that he might have been in pain.

His tongue absently stroked the outer edge of her ear before he whispered his reply. "No. It is as natural to me as breathing. I can shift into an owl as well, but it is a much harder thing to do. I prefer the wolf."

It was hard to think when Cris was thrusting his tongue into her ear. She sighed as his teeth nibbled at her earlobe, tugging gently before returning to trace the whorls with his tongue.

"I want you." His dark, velvet voice filled her with need even as his hands slowly glided over her shoulders and down her back before coming to rest on her behind. "Here." He gripped her ass and pulled her close. She could feel the steel of his arousal against her stomach. "Now."

For better or worse, Johanna knew she'd made her choice. Man, wolf, or vampire, he was Cris and he was hers. "Yes," she sighed as she leaned closer, rubbing her breasts against his chest. "Right now."

Chapter Six

∞

Cris bent down and wrapped his left arm around her upper thighs. Straightening, he tossed her onto his left shoulder. Her head and shoulders hung down over his back while her legs dangled down his front. His move surprised Johanna and she gasped and bucked slightly as he carted her towards the woods.

Cris gave her a swat on the backside when she continued to struggle, trying to free her hands that were pinned between their bodies. "Settle down." As he walked the short distance from the road, his large hand smacked her once again before caressing her behind through the fabric of her skirt.

The heat from his hand shot straight to her sex, making her squirm even more. His laughter was dark and sensual as he gave her bottom another sharp smack. This time his fingers stroked between her legs, pulling the material of her skirt tight. Johanna pushed back against his hand, wanting his fingers on her. Frustration built as she was unable to get the close contact she needed.

His hands stroked down over her legs until he was gripping the hem of her skirt. With one motion, he ripped the back of the skirt open all the way to the waistband, popping the button off at the top. The cool night air hit her bare legs as he tore the fabric away from her body.

Intellectually, Johanna knew that Cris would never hurt her. But there was something thrilling and slightly scary about being carried off by such a large, powerful man for his sexual pleasure. Hanging over his shoulder like she was, she was certainly getting a great view of his backside. And Cris had a prime ass. Her mouth watered as she watched the flex and movement of it as he strode to whatever destination he had in mind. She longed to nibble and bite his firm behind.

This time his hand stung when it hit her behind. "Cris," she gasped, but it soon turned to a moan as his fingers stroked the crotch of her panties. Johanna knew they were already damp and getting wetter by the second. She could feel her cream coating her sex, readying her for him.

In one quick motion, Cris stopped and lifted her off his shoulder. After being upside down for so long, she swayed slightly, trying to get her bearings. She looked around, but had no idea where they were. Tall trees surrounded them, but they were in a small clearing and the moon was shining directly down on them.

Cris stood with his hands on his hips watching her. She licked her dry lips as he ran his gaze over her body, paying particular attention to her bare legs. Her bottom throbbed slightly and her pussy creamed in anticipation of what was to come.

"Strip." Folding his arms across his massive chest, he braced his feet apart and waited. The night was quiet except for the swish of the wind through the trees and the occasional hoot of an owl.

Uncertainty filled her and she hesitated. If she hadn't been watching him so closely, she would have missed the sadness that flashed in his eyes. It was gone as quickly as it came, hidden behind an impassive gaze of green.

She'd hurt him and was dealing with a slightly wounded beast. Cris could be quite sophisticated at times, but he could also be very primal and untamed. If she wanted to be with him, she would have to accept all parts of him.

Not taking her eyes off him, she shrugged off her jacket and let it drop at her feet. Raising her hands to her blouse, she slid one button from its hole. Goose bumps covered her body as she slowly worked her way to the bottom and slipped the blouse over her arms, leaving her feeling very exposed.

Cris said nothing, but she could hear his breathing getting heavier and louder. His cock jutted out in front of him, flexing slightly as she raised her hands to her bra. Emboldened, she cupped her lace-covered breasts and molded them with her hands. Her legs were shaky as she rubbed her tight nipples through the fabric. A low moan broke from her throat as heat shot from her breasts to her sex.

"Finish it."

Reaching between her breasts, Johanna unhooked her bra. Rolling her shoulders, she allowed the straps to fall over her shoulders and down her arms. It fell to the forest floor, forgotten as she felt his eyes devour her naked breasts. Hooking her fingers in the waistband of her panties, she shimmied her hips as she pushed the scrap of fabric down to her ankles. Stepping out of them, she stood quietly and waited. The slight breeze licked at her skin and her nipples pebbled even tighter.

"Come here."

Taking the few steps needed to reach him, she pressed her breasts against his chest. The hard points of her nipples stabbed at his chest and she felt his muscles flex as she rubbed her breasts against him.

His cock was hard and hot against her stomach. Reaching down, she wrapped both her hands around it, marveling at its sheer size and length. Gliding them over his length, she rubbed one of her palms over the tip, spreading the fluid that had seeped out from the tip. Her damp hand slid easily back down over his cock from tip to base.

Groaning, Cris buried his hands in her hair and tilted her face up until she was looking at him. His face was stamped with need. His eyes were dark mirrors of desire, his nostrils were flared, and his lips were pursed in a hard line. He looked like a man in agony. "I cannot be gentle."

Johanna pumped her hands up and down his cock once again. "Whatever you need."

Lifting her up, Cris buried his face in her breasts while he walked towards a large tree. The sudden motion startled her and she dug her fingers into his shoulders and wrapped her legs around his waist for support. Every step Cris made caused his cock to rub against her clit. Johanna clung tighter to him, wanting the contact to deepen.

It was darker in the shadow of the tree and Johanna could feel the rough bark against her back as Cris pushed her against the trunk. The movement upset an owl and it hooted and flew from the branches above. At any other time, Johanna would have been keen to see the creature, but she just didn't care about anything at the moment except Cris.

Johanna tried to raise her body high enough to get his cock inside her, but she was pinned between Cris and the tree. She couldn't get enough leverage to do that, but the slight up and down motion allowed her to rub her damp sex against his erection.

Stroking her clit against his cock made her even hotter. She could feel her creamy outer lips coating him as she pleasured herself. Cris gripped her ass in his large hands, spread her cheeks wide and raised her high. Flexing his knees, he drove his cock to the hilt. Johanna arched back, feeling the bark of the tree scrape her back.

Cris nipped and sucked at her breasts, holding her easily in his grasp. Johanna tried to move, but she was helpless, impaled on his cock. Cris kept his hands anchored on her ass, not allowing her any motion.

Arching her back, she pushed her breasts closer to his mouth. Cris laughed and caught one of her tight nipples between his teeth and flicked it with his tongue. He teased one breast and then the other.

"Cris." Johanna moaned his name as she tugged his head up to hers. Peppering his face with kisses, she desperately tried to move, jerking her hips forward.

Holding her easily with one hand, he tugged one of her hands away from him and raised it high, wrapping her fingers around a thin branch. When he was sure she had hold of it, he captured her other one and raised it as well. "Hold tight to the branch and don't let go."

She nodded, her face brushing his. Cris turned his head and caught her mouth with his. Plunging his tongue deep inside, he kissed her breathless. She was gasping for breath when he finally pulled away and buried his face in her neck.

His fingers tightened around her bottom as he bent his knees and lifted her. He pulled her back down at the same time he straightened his legs, driving deep into her. Her inner muscles clenched around his cock as he pulled almost all the way out of her. Driving back even harder than before, he buried his cock to the hilt.

Johanna could feel her hot pussy wrap tight around him each time he drove into it. He set a pounding rhythm that had her gasping for breath. With her fingers wrapped tight around the tree branch, she hung on and rode out the storm. Her breasts bounced with each stroke, making them ache for Cris's touch.

Her cunt clenched harder with each thrust. His skin slapped against hers, music on the night air, as she hung onto the tree for support. Cris was relentless, not stopping for a moment. If anything, his thrusts seemed to get harder and quicker. Johanna didn't know how much more she could take. Every cell in her body was screaming out for release.

Digging her ankles into his behind, she slammed down hard on his cock with every upward thrust he made. A bead of sweat slipped down her temple as she tightened the inner muscles of her cunt around him.

Cris growled and hammered into her over and over again. Tilting back her head, she dug her nails into the tree bark, screaming as she finally came. Her muscles flexed and closed around his cock as he continued to pound into her.

"Don't let go." His guttural command had her hanging on even tighter. She felt his teeth scraping her throat and tilted it back even further. Growling, he sank his teeth into her flesh and drank.

Even though she'd just come, Johanna felt a familiar heat as her pussy clenched once again. Spasms of pleasure rocked her body, as Cris gave one final thrust and came on a moan of pleasure. He removed his teeth and licked at her neck as he continued to hold her close.

Johanna took a deep breath and the scent of sex and pine filled her nostrils. She shivered as the cool night air dried the sweat from her skin.

"You can let go now." Cris's voice sounded amused and Johanna was slightly bemused to discover that she was still clutching the branch. She released her grip and dropped her hands to his shoulders.

Carefully, Cris lifted her off his cock, which had hardened once again, and stood her in front of him. Picking up her blouse, he shook it out before helping her to slip it on. Her skirt was useless, so she picked up her jacket and wrapped it around her waist, tying the sleeves together to keep it up. She scooped up her underwear and stuffed it into the pocket of the jacket. Looking around, she spied what was left of her poor leather shoes and slipped them over her feet.

Cris said nothing as he wrapped his arm around her and led her out of the woods and back towards the castle. She sensed that he didn't want to talk any more than she did. In truth, after what she'd just gone through, she was content to just enjoy the sensations still coursing through her body. She knew they'd have to talk, but right now it was enough that they were together.

Her leather briefcase was lying abandoned in the middle of the dusty road. "I can't believe I forgot it," she murmured under her breath. Cris said nothing, but waited as she bent down and picked it up. They continued on in silence, back up the path, across the courtyard, and into the castle.

It was only when the door slammed shut behind them that she found the courage to begin seeking the answers to her many questions. "Please explain to me how our relationship has been possible all these years? There are so many things that I need to understand."

Cris pried the briefcase out of her clenched hand and dropped it to the floor. He nodded, but continued to guide her past the study to a set of worn stone stairs. At the bottom, he scooped her up in his arms and carried her up the long flight of steps. She snuggled closer as his familiar shape and scent filled her senses. His face showed no emotion, but his muscles were tight as he walked. She could sense his emotional turmoil, but now that the crisis had passed, his mind was closed to her once again.

Taking a deep breath, she continued her line of thought. "How is it that you can read my mind? It's not fair, you know." Looping her arms around his neck, she placed her head on his shoulder and nuzzled his neck. "You know my thoughts all the time, but I catch only rare glimpses of yours."

"Be thankful that you cannot read my mind." His words made her shiver, but now what she felt was desire, and not fear.

At the top of the stairs he turned right and walked down a dimly lit hallway. The walls looked as if they were covered in artwork, but she couldn't quite make out what they were. "I'll give you a tour tomorrow," he told her as he strode into a large room and pushed the door closed with his booted heel.

"See what I mean?" she complained. A moment later, that thought was forgotten as she peered around the room, unable to contain her natural curiosity.

The huge bed in the center of one wall made it obvious that this was his bedroom. It was a study in masculine opulence and suited him well. All the furniture was large, obviously hand-carved, and quite old. The bed was draped with yards of rich burgundy velvets and brocades. A set of bed curtains was pushed back so she could see the piles of overstuffed pillows that lay there. The stone walls were covered with a variety of tapestries and artifacts, including an enormous jewel-encrusted sword that was mounted directly over the fireplace. A low, lacquered table sat in front of the roaring fire, which was the only light in the room, and on it sat a bottle of wine and two crystal glasses.

Cris carried her to the far side of the room where she noticed another door. It was a small room with an old-fashioned bathtub that was steaming with hot water, the smell of lavender tickling her senses. Plush white towels sat on a low stool next to the tub, and a heavy brocade robe hung on a hook by the door. He stood her next to the tub and began to unbutton her blouse. Peeling it down over her arms, he dropped it to the floor at her feet.

Cris surprised her by falling to his knees in front of her, wrapping his arms around her waist, and burying his face between her breasts. His tongue was moist and hot as he wove a path around both breasts before licking her nipples into hard points. Johanna felt the familiar heat rise within her.

It was the night of the full moon and they'd just had sex outside under the moonlight sky. It had felt like the first time, which was ridiculous, considering how many times they'd made love in her dreams over the years. But the truth was that she was thirty years old, and she'd never had sex with a man except Cris. No other man in her day-to-day life had ever been able to measure up to him and what he gave her. Her legs shook as she stood half naked in front of him.

He rubbed his face over her breasts and belly, tickling them and making her laugh. "What am I to do with you?" Cris asked, his tone tender and playful all at once. "I have known you as no other man has. There is no need to be nervous of me." He continued to work as he talked, untying the sleeves of the jacket from around her waist and peeling it away from her body. She stood naked in front of him. Even kneeling on the floor, he was overwhelming.

His hands trailed up the back of her legs from her ankles to her thighs, making her sway with desire. Everywhere he touched, she felt the flames of desire licking her. His large palms covered her bottom and he squeezed both globes tight, massaging them. Moving closer, he nuzzled through her pubic hair, his tongue stroking the hot, moist folds of her sex. She grasped his shoulders for balance as her blood began to sizzle. The need to have him grew deep inside her.

He growled and sat back on his heels, his eyes glowing hot with desire. He shook himself and lowered his head. "Bath," he hissed from between his clenched teeth. Turning her, he pushed her towards the tub.

For a moment she almost protested, but it looked so good, and she felt sore and dirty after her ordeal. Gingerly, she climbed over the side of the tub and sank down in the fragrant water. The hipbath curved up behind her back and she leaned back against the cool porcelain and closed her eyes. The picture of Cris kneeling on the floor was still burned into her mind. Her knees bent slightly as the tub was not long, but it was extremely comfortable, and she felt the hot water relaxing her aching muscles.

She sensed him leaning over her and parted her lips in anticipation. His tongue dipped inside, tasting and teasing hers. Wrapping one hand around her head so she couldn't escape him, he laid claim to her very soul with his hot carnal embrace.

She sucked his tongue and kissed him with abandon. "I want you," she moaned, when he began to nibble on her lips. The sound of her voice seemed to jolt him and he pulled back and stood by the tub.

"Bathe first. Then if you still want me, come to me." He was gone before she could think to reply to his outrageous statement.

"If I still want him," she muttered before she held her breath and sank beneath the water. Gasping as she surfaced, she grabbed a cloth and began to scrub. All thoughts of a leisurely bath were gone now as she quickly finished washing the dust from her body.

"What does the man want? A gilded invitation? I should have just pulled him into the tub with me." She glanced at the small tub. "On second thought, maybe not."

Standing, the water cascaded down her body. She grabbed one of the towels as her body shivered. Carefully, she stepped out of the tub, dried herself off, and grabbed the robe off the hook, stuffing her arms into the sleeves. She didn't bother to belt it, so it flowed behind her as she stalked into the other room.

Chapter Seven

ಬಿ

Johanna strode across the room and stood beside the bed with her arms folded under her breasts, which pushed them up slightly. She wasn't overly large in that department, so she figured it couldn't hurt, and she knew Cris agreed when his eyes seemed to devour them.

The heat from his gaze evaporated any water drops left on her body, and her whole body softened as a lethargic heat filled her. She shook her head to try and break away from his sensual snare.

Cris was sprawled naked across the crisp white sheets with his hands crossed behind his head, his large body taking up most of the space. Even in repose, the muscles of his chest and arms were sleek and hard. The tufts of soft hair under his arms and across his chest should have made him look softer, more vulnerable. Instead, with the trappings of civilization removed, he appeared even more dangerous. He seemed to be totally relaxed, but she wasn't buying it. She stared pointedly at his erect cock and it twitched slightly in response. "Well?"

He didn't even pretend to misunderstand. "You know what I am." He waited until she nodded before he continued. "But you need to know how it will affect you." Patting the covers next to him, he urged her to sit. Not bothering to close the robe, she climbed onto the bed and sat cross-legged facing him, waiting.

"I am a Dalakis." His eyes glowed red as he stared right into her very soul. "We are different. My family have always been vampires and have lived here for thousands of years. I have heard of other families of vampires, but like us, they keep to themselves, struggling for their own survival. Now there is only myself and my two brothers, Stefan and Lucian."

He held up his hand to stop her before she could speak. "Let me finish first, then I will answer all your questions." She nodded and he continued.

"I am immortal. I need blood to sustain me. But," he hurriedly reassured her, "I do not kill others to live, but take only what I need to survive. It is different from the old days. Centuries ago, we killed often to protect ourselves and our people." His features hardened, "And I would kill again in a heartbeat if you were threatened." With an obvious effort he forced himself to relax. "Today, we even store blood for emergencies, much like a blood bank."

He rolled to his side and propped himself up on one arm. His other hand reached out to tease the flesh on the inside of her thigh. The up and down motion of his fingers was making it extremely hard for her to pay attention to his words.

"Prolonged exposure to sunlight, a stake through the heart, or beheading will kill me. Nothing else. Well, nothing except perhaps love."

That comment had her full attention. "What do you mean?"

"Dalakis men love only once in their lifetime. It is their gift and their curse." His smile was tender as his hand caressed her cheek. "You were a gift from the heavens when I found you, but you were so young. I could not take you or ask you to join me then. So, I lived but did not fully live. To find you and not have you was a torture beyond what you can imagine. After six hundred years of living, to have you so close—" he broke off and sighed deeply, shaking his head at the dark memories, "—but yet not to have you."

Johanna opened her mouth to speak, but Cris placed a finger over her lips. "Many have given up in despair and faced the killing midday sun rather than live any longer without finding their true love. Others have done the same after being rejected. Now it is your turn to choose."

He sat up in bed and took both her hands in his, squeezing them gently. "Whatever your choice, I will honor it. I give you my word as a Dalakis."

Leaning forward, he kissed her forehead, her cheeks and then her lips. She clung to his hands, half-fearful now. She sensed that his word was not something he gave lightly and that he would die before dishonoring it.

"You are right, little one." He laughed, and it was a bitter sound. "I would choose death before dishonor, but that is not your concern. If you wish to stay with me, you can live out your normal life here at the castle and I will cherish and protect you for as long as you live. And when the time of your death is upon us, I will join you."

"No!" she gasped, squeezing his hands so tight that her knuckles turned white. Her heart pounded with grief at the mere thought of his death.

"Or," he continued as if she hadn't spoken, "I can change you so you become as I am. You would be vampire, but your life would be linked with mine. If I die, then you too will die. You would be susceptible to the other dangers as well. But I would be by your side for eternity, and no other man living or yet to be born will love you as I will. Your happiness and protection are my life's work and my life's joy."

Johanna was speechless when he finished. She could feel the tears tracking down her cheeks, but she could not tear her gaze from his beloved face. His features were impassive as he sat there, a beautiful bronze nude statue, waiting for her to decide his future.

In the light glowing from the fireplace, his harsh countenance and glistening muscles made it easy to picture him wielding the massive sword that hung over the mantle. She could easily imagine him astride a horse in the fifteenth century, defending his home against all enemies. He was a warrior without equal. Yet he had laid his heart bare before her and now stoically awaited her decision.

Coming to her knees in front of him, she slipped the robe from her shoulders before wrapping her arms around his neck and gently kissing his lips. The muscles stood out on his arms and chest with the effort it took to keep himself still. "I know there is still so much I have to learn and understand. But I know what is in my heart." Taking one of his hands in hers, she placed it gently over her heart. "You're a part of me and we belong together. Forever."

Johanna paused for a moment and then uttered the words that would change her life eternally. "Make me like you."

As if unleashing a tethered beast, he pounced on her. Before she could take a breath, she was flat on her back and his mouth covered hers in an all-consuming kiss. Wrapping her arms around his broad shoulders, she gave herself into his keeping, not knowing what was coming, but trusting him with her very life.

His hands were everywhere as he ran them up and down her entire body as if committing every inch of it to memory. They traveled up her arms, teasing the sensitive skin on the underside. The skin on his hands was slightly rough and made her shiver as she imagined them on other parts of her body. He didn't linger, but traced the veins in her neck and leaned over and nipped at the fluttering pulse at its base.

From there, he continued down her torso, outlining her breasts and every single rib as he made his way to her hipbones. She moaned and eagerly parted her legs when he grazed her pubic bone, but he ignored the invitation and continued to trace a path down both legs to her feet. Her hips rolled on the bed and she could feel the aching need for him inside her.

"Cris." His name was both a command and a plea. Her whole body felt like liquid fire, raging out of control.

"Shhh," he whispered as he sat up in bed and pulled her feet into his lap. She wasn't sure what he was going to do until he leaned over and began to nibble on her toes. His large hand held her foot steady as he made his way from her little toe to her large one, first licking and then sucking on each one.

Johanna collapsed back against the pillows and let the pleasure take her. Never in her life would she have thought of her feet as an erogenous zone. Obviously, she had a lot to learn.

"Oh my god," she panted as he moved up her ankle and calf. Her chest was heaving as she gasped for breath. Meanwhile, he was nibbling his way past her knee and up towards her inner thigh.

Reaching down, she grabbed him by the hair and tugged him towards her moist, eager pussy. His laughter was wicked as he ignored her efforts and instead ran his tongue in the crease at the top of her leg. She almost shot off the bed.

Cris gripped her inner thighs in his hands and held her wide open for his inspection before lowering his head and tasting her hot, wet flesh. Johanna grabbed the covers in her hands, trying to anchor herself as pleasure washed over her in waves. His sharp teeth carefully nipped her clitoris as his tongue flicked over the distending nub.

For a moment, every muscle in her body was clenched tight as she was poised on the edge. He knew it too, as he looked straight at her before pressing his tongue hard against her clit and showing his teeth in a feral smile.

She shot over the edge and could hear herself screaming as pure fire shot through her entire body. Her body jerked and heaved as her orgasm consumed her. When it finally subsided, she felt as if she didn't have a bone in her body, she was so relaxed.

Cris shifted until he was lying beside her and pulled her into his arms. Rubbing her nose against the hair on his chest, she snuggled tight in his embrace. Contented, she nuzzled one of his flat brown nipples before sucking it into her mouth and nibbling on it. His arms tightened and one of his hands cradled her head closer to him.

Pleased with her efforts, she could feel his erection pushing against her leg, so she wrapped her hand around him and began to pump. His hips jerked forward in a reflex action as her other hand reached beneath him to caress his testicles, which were drawn tight to his body.

"Are you sure?" His question amazed her. Even at this stage, he was still concerned only about her.

"Yes, I'm sure." She punctuated her statement by peppering kisses across the broad expanse of his chest. Leaning back, she met his hungry gaze. "I love you."

"It is time then." Cris sat up in bed, forcing her to release her grip on him. Kneeling up on the bed, he pulled her to him. "Mount me."

Johanna licked her lips in anticipation at the sight of his hard, thick cock and gingerly threw one leg over his knees and began to lower herself. Inch by inch, she took him into her. Her inner muscles squeezed him, and she could feel the fire growing deep within her again. Gripping his shoulders for support, she seated herself to the hilt, squirming around for a minute to get comfortable.

"Enough, woman." He grabbed her hips and held them tight as he gave her a ferocious glare. She responded by reaching behind her and squeezing his balls.

Cris moaned and lowered his mouth to her breasts, feasting on them. His tongue was hot against her skin and she could feel his teeth scraping across the skin. She felt the scorching caress between her legs as she got wetter and the need to move grew too great to ignore.

Rotating her hips, she pleasured them both. Her nipples were hard and aching and her breasts felt heavy and needy as he continued to play with them. "Now," she pleaded.

As if he had only been waiting for her signal, Cris licked a hot trail from her breasts to her neck before allowing his teeth to sink into her. As he fed from her, she could feel each sucking motion between her legs. All his emotions, as well as her own, pummeled her, and the overwhelming desire engulfed her as she came long and hard. Her body gripped his cock tight as she came, but he was still rigid inside her when she finally collapsed against him. She lolled against him, feeling sated, yet still pleasantly aroused.

He continued to drink from her until her vision blurred and all consciousness began to fade. She knew she should be afraid, but instead she was filled with a feeling of rightness and completion. If he needed all her blood to survive, she would gladly surrender every drop to him. That was her last thought as darkness greeted her.

Chapter Eight

ॐ

Cris felt her heart beat grow slower and slower. It pulsed one final time and then stopped. Forcing himself away from her neck, he used his tongue to close the small wound. His fingernails tore at the skin of his chest, slicing the flesh and opening up a large gash. As the blood flowed, he pushed her mouth towards the life-giving liquid. Reaching deep into her mind, he willed her to drink from him. If she did not, if some natural instinct kicked in and prevented her from doing so, then they were both dead.

"Drink my love," he urged her, with words as well as with mental commands. Rubbing her lips back and forth against his bloody chest, he felt his hope slowly dying as she just lay limply against him. Fighting for both their lives, he bent all his concentration and skills towards getting her to drink from him. Long minutes passed as his blood trickled slowly but steadily down his chest, and still she did not move.

Swallowing hard, he forced himself to face the inevitable— he had pushed her too hard. She was still so young, and he had wanted her too much. Her death was on his hands. "So be it." His acceptance echoed throughout the room. She would not face it alone. His life was linked to hers now and he would join her in death rather than live without her.

At the very moment of his thought, he felt a tentative movement against his chest. Hope renewed, he begged, pleaded and commanded her to drink. It was slow at first, but within a moment, she was sucking slowly, but steadily. He raised his eyes to the heavens in thanks even as he felt a lone tear streak down his face.

She drank steadily until he sensed she'd had enough. Gently, he eased her away from him. As she stared at him with her lips coated in his blood, he could feel his desire rising to a feverish pitch within him.

"Close the wound with your tongue," he instructed her. His voice was harsh and barely recognizable to himself, but his emotions were running high and his need for her was riding him hard. Both the beast and the man were ready to claim their mate. She was his now. Forever.

As soon as the wound was closed, he kissed her, licking all traces of his blood from her lips. Eagerly, her tongue dueled with his and for a moment the sheer joy of her eager acceptance filled him.

His need for her consumed him. The need to claim her in the way of his people, and thereby tie her to him forever, was all that mattered now. Lifting her off his throbbing cock, he laid her facedown on the bed. Raising her slightly so she was on her hands and knees, he mounted her from behind and pushed himself all the way inside her.

With his hands wrapped tight around her waist, he widened his stance until her legs were spread wide. He reveled in his dominance of her, needing her to surrender to both him and her passion. Her hot sheath pulsed around his stiff cock and he ground his hips against her ass, pleasuring them both.

He sensed her surprise, then her acceptance, and finally her rising passion. More than anything, he wanted to reassure and comfort her, but instincts older than time were controlling him now. She was his and he had to claim her. "My woman." His guttural words rang through the room as he pulled almost all the way out before surging deep inside her once again.

Her wet heat welcomed him and he felt her move her bottom to meet him as his cock continued to plunge deep within her. Johanna's acquiescence fueled his passion and he lost himself in her, thrusting in and out of her welcoming body. Leaning over her, he sank his teeth in the back of her neck and tasted her blood. Her pussy clamped down hard on his dick, driving him to the very edge.

He wanted to prolong the sensations, but he could feel himself coming. When it hit, his orgasm was so overwhelming that it seemed as if he was emptying his very soul into her. As he poured his seed deep inside her, he felt her muscles clamp tight around him as another orgasm enveloped her.

Aftershocks of pleasure surged through his body as he extracted his fangs, and closed the small wound on the back of her neck before collapsing on top of her. He covered her entire body with his, sheltering her with his bulk. He nibbled at the nape of her neck as he always did in her dreams. She laughed softly, but didn't move.

They lay there in a tangle of limbs and spent energy for a long time before he found the strength to withdraw from her. She moaned in protest, but he ignored it and rolled her into his arms, cuddling her tight. Hence forth, she was his for all eternity.

"What comes next?" The sound of her sleepy voice surprised him.

"What do you mean?" He pushed a stray lock of hair off her face so he could see her better, hearing the slight tremor in her voice.

"Am I like you now? A vampire?" She paused for a moment before continuing, more thoughtful now. "I don't feel any different. Am I changed?"

"No, it's not finished yet." Smoothing her hair back, he kissed her lips lightly. "We will sleep at dawn and when you awake tomorrow evening it will be done. There will be some discomfort as your body adjusts itself, but I will be with you."

"What do you mean, discomfort?" She tugged on his chest hair. "And why didn't you mention that little detail before?"

He laughed at her spirit. "It is little when you weigh it against eternity."

Her gaze softened and she smiled at him. "I'm woman enough to handle a little pain if it means we can be together. What we share is worth any price."

Cris smiled as he cupped her precious face. "We will be together and I have much to teach you."

He laughed suddenly. "You have two brothers now, you know. They are good men, but are very overbearing and will drive you absolutely crazy trying to keep you safe and protected at all times."

"Really!" she laughed. "I can't wait to meet them." He could hear the excitement in her voice and it was contagious. "How soon do you think I'll get the chance?"

"You already did." He gave a soft laugh at her look of surprise. "I'm not the only member of my family who can shapeshift. Those two wolves were not happy you were leaving me."

Johanna reared back in surprise. "Those wolves were your brothers? But they attacked me."

"No, my love. They merely wanted to keep you from leaving me. Never would they have harmed you." Her scowl of displeasure made the corners of his mouth tilt up as he anticipated the tongue-lashing she would give his brothers. "I'm sure they will give us a few days before they come to visit, but I would not count on more than two or three at most. I'm sure they are most eager to meet you."

Absently, he tugged her back into his arms. "First thing tomorrow evening, you must call your company and quit your job."

"I hadn't quite thought that far ahead yet." Her voice was quiet as she drew circles on his chest with her index finger. "There'll be a lot of changes in the days ahead."

"Do not worry," he reassured her. "You have the entire Dalakis fortune at your disposal, and your talent for business will not go unused."

"You'd trust me to handle your fortune?" Johanna sounded totally bewildered as she raised her head to look at him.

The surprise in her voice amazed him. "Of course. You are the Dalakis bride. I am the oldest brother and you are now the matriarch of the family, such as it is."

"What a challenge..." Johanna trailed off, lost in thought for a moment. Cris could almost see the wheels turning in that nimble brain of hers. "We'll have to travel back to Chicago so I can close up my apartment and arrange for my things to be shipped."

"That is no problem. I have a private plane that will take us whenever you are ready."

"Now why doesn't that surprise me?" she laughed.

She was quiet for a moment before she spoke again. "As the head of this family, the first thing we need to do is try and find brides for your brothers. If this family is to grow and prosper, we need children." Her eyes widened suddenly. "How come I never got pregnant? We've been having unprotected sex for twelve years! Do we even have children in the conventional way?"

Cris shook as laughter welled up inside him. Unable to contain it, he laughed until tears came to his eyes. "They will love you and be terrified of you all at once."

"Yes, well..." she trailed off looking slightly disgruntled at his laugher and embarrassed by her own exuberance.

"You are amazing." Unable to resist her delicious flavor, he nipped at her neck for a taste. "Do not worry. Everything will come in time." As the first drop of blood hit his tongue, he was instantly aroused again.

Johanna twined her arms around his neck and arched her hips towards him. Cris healed the small puncture mark with his tongue before kissing a path up to her mouth. "There are many hours yet until we must seek our rest at dawn," he murmured against her lips.

"And I bet you know just how to spend them." Her hand glided down his chest until it captured his growing cock.

Loving the feel of her around him, he thrust his hips closer. "I can see we will agree on all things."

She laughed. "Definitely not on all things. But certainly on the things that really matter."

All need for talk was forgotten as they came together once again to celebrate the start of their new life together.

Chapter Nine

ဆာ

Two nights later, Johanna strolled into the formal dining room. It was a monstrous room, with a large stone fireplace that currently housed a roaring blaze. A twenty-foot trestle table made of oak sat in the center of the room and was surrounded by heavily carved chairs. Cris was seated in the most ornate of the chairs at the head of the table.

Johanna was finally feeling like herself again. Well, an improved version of herself. It amazed her how much keener all her senses were now. At first, it had been totally disorienting to try and sort through all the noise, but Cris had taught her how to control her superior hearing. Everything was heightened, including touch. Sex was incredible since the change. Not that she'd gotten much yesterday.

She shuddered when she remembered last night. Her entire body had been burning when she'd awoken at dusk. Rolling to her side, she'd curled herself in a ball, grasping her stomach tight. It felt as if someone had set her entire body on fire. Every organ and muscle was rocked with spasms of pain. Talking had been beyond her and it had taken every ounce of her strength just to breathe.

Cris awoke immediately and wrapped his arms around her. The pressure had been too much for her poor stomach. "Sick." She forced the word from between her lips, but Cris was already in motion.

Plucking her off the bed, he hurried into the small bathroom with her and knelt in front of the toilet. "Your body needs to purge itself of human waste." Holding her gently, he positioned her head over the porcelain bowl.

Johanna was appalled at the thought of heaving up her stomach in front of him, but in the end her stomach had its way. Unable to stop herself, Johanna was violently sick for three hours straight. Every time she threw up, Cris swore. It was so ridiculous that she would have laughed if she'd had the strength.

When it was finally finished, her hair was plastered to her head with sweat and her entire body felt sticky and dirty. At her insistence, Cris had filled the hipbath with hot water and helped her into it. She'd found it unbearably sweet, the way he'd sat next to the tub holding her hand, while she'd allowed the hot water to clean the sickness from her body.

She felt incredibly shaky and tearful when he'd lifted her from the bath and dried her with a thick, heated towel. He'd even held her in his arms while she rinsed her mouth and cleaned her teeth. After that, he'd carried her back to bed and tucked her under the covers.

The poor man looked worse than she did and fell into bed beside her. Pulling her into his arms, he curled his body around hers and explained many of the changes in her body to her. He anticipated many of her questions, answering them before she could ask them. Eventually, she'd been unable to stay awake any longer, and they'd both slept. It was just before dawn that they'd awakened long enough to make love before falling asleep for the day.

When she'd awakened tonight, she'd been alone in the massive bed, but she hadn't been worried. By opening her mind and scanning the castle, she knew that Cris was in the dining room sitting at the table, waiting for her.

Rising from the bed, she stretched, feeling better than she had in her entire life. Draped over the end of the bed was a beautiful long dress made of plush green velvet. She looked around, but there was no sign of her underwear and all her other clothing had been ruined and discarded. Unable to resist the luxurious dress, she'd stepped into the dress, pulling it over her hips. The sleeves were long and the bodice laced up in the front. It fit her perfectly.

Totally naked under her dress, she somehow felt more exposed than if she was truly naked. The fabric swished against her legs and the tight bodice rubbed against her breasts, causing her nipples to pucker into hungry buds. Johanna licked her lips in anticipation. Her pussy throbbed with need at the mere thought of Cris. She was hungry for her husband in more ways than one. And she did consider him her husband, even if there hadn't been a formal ceremony yet. What they shared went far beyond a normal marriage.

She had no shoes, but her feet weren't cold as she padded out of the room and down the hallway. Thick carpet covered the center of the stairway and Johanna enjoyed the sensation under her toes as she made her way towards the dining room. She stopped in the doorway, amazed as always that this gorgeous man belonged to her now, just as she belonged to him.

Sitting back in his massive chair at the head of the table, Cris looked every bit the lord of the manor. It struck her then that this was no pose. He was lord of this castle and had been for centuries. The thought was intimidating and arousing at the same time. He turned his head slowly and a look of pure male satisfaction glittered in his eyes when he noted what she was wearing.

His heated perusal left no doubt that he wanted to fuck her again. The man was insatiable and Johanna was quickly finding that, when it came to Cris, so was she. Taking her time, she sauntered towards him, her feet practically gliding across the stone floor until she was standing beside his chair.

Bending down, she rubbed her breasts against his shoulder as she traced the outline of his ear with her tongue. He reached for her, but she skittered backward just out of his reach. "Good evening, my lord."

His eyes practically glowed and she could feel the heat radiating from his massive body. "Good evening, my love. I see you found the dress."

Johanna rubbed her hands over the bodice, lifting her breasts as she did so. "Thank you. It's beautiful."

"No, the dress is adequate. *You* are beautiful." Cris shifted in his chair and she could see the large bulge in the front of his pants straining for release. Her man was very aroused and more than ready for her.

Teasingly, Johanna unlaced the front of the bodice, spreading the fabric until it framed her small breasts, plumping them up and pushing them forward. His eyes never left the soft mounds as she pinched their tips. Her mouth parted on a low moan and a gush of cream coated the lips of her sex.

"Come here."

Swinging her hips, Johanna danced away from him. "But I'm hungry."

"So am I." Cris pronounced each word slowly and precisely, leaving her no doubt that he was hungry for her.

Hunger rose from deep within Johanna, unlike anything she'd ever experienced. She wanted, no needed, Cris to take her now. Johanna felt her fangs growing and licked her lips. Not hesitating, she lifted herself up onto the table in front of him and raised her skirts to her waist.

He sat back in his chair and raised an eyebrow. "Put your feet flat on the table and spread your knees wide." His tongue came out to stroke one of his fangs. "I want to see your cunt. Are you hot for me? Are you wet for me?"

Pushing back slightly until her bottom was securely on the table, Johanna raised each foot and placed both heels flat on the table. Widening her knees, she pushed her legs wide open, letting him see all of her. As she sat there totally exposed, she could feel the trickle of her juices flowing from inside her pussy, down the outer lips, and disappearing into her behind.

Reaching out a single finger, Cris stroked the sensitive flesh before bringing it back to his mouth and licking it. "You belong to me now."

"Yes." Using one of her hands for leverage, she pushed the other one between her legs and stroked her aching sex.

Cris captured her hand in his, not allowing her to pleasure herself. "Tell me what you want."

"You." She moaned as she tried to pull her hand from his grasp. She might be stronger now that she was a vampire, but she was no match for Cris.

"What do you want me to do?"

"Fuck me, Cris. Now." She stopped trying to pull her hand away from his and instead tried to push his hand closer to her damp flesh.

His dark, satisfied laughter washed over her and he pushed out of his chair and stood. Opening his pants, he released his cock, which was huge and red. Gripping her knees in his hand, he held her wide as he probed for her opening. One slow inch at a time, he sank into her waiting depths.

Johanna moaned with pleasure as she lowered her upper body back over the table. Now that her hands were free, she covered her breasts with them, reveling in the feel of the tight nipples stabbing her palms as she rubbed them.

Cris reared back and drove hard, stopping once again when he was buried to the hilt. "You are my one true love."

Johanna intentionally squeezed her inner muscles around his throbbing length. "And you're mine."

Cris's eyes darkened as he laid one hand on the table by her head for leverage and wrapped his other arm around her waist. "Forever." Pulling back, Cris began to fuck her. Hard. It was if he felt he needed to reassure himself that she was real and that she was his. Johanna reveled in his possession, needing their intimate connection as much as he did.

The table groaned beneath her as she bucked and arched on its hard surface as he rode her. She turned her head to one side and watched the flames leaping wildly in the fireplace. Their shadows moved in a raw, primal dance on the wall. Reaching up, Johanna pulled his head down to her even as she hooked her legs around him and held him tight.

Cris buried his face in her throat, nuzzling it before moving to her shoulder. Cradling her head in the palm of one hand, he held her mouth to his throat. His fangs sank into her the same moment that she sank hers into him. While he continued to thrust in and out, the table creaking in distress, they shared each other's blood.

It was the most incredible thing that Johanna had ever experienced. More intimate and intense than any of their previous lovemaking. Johanna's whole body tightened, and for a second she was suspended between need and pleasure. Cris stroked hard into her once more and she went over the edge.

Her entire body jerked as she came. A gush of liquid flowed from her pussy as she continued to suck from his neck. She could feel the sucking motion of his mouth on her neck all the way down between her thighs as if they pulsed to the same powerful rhythm. Johanna pulled her fangs free from his flesh and licked his neck.

Cris's entire body heaved and shuddered. He withdrew his teeth and gave a cry, pumping his cock into her until it was empty. Leaning forward, he licked the puncture marks on her neck, closing and healing them in one motion. Resting his head on her chest, he lazily licked at one of her nipples, making her moan once again.

"We can come back later." The new male voice was quite amused and very close.

With a panicked look at towards the door, Johanna gave a shriek and pulled the bodice of the dress closed, smacking Cris' nose as she did so. Cris swore and reared back, glaring at the intruders. "You have terrible timing."

Cris withdrew from her body, but was careful to make sure the fabric of her dress covered her. Casually, he adjusted his pants and refastened them. His face softened as he took in her disheveled state. Ignoring their guests, Cris helped her lace her gown shut, ran his fingers through her hair and gently lifted her from the table so that she stood beside him.

Johanna was almost too embarrassed to look at their guests. She had a good idea who they were, and this was not how she envisioned this meeting. Cris caught her chin in his hand and tilted her face upward. He kissed her lips, sensually moving his over hers.

The sound of a male clearing his throat interrupted them. "I am most sorry to have to interrupt your lovemaking, madam, but as we are leaving tomorrow, we wanted to meet you before we left."

Cris sighed and turned her towards the voice. Two men stood side by side, not far from the table. They both had long black hair and vivid green eyes, just like Cris'. "May I present my brothers, Lucian and Stefan."

Johanna noted that Stefan was slightly taller than Lucian. They were both dressed formally, and Johanna wasn't sure if she should offer her hand or curtsy. She smiled nervously and decided to be herself. Sticking out her hand firmly, she offered it to Lucian first. "Hi, I'm Johanna."

Picking up her hand, he kissed the back of it before passing it to Stefan, who also kissed it. Not the handshake she'd expected, but it tickled her all the same. Her smile warmed.

Cris wrapped his arms around her waist pulling her back against his body. She could feel his still-hard erection poking her behind, and snuggled back closer to him.

"This is Johanna Harker, my love and my life. I present to you the Dalakis bride." Cris leaned down and captured her lips in a searing kiss.

The sound of male laughter echoed in the big room, followed by the sound of a door being pulled firmly shut.

LUCIAN'S DELIGHT

જી

Dedication

To my husband who shares my love of vampire lore and all things gothic.

Thank you for your support and input and for caring as much about the Dalakis family as I do.

And to the many readers who have fallen in love with the Dalakis brothers, thank you for taking these remarkable men into your hearts.

Chapter One

ဆာ

Run!

The thought exploded in her brain like a blinding flash of light.

Run!

She was frozen in place like a deer caught in the headlights, not knowing what to do, where to turn. Then suddenly, she was in full flight, racing through the darkness, fleeing for her life. Her heart was pounding so loud it drowned out the footsteps behind her, but she knew her pursuers were there. Unknown monsters chased her, wanting to run her to ground for the sheer pleasure of doing so.

Muscles straining, lungs burning, she redoubled her efforts, racing on through the dark, lamp-lit night searching for a place to hide. Looking for a sanctuary.

Up ahead, she could barely discern the outline of a wrought iron fence and she sprinted towards it. The swift tapping of shoes on the pavement behind her spurred her to go faster. She risked a glance over her shoulder, but couldn't see anyone behind her. But she knew they were there. They always were.

The tall, solid bars of the old iron structure came into view and for a moment she panicked. Where was the gate? Tears slipped from her eyes, a combination of the whipping wind stinging them and her rising level of frustration and fear. Dashing the tears away with the back of her hand, she kept running while her eyes frantically scanned for any opening in the fence.

There had to be a gate. There just *had* to be. The scattered, dim streetlights did little to cut through the dark gloom of the night. Just then the clouds above parted enough to allow a small sliver of moonlight to shine down. It wasn't much, but it was enough.

When she finally saw the rusty old gate that hung partially open, leaning precariously on hinges, she wanted to shout with relief but she could barely gulp in a breath.

Skidding to a stop, she gripped the iron bars and tugged slightly. Stuck. The stupid thing was jammed. Despair threatened to overwhelm her and she leaned on the gate for support as she eyed the opening. Sucking in her breath, she began to squeeze herself through the small space, ignoring the discomfort as her breasts were compressed against her chest. It was tight and for a moment she thought she might not fit.

Clamping her lips together, she swallowed hard and made herself focus. Angling her body, she pushed herself, ignoring the pain as a piece of metal gashed her back. Then she was through, stumbling when she finally popped out on the other side, falling towards the ground.

Rocks and dirt scraped the palms of her hands as she kept herself from sprawling facedown onto the ground. Pushing away from the hard-packed earth, she ignored the pain and kept running. She had to find a place to hide somewhere that they wouldn't find her. It was only when she started searching her surroundings that she realized where she was.

Tall majestic statues rose high against the blackness of the sky. They were probably beautiful in the light of the day, but in the darkness of the night they took on a threatening aura. White, crumbling stone littered the path as row after row of family tombs lay in front of her. *A cemetery.* She was in one of the older, dilapidated cemeteries that littered the city.

Metal grated against metal. She could hear the sound of several men swearing as they wrenched the gate fully open. There was no time left. She pitched herself into the unknown, slipping as quietly as she could among the tombs.

Perhaps there was safety among the dead.

Crouching behind a large graying mausoleum, she held herself still, quieted her breath and tried to hear over the pounding of her heart. They were out there somewhere and they were hunting for her.

She could sense their perverted pleasure permeating the air. They were feeding off her fear, anticipating what they would do to her before they killed her. She shuddered and her stomach rolled at the thought of being raped by these three men before she died. And she *would* die. They would not let her live.

Anger flooded her body, pushing away the chains of fear. She would outsmart them or she would go down fighting. There was no way she would go easy, like some lamb to the slaughter. She was a Deveraux and Deverauxes were fighters and survivors.

She couldn't hear them now, but she knew that they were out there. Looking. Searching. They would not give up the hunt easily. But if she could slip out while they were searching the cemetery for her, she had a chance. They didn't know who she was, so if she eluded them this night, she was free.

Taking a deep breath, she calmed her body and her mind, and began to move. Stealthily, she slipped behind the stone mausoleums. Slowly and steadily she crept, stopping to listen every few steps. The gate was in view once again. This time it was wide open, and there was no one in sight.

Freedom was only steps away. She exploded like the shot out of a gun. One second she was still, the next she was almost at the iron gate.

Almost there.

She could taste success. Her hands reached out in front of her as if she could grasp her freedom and hold it —

Flying.

Suddenly, she was airborne, her body weightless as it flew through the air. There was no time to brace herself as she crashed down against the stone and dirt. Her head bounced off the hard ground and the breath was knocked out of her body. She lay there, dazed, hurt and confused.

He loomed over her, his body blocking what little light there was. His laughter echoed through the graveyard, low and sinister.

She dug her heels into the dirt, scrabbling backwards to escape him, but he reached down and grabbed her foot. Pulling hard, he yanked her towards him. "I've got her!" he yelled as he dropped to his knees and shoved her legs wide open.

She wanted to scream, but her throat had closed up with fear and the only sound she could make was more like the low moan of a wounded animal. Letting go of her legs his hands moved roughly up her body as he tore her blouse open and shoved her bra out of the way. She forced herself to ignore what he was doing to her. Because she wasn't fighting him, he would think that she was paralyzed with fear. Defeated.

Detaching herself from what he was doing to her body, she curled her hands into fists and struck hard and fast. Her arm shot straight towards his throat, her aim perfect. The weight left her body as he toppled off her, gasping for breath. Rolling to her side, she tried to drag herself to her feet.

But it was too late.

Flesh met flesh as the back of a man's hand cracked across her face and she tasted blood in her mouth. Falling back into the dirt she knew that this time there was no way out. She could hear them all swearing and arguing in the background, but she no longer cared. Deep in her mind, she cried out for help and was shocked when she got an answer.

"Who are you?" a calm, soothing male voice inquired.

"Delight Deveraux," she replied immediately. It never occurred to her not to answer the voice. As it washed over her, some of the pain receded, and she wanted desperately to hear it again.

There was silence for a long moment and despair filled her. Somehow the loss of his voice was worse than what was happening to her physical body. Delight could feel the men stripping off her shirt and squeezing her breasts, bruising and brutal as they mauled her. But it was almost as if that was happening to someone else. She was focused entirely on the voice in her head, trying to bring it back.

Her head fell to one side and she opened her eyes. A lone flowerpot sat in front of the tomb across from her. Their lovely blossoms were barely visible and looked black in the dark, yet they comforted her as she prepared to die.

"I am coming." The voice flooded her entire body with strength.

She heard the rasp of a zipper as one of her assailants knelt between her knees and shoved her thighs wide open. Acting on instinct, she drew back her leg and kicked him in the chest, knocking him backwards with her unexpected assault.

"Bitch," he swore as his fist came towards her. She closed her eyes and braced herself for the pain.

It never came.

Screams rent the night. High-pitched, terrified and male.

Rolling to her side and curling her body for protection, Delight squinted into the darkness but couldn't see anything. The sounds stopped abruptly. The silence was more frightening than the screams.

The darkness parted like a curtain and he was suddenly there in front of her. His eyes blazed like fire and pure menace radiated from every pore of his body. She glanced away, shaken by the intensity in his gaze.

Out of the corner of her eye, she could see the still body of one of her attackers. His sightless eyes were wide open, staring up at the night sky. Blood flowed from a wide slash in his neck and soaked into the ground around his head.

"Don't look at them." His softly spoken command made her flinch. This man was lethal in a way her assailants could never be. He was power. He was judgment and death.

Yet, his hands were gentle as he turned her onto her back. She could feel him touching her, soothing her aching flesh. It took her a moment to realize that he was dressing her, covering her naked body with her clothes. The reality of her ordeal began to sink in and she began to shake. The dark stranger sat down on the ground next to her and lifted her into his lap as easily as one would a child.

Biting her lip, she tried to hold back the tears that threatened. But then he stroked her bruised cheek with his fingers. Ever so softly, his lips grazed her wound. She was lost.

Huge sobs welled up inside her and spilled out of her mouth, their tortured sounds too loud in the quiet of the cemetery. Her entire body shook as she released her fear and pain.

Strong arms wrapped around her as he pulled her tighter into his embrace. Heat radiated from his massive body and she snuggled close to him, needing his warmth and comfort. He said nothing, but his chest rumbled as he made low comforting sounds.

Safe.

He made her feel safe in a world gone mad. She owed him her life. She had called and he had come. Time had no meaning as she poured out her tears. When she was finally spent, she sniffed and scrubbed her hands over her face before finally raising it to look at her savior.

The moon came from behind the clouds, illuminating his face. Long black hair fell over his shoulders in a silky curtain, framing a face that was harsh, yet beautiful in its own way. His cheekbones were chiseled, his forehead high, and his lips thin. But it was his eyes that captured her. A brilliant emerald green, they were hard and cold as he looked out over the night, but the moment he sensed her gaze on him, they changed. Heat radiated from their depths as he raised his fingers to her face and carefully brushed away the remains of her tears.

Something about this man called to her on a very deep physical and emotional level. Delight knew that she was still shaken after her ordeal and that the last thing she should want was a man's hands on her body. But her body wasn't listening to her. It was totally illogical, but this stranger made her feel protected, cherished, and wanted.

Slowly, he lowered his head. His lips were gentle as they covered hers. He tasted and nibbled every inch of her lips as if he had all the time in the world.

It was she who needed more. It was crazy, but she wanted him. His touch and caress would wipe out the stain of the men who had hurt her and make her feel whole again.

Her lips parted on a sigh as she raised her head towards him, offering him more. Delight could feel his smile against her mouth just before his tongue slipped inside. Sighing, she opened her mouth to him.

His tongue tasted her, mapping out every contour and finding every crevice. Delight lay in his arms, surrendering to the bliss. Cradling the back of her head with his hand, he held her securely as he kissed her. She leaned easily into his strength, trusting him to support her.

The muscles of his chest rippled under his shirt as she skimmed her hand over his torso. Continuing upward, she slid her hand behind his neck and urged him closer. When her tongue stroked his, he moaned deep in his chest, and she shivered as the sound vibrated throughout her entire body. Their tongues tangled slowly, a dance of seduction meant to entice and not to frighten.

Delight could feel his erection growing as it pushed against her leg. She should have been afraid, even disgusted after what had just happened to her. Instead, she felt an answering arousal well up deep within her. Her panties dampened as her body softened in preparation for receiving him. The inner muscles of her sex clenched as if begging for his cock. Her breasts swelled and her nipples tightened to aching points. Never had she been aroused so quickly or thoroughly in her life.

He coaxed her tongue into his mouth and then he sucked on it, drawing it deeper to him. Delight was immediately addicted to the slightly coppery taste and began to explore his mouth. He angled her face so that he could deepen the kiss. Her entire body was humming as she gave a little sound of encouragement.

His large hand cupped her breast, covering the soft mound completely. Squeezing gently, he moved his palm over the tip in a slow, easy circle. Delight tipped back her head and moaned. The moment her lips lost contact with his, he peppered her forehead, eyelids, cheeks, nose and chin with gentle, seductive kisses.

When his hand moved towards her other breast, she moaned again, this time in anticipation of the pleasure. She squirmed, trying to get closer to him, rubbing her thigh against his erection, loving the feel of his large cock against her leg.

His lips nuzzled her neck, nipping at her delicate skin. Desire pulsed from her swollen pussy to her breasts as she tilted her neck back, offering herself to him. She could sense his pleasure as she used the hand on the nape of his neck to pull him closer. Arching backwards, she was so lost in the pleasure of her arousal that the pain struck her unawares.

Crying out, she pulled away as pain shot through her back and shoulders. Her body went hot and then cold, and she could feel the clamminess of her skin as she broke out into a sweat.

He swore. Holding her carefully, he waited until the pain had subsided once again before pushing a damp strand of hair out of her face.

"I should not have forgotten your injuries. Forgive me?" His words were formal and tinged with an accent she couldn't place.

Although it was hard, she offered him a weak smile. "It's not your fault. I forgot them myself for a moment." But the moment was gone and memory flooded through her. She tried to sit up, but he held her easily, his arms velvet manacles around her.

"Why are you in my dream?" His words shocked her as understanding began to clear the cobwebs of her muddled mind.

"You're in my dream," she informed him.

He arched one his black eyebrows and gave her a superior male look. "I think not."

Delight had been having a variation of this nightmare for the past eight years. She was one of those few people who were able to master lucid dreaming, giving her the ability to be aware and exercise some control over them. Once she was fully cognizant of the dream, she always managed to wake herself up before they raped and killed her. Being chased and beaten was bad enough, even if it was just a dream.

But not tonight. Tonight had been different. This time the dream had been more real, more vicious and had continued long past its usual ending. She had been unable to stop it and had panicked.

Then he had come. Like some knight of old, he had rescued her and then claimed her as the spoils of victory. Now he had the nerve to tell her it was his dream, not hers.

"I've had the same dream for years." Even though every inch of her body hurt, it was still screaming with arousal. Ignoring it, she forced herself to continue. "You're definitely in my dream." She poked him in his chest for emphasis, but it was like hitting steel. There was definitely no give in this man's chest.

"This is unusual." He frowned down at her as if this was somehow all her fault.

She just shrugged at him. As much as she wanted to stay with him and explore the sexual possibilities with him, Delight knew that it was time to wake up now. She desperately needed to put this dream behind her and find her equilibrium.

"I have to go now." She tried once again to ease out of his arms.

"No." There was a note of desperation in his voice that had not been there before. "If you're real, then you are the one."

The intensity in his eyes began to scare her. They were turning from green to red right in front of her. The power that had been leashed suddenly lashed at her from all sides. Ignoring his pleas to stay, she clapped her hands over her ears and began to scream out loud. "Wake up! Wake up! Wake up!"

Chapter Two

ॐ

As she bolted upright in bed, Delight could swear she heard his anguished cry ringing in her ears. She reached out with her mind, suddenly afraid to lose all contact with him. But it was too late. He was gone. Their connection had been severed as if it had never been. She felt empty inside, like something special and important had been lost.

Falling back against her pillows, she rolled over and buried her face against them. She could feel the dampness of the tears she'd cried drying on her cheeks and the phantom pain in her back as it slowly disappeared.

Half an hour later, she rolled over and dragged her aching body out of bed. She felt totally exhausted and drained by her nocturnal activities. Who knew that a dream could be so real or so vivid? And it was just a dream. Common sense had seeped gradually back into her mind. Now all she needed was a shower and a cup of hot, steaming coffee to put her back to rights.

Wandering over to the window, she gazed out over the city she'd called home her entire life. The sun was rising for another day and it hung like a bloody orb in the sky, tingeing the city in red. Delight couldn't shake the feeling that it was a bad omen of things to come. New Orleans. The city of ghouls and legends and superstitions. There was no other place like it in the world.

Delight shivered even though the air wafting through the open window was warm. Rubbing her hands up and down her arms, she turned and padded silently to the connecting bathroom. She showered quickly, wrapped herself in a towel and returned to her bedroom to dress.

All the while, a pair of green eyes haunted her. Every time she closed her eyes, his face was there in front of her, waiting for her. She laughed as she dragged on a pair of panties and a matching bra in a pale mint color. The stranger in her dream certainly fit the criteria for being a dream-man. Handsome in a rugged way, he exuded an aura of sexuality and power. Definitely a man way out of her league.

Grabbing a long linen skirt in a light beige color, she topped it with a crisp, sleeveless white blouse. Examining herself in the mirror, she was pleased that her restless night didn't show on her face. Her hair was cut in a short style that fell easily into place every morning when she washed it. Its sandy brown color went well with her pale blue eyes. They were her best feature in an otherwise plain, heart-shaped face. Her lips were average, not too thin, not too thick, and her nose tilted upward just a smidgen.

Average height, build, and weight summed up everything about her as she frowned at her reflection. The only thing that was a little better than average was her breasts. At least they were a respectable thirty-four C-cup. At twenty-eight, she had long since accepted herself the way she was.

Sighing, she went to the closet and pulled out a pair of beige loafers and slipped her feet into them. Just because she was only five-foot-five didn't mean she wore heels. When you were on your feet all day like she was, comfort was the only thing that mattered.

Delight had one hand on the doorknob when she swore softly and stomped back over to her dresser. Picking up a tube of lipstick, she swiped the light shade across her lips. It didn't show up very much, but the rosy color flattered her features. It was more for her than for anyone else, giving her a sense that she was donning her professional armor so she could face the day a little more easily.

With a nod in the mirror, she turned and left her room. She was going to check her brother's room as she passed by, but she could hear Chase rummaging around inside. She thanked God every day that her brother was different from most other eighteen-year-olds.

Responsible, polite, hardworking, and a joy to be around, Chase had been her sole responsibility for the last ten years since the death of their mother to an unexpected fatal heart attack. Their father had abandoned them years before and neither of them thought about him much. He simply hadn't ever been a part of their lives.

Delight hurried down the back stairs. She could smell the coffee wafting on the breeze and she knew that Miss Nadine was already up and hard at work. Stopping at the bottom of the stairs, she smiled as she watched the older woman bustling around the kitchen.

Miss Nadine might be in her mid-sixties, but nobody had better suggest that she was old, or they'd get a tongue-lashing that they'd never recover from. Tall, thin, and full of energy, she worked nonstop from morning until night. Her face was long, but her mocha-colored skin was surprisingly smooth and unlined, except for the laugh lines around her mouth and eyes. Always smiling, she kept her thick black hair swept up in a fashionable chignon. She looked more like an aging movie starlet than someone's grandmother. Her chocolate-brown eyes were shrewd, her heart was as big as an ocean, and Delight loved her like a mother.

Ten years ago, she'd shown up on the front doorstep of Miss Nadine Grande's Bed and Breakfast with little Chase's hand clasped tight in hers. Boldly, she'd knocked on the door and announced that she was there about the live-in position of maid/cook/waitress. Delight had worn some of her mother's makeup, trying her best to look older than her eighteen years. But the truth was, she was desperate. Their mother's death had left them in dire straits. They were being evicted from their apartment at the end of the month, and if she couldn't find a job she would lose Chase to a foster home.

Miss Nadine had taken one look at her and ushered them into the kitchen where she proceeded to feed them breakfast all the while dragging their entire life story out of them. She did it so smoothly that the story had been tumbling from Delight's lips with no way to stop it. Chase had started crying quietly and Delight had picked up her young brother and headed towards the door, knowing she'd blown one of her few employment opportunities.

She'd never made it out of the kitchen.

Miss Nadine's no-nonsense voice stopped her in her tracks, asking her if she could start immediately. They'd packed their belongings and moved into the small attic apartment of the three-story bed-and-breakfast that very day. Delight had worked hard to make sure that Miss Nadine never regretted her decision. The job had been perfect for her, and the two women had forged a deep friendship.

Chase had benefited the most. Delight was able to be there for him when he got home from school every day. She was able to participate in his school activities while providing a roof over his head and food on the table. But even as a child, Chase had done his share of work around "The Grande", as they all called it. Now at eighteen, he worked part-time at an art supply store during the school year, keeping himself in pocket money and art supplies. He was a talented sculptor and worked in wood, stone, and metal, selling his creations down at Jackson Square.

"You gonna stand there all day or do you want some coffee?" Miss Nadine's smooth tones cut through Delight's thoughts like a knife, making her hurry into the kitchen.

"Sorry I'm a little slow this morning." Delight hated that she'd slept late. It was only seven, but she was usually helping in the kitchen by now.

The older woman just glared at her as she whipped the batter for her famous pecan pancakes. "You work too hard, child." Plunking the bowl on the counter, she shook her spoon at Delight. "Here all day and then bartending at that fancy restaurant four nights a week. You need to get out and have some fun. Maybe have a social life." Grumbling, she tested the griddle before pouring some batter on its hot surface. "When was the last time you had a date?"

Delight opened her mouth to speak and slowly closed it. She thought and thought.

"There you go," Miss Nadine said as she watched the pancakes cook. "Child, I date more than you do and that's just not right."

"I just haven't met anyone that interests me." Even as she spoke the words, the man from her dreams popped into her head. Just the thought of him sent a shiver down her spine and made her feel all hot and bothered. She could feel the moisture between her legs making her panties damp, and suddenly her nipples had become hard pebbles pushing against the cups of her bra. To hide her discomfort, she hurried to the cupboard, pulled down a mug, poured herself a cup of coffee, and took a fortifying sip.

Keeping her back to Miss Nadine, who usually saw way too much with those laser brown eyes, she went to the refrigerator and pulled out fresh fruit. Carrying it to the counter, she began to section oranges with the ease of long experience. "Besides, I make good money at Etienne's and the tips are good." Wielding the knife like a machete, she attacked the bananas next. "Chase wants to go to art school and he's too talented not to get the opportunity."

"And what about you, child?" The soft words struck Delight like a cruel whip, lacerating her soul.

Swallowing hard, she tossed the fruit into a large glass bowl and began to pluck green grapes from the bunch. "I'm fine just the way I am." And she was, she reminded herself, blinking back tears.

Miss Nadine opened her mouth to speak, but the moment was lost when they heard the stomping of large sneakers down the back stairs. Chase came to an abrupt halt when he entered the kitchen. He looked from one woman to the other before proceeding with caution into the room. "Everything okay?" His voice was casual, but his expression showed his concern.

Chase had always been sensitive, even as a child, and Delight knew that was part of what would help him become a great artist and an even better man. Walking over to her little brother, she tilted her head back and peered into pale blue eyes that were just like her own. Her little brother was over six feet tall and filling out more and more every day.

Reaching up, she patted him on the cheek. "Everything is fine. Now have breakfast so you won't be late for work." Now that school was out for the summer, he was working full-time at the art store and working on his own sculptures in his spare time.

"You're sure?" Catching her hand in his much larger, rougher one, he gave it a squeeze.

"I'm sure," she smiled up at him. All she wanted out of life was for Chase to be happy and be able to pursue his art. Life was flowing just the way she wanted it to, and if sometimes she was a little lonely and wanted a little more from life, well that was just too bad. Her life had been a good one so far and she wouldn't change a single moment of it.

"Stubborn," Miss Nadine muttered under her breath as she flipped pancakes onto a large plate and handed them to Chase.

"And don't you forget it," Delight taunted. With the sun shining in through the kitchen window, making patterns of light and shadow on the wall, and the three of them together, she felt the last remnants of her nightmare fade away.

And when she heard the sound of footsteps on the front stairs, she hurried out of the kitchen to bid one of the guests good morning as she led him into the dining room. Another normal day was about to begin.

Chapter Three

ജ

Lucian Dalakis came completely awake in the blink of an eye. One moment he was in a dead sleep, the next he was wide awake, alert and totally aware of his surroundings. Lying in his large, luxurious bed that had once belonged to a Russian prince, he mentally scanned his home. None of the doors or windows had been tampered with and every stick of antique furniture was in its place. Everything was as it should be. He was alone.

The remnants of his dream played over and over in his head like an unending loop. The dream had hit him as soon as he'd closed his eyes just before dawn. He could enter other people's dreams at will, but it was rare for his kind to have dreams of their own. So when it did happen, he paid attention. He prided himself on his cool, urbane demeanor and his control. But in his dream, he'd had neither.

When he'd first heard her cry, it was as if someone had stuck a knife in his heart. Her pain was his pain. Then his anger had stirred like a sleeping beast suddenly unleashed. It was unlike anything he'd ever experienced. He wanted—no, needed—to kill those men who had dared to put their hands on her body. Dared to hurt her. Even now, his fangs lengthened and his hands curled into fists at the mere thought.

Taking a deep breath, he slowly unclenched his fingers and forced himself to relax. It was only a dream. Even as he told himself that, he knew that he didn't believe it. It was more than a dream. She was as real as he was and she was out there in the city. Alone. Unprotected. Waiting for him.

He could still taste her on his lips. A combination of honey and sweet woman. His tongue flicked over his teeth, savoring the flavor. Lucian had lived a long, long time and had made love to many women—all kinds of women. They fascinated him with their soft skin, scent, curves and hollows. But never had he felt such a need in his life as he did for this particular woman.

Delight. Her name suited her. Delicate features gave her an ethereal air, and her pale blue eyes shone out of the face of an angel. She'd worn no makeup, and hadn't needed any. Even though she'd been pale with fear, her skin was smooth and soft. Her short, light brown hair framed her face to perfection. But her body was a surprise. She was average in height, and slender with subtle curves. But her breasts were lush and full, more than capable of filling his large hands. His fingers itched to stroke and caress the soft mounds of flesh and pluck at her nipples.

Just thinking of her made him hard. His cock was long and thick and throbbing. If she were here next to him, he'd already be buried to the hilt in her moist, welcoming heat. She'd be so damned sweet. He'd try to take his time, to draw out the pleasure, but he was doubtful that he'd last long the first time he fucked her. It would probably be hard, fast and over much sooner than he wanted.

But the next time he would take his time and savor every delectable inch of her supple body. She'd been eager in the dream, reaching for him, pulling him closer. Closing his eyes, he pictured her naked, spread out before him on his bed like a sumptuous banquet just waiting to be sampled. She would arch her back, pushing her breasts towards him while she opened her luscious thighs, offering herself to him.

Her pussy would be hot, moist, and pink as blood flowed to the area, as she grew more aroused. He could imagine his tongue tasting the soft, slick folds. Her skin would taste salty and divine. For an appetizer, he would nibble on her breasts, enjoying their texture and shape while teasing her rosy nipples into even tighter buds of desire.

While his mouth was pleasuring her breasts, he would touch her entire body, stroking and examining every inch, until there wasn't one part of her that he didn't know intimately. Only when she was a mass of burning desire would he touch her clit.

Softly at first until she cried out and begged him for more. She'd spread her legs wide and arch her back frantically off the bed, pleading for him to take her. Begging for him to fuck her.

He'd tell her to roll over and offer herself to him. That was the way he wanted to take her. From behind, he could mount her and fuck her until they both found the release they needed. Delight was a feast for the senses, just waiting for him to take the first bite. And he would. Because as much as he wanted to fuck her, he wanted to taste her even worse.

When he was fucking her from behind, he would lean over her, trapping her body beneath him. Her neck would be exposed and vulnerable to him. As he pounded into her from behind, she would arch back to meet him, offering him everything. Then he would graze his teeth over the back of her neck before sinking his teeth deep and drinking from her.

Sweat rolled off his body as his cock jerked. Beads of liquid seeped from the tip as he imagined how tight she would be. Her pussy would clamp down hard on his cock even as he rode her hard. Wrapping his fingers around his cock, he pumped his hand up and down all the while imagining himself buried inside Delight's welcoming body. Her heat would be incredible as it surrounded him.

Lucian could almost hear her moans of pleasure as he imagined clasping her breasts in his hands and rolling their tight buds between his thumbs and forefingers. She was his to take however he chose, whenever he chose. Tipping his head back, he groaned with pleasure as his fist continued to slide up and down his hard length.

His testicles drew up tight to his body and he could feel the blood pounding through his veins. Lucian craved her taste like a dying man in a desert yearns for water. His fangs ached for just a sip of her sweet blood.

Alive. She made him feel so damned alive. His hand continued its frantic pace and his breath caught as he came. Liquid gushed over his belly and chest. Groaning, he milked his cock, drawing out every ounce of pleasure. When he was finally spent, he sank back against the pillows. Replete, but not satisfied or relaxed. If anything, he was even more tense than when he'd awoke.

He could still smell her blood. Her attackers had hurt her in the dream, drawing her precious blood from her body. Lucian growled low in his throat and his eyes snapped open, blazing like green fire.

Delight was his and he would kill anyone who hurt her.

Throwing back the covers, he rose from his bed. Unconcerned by his nakedness, he stood on the platform that the bed sat on and wiped the cum off his stomach with the corner of the sheet.

Stretching his arms over his head, he stepped down to the floor and padded towards the thickly shuttered window, his muscles rippling with every movement he made.

Pressing a button that was hidden under the windowsill, he waited as the heavy metal shutter rose silently, exposing the night to his view. She was out there. Somewhere. This was his city and he would find her.

If she wasn't a dream, then she was the one. The one he'd been waiting for his entire life, but had given up hope of ever finding. If she was real, then she was his curse and his salvation. His destiny. His only chance to love. For over five hundred years he had waited for her, all but giving up hope.

But now, for better or worse, his life was changed. It was no longer his own, as his very life-force was now linked to hers. It was the curse of his family. The Dalakis curse. Passed from father to son throughout the eons of time. Dalakis children were always male and the curse was theirs from birth. To love only once in their lifetime. They did not choose who to love, but rather it was chosen for them by nature or by God—which, he wasn't sure.

Many of his family had given up in despair and faced the killing midday sunlight rather than live through the long years without finding their one true love. Others had done the same after being rejected by their chosen love. Still some had joined their chosen mates in death after living a human lifetime.

It took a strong woman, and a rare one, to take the chance of the conversion. To risk dying so that she could be reborn as a true Dalakis bride. A vampire bride. To then live in the night as he must, to survive on blood and be feared and misunderstood. It was not a life most women chose. And there was no forcing her. A Dalakis male had to accept his mate's choice. It was hers to make. But that didn't mean that a Dalakis male wouldn't do everything in his power to convince her to accept him. And he had many powers. Seduction but one of them.

What had seemed like an impossible dream was now a possibility. His older brother Cristofor had claimed his own woman recently. His new sister-in-law, Johanna, was indeed a prize and a credit to the Dalakis family.

A rare smile crossed his harsh features as he pictured his brother's bossy little wife trying to manage all of them. She was taking her role of family matriarch very seriously and if she caught wind of the fact that Lucian was on the trail of his own woman, she and Cris would be here in New Orleans within twenty-four hours.

That, he didn't want. For one thing, Cris and Johanna were still on their honeymoon. And for another, he much preferred to pursue Delight himself without family interference. He had no way of knowing what her life was like or what obstacles they both might face.

His head jerked up as he sensed an intruder. Sensing who it was, he relaxed and gave a chuckle of self-deprecation. He wouldn't be able to escape all of his family interference. Sending out a mental command, the door unlocked and swung open as his visitor approached.

"Are you all right?"

Lucian turned and faced his younger brother Stefan, who lounged in the doorway. It was almost like looking in a mirror. They were much alike in looks except that Stefan was a little bit taller than he was. They both had the same harsh, Dalakis features and brilliant emerald green Dalakis eyes, but they were as different as day and night.

He was more controlled, urbane and old-fashioned than Stefan. Lucian's home in the French Quarter reflected his taste. Decorated tastefully with antiques and items of quality, it had a refined air about it. He liked classical and jazz music, and drove a luxury sedan.

Stefan owned the house next door to his and it reflected his unique personality. Filled with every electronic gadget known to mankind, it was furnished with sturdy, comfortable wood furniture. His brother listened to rock and country music, and drove a big black pickup truck.

"I'm fine." He answered because he knew that his brother had the patience of a saint and would stand there all night waiting for him to answer.

"You dreamed." Stefan moved further into the room, coming closer but still giving Lucian his space.

"How did you know?"

Stefan shrugged his large shoulders that were covered in a plain white, cotton T-shirt. He propped his hands on his jeans-covered hips and cocked his head to one side as he stared at his brother. "I can't explain it. I just knew that you dreamed and that it was important."

Lucian ran his fingers through his long hair, pushing it out of his face. "She's out there." Turning, he looked out over the twinkling lights of the city. He could feel the tension rolling off Stefan in waves as he waited for him to continue.

"What is her name?" Stefan's words were almost a reverent whisper.

"Delight Deveraux." Her name rolled off his tongue easily. He could hear Stefan repeating the name under his breath. "Now I just have to find her."

"What do you want me to do?"

Lucian closed his eyes and gave silent thanks to his brother. All three brothers were close and there was never any hesitation or doubt that one would come to the aid of the other. "Nothing for now."

He held up his hand to stop his brother before he could speak. "First, I must find her. I may need your help later, but for now there is nothing anyone can do."

Stefan gave a little laugh. "You might want to get dressed before you go looking for her."

Lucian looked down at his naked body, not surprised to find himself semi-aroused yet again at the thought of Delight. "Hmm. You're probably right."

"I'll wait for you downstairs and we'll go hunting together."

Before he could speak, Stefan was gone. His younger brother had a surprising stubborn streak and Lucian knew that he would have to let him help with the search for a few hours before he'd be able to go off on his own. As he padded to the bathroom to take a shower, he reflected that it was good to have family.

Chapter Four

ဆာ

"Why did I agree to stay late?" Delight didn't expect an answer, as she was one of only two people left in the restaurant. It was just after two in the morning and most of the staff had left a half-hour ago.

Tossing her pen and clipboard on her boss's desk, she rolled her tired shoulders. She really didn't have any choice in staying late. She needed the money that working at a fancy restaurant like Etienne's gave her. Being a bartender in such a swanky place meant decent pay and tips if you were good at your job.

And she was very good.

Because she was unassuming, people relaxed around her. That fact, coupled with her ability to read people, made her a natural at her job. She instinctively knew when people needed to chat and when they just wanted to be left alone. She mixed, poured and served drinks quickly and efficiently, all the while keeping track of who was drinking what.

What she didn't like was the fact that the manager, James Brenner, had a tendency to ogle the female staff and abuse his position of authority. Like tonight. She'd been almost out the door when James had decided that they needed a full inventory of the liquor and wine stocks.

Swallowing her anger, she had gone off to the wine cellar to count bottles, taking care to lock the door behind her. She wasn't stupid and wasn't about to chance being caught unaware by her groping boss.

But now she was finished her last shift for the week and more than ready to go home. Rolling her shoulders to release the tension, she strolled back to the employee's locker room and gathered up her belongings. Tugging her light cotton sweater over her crisp white blouse, she looped her small purse over her head and shoulder and went in search of her boss. She wasn't even sure if he was still here, but she'd check with Chuck, the night janitor, before she called a cab to take her home.

It had been a good night at work and she had fifty dollars in tips tucked in her pants pockets. She hurried down the corridor, relieved to hear voices in the distance. Etienne's was usually a bustling establishment filled with music, chatter and laughter. But this late at night, it was quiet, kind of creepy and covered in shadows.

Delight slowed as she approached the main dining area. From the sound of the voices, it was obvious that someone was having a fight and the last thing she wanted was to get caught in the middle of some dispute. Creeping down to the end of the hallway, she peeked around the corner.

Two big men flanked her boss while another stood in front of him. At first glance it looked to be no more than four men having a heated conversation. Then one of the men shifted and Delight noticed the gun.

"I can pay. I just need more time." Sweat rolled down James Brenner's face as he pleaded for his life.

"You've had time." The man with the gun shook his head regretfully.

James tried to pull away, but the two goons on either side of him held him in place. "I'll pay more."

Delight was frozen in place, not knowing what to do. She was afraid to move, not wanting their attention turned on her, but she had to do something to help. She glanced towards the bar and almost cried out. A pair of legs stuck out from behind a table with a mop lying next to them. Chuck. It had to be Chuck, and she couldn't tell if he was dead or alive. Her head snapped back to the scene in front of her. The fear in James' voice grew as he pleaded with the man who seemed to be in charge.

"If only it was just the money, James." The man with the gun was speaking. With his stylish hair and fashionable clothing he looked more like a banker than a killer, but there was a cruel look on his face that said he was enjoying James' fear.

Shivering, Delight pulled back deeper into the shadows. She would sneak back to the office and call the police. "You should have kept your mouth shut about Mr. Prince's business."

"I didn't say anything." James fell to his knees in front of the man. "I didn't talk." He was crying now. She could see the tears falling freely down his face. Her knees were shaking as she moved a step back towards the office, her eyes never leaving the scene in front of her.

"That's not what Mr. Prince heard." The man raised the gun and fired it once. James swayed for a moment before falling facedown on the floor with a heavy thud.

Delight gasped, slapping a hand over her mouth to stop the sound. But it was too late. Three pairs of hostile eyes snapped in her direction and then the man with the gun smiled. It was a truly dreadful smile. One that said he had enjoyed what he had just done and was looking forward to dealing with her.

"What have we here?"

The sound of his voice snapped her out of her trance. Turning, she raced down the hallway and into the kitchen. Reaching out her hand, she slapped off light switches as she went. She could hear the men swearing and banging into things as they chased her, but she didn't dare look back. She ran straight through the kitchen and out the back emergency.

The alarm sounded the moment she opened the door, and she could only pray that help would come and that it wouldn't be too late for her and Chuck. There was no hope for James Brenner. He was dead.

She turned the corner of the alleyway just as she heard the restaurant door slam open behind her. "Come back here, you little bitch!"

Delight continued running. She wasn't long-legged, but she was fast. And she was running for her life. Ignoring the pain in her side and chest, she gasped for air. Her lungs were burning, her body starved for oxygen, but she never faltered.

Usually there were people on the streets all hours of the day and night, but for some reason they seemed almost bare. She raced past a drunk passed out against a building. Common sense told her to run into the first open business and get help, but a small voice inside her head told her that the men chasing her would kill whoever helped her.

It was just like her dream except for one major difference. This was real. Her boss had just been murdered in front of her, three men were chasing her, and when they caught her, they were going to kill her. Instinct had her racing towards St. Louis No. 1 Cemetery. It was close to home and fairly familiar to her. If she could lose them there, among the maze of tombstones and mausoleums, she could slip back out, run home and call the police.

She only wished that the stranger from her dream were here. She could use a knight in shining armor about now. Mentally, Delight sent out a plea for help and was shocked when a voice in her head replied. "Where are you?"

The lack of oxygen and fear must be causing her to hallucinate. It was the only explanation she could come up with. Sucking air into her lungs, she continued to run.

Her shoes pounded the pavement, and her breathing was ragged. It was hard to hear over the pounding of her heart, but she knew that the men were right behind her. She could feel their evil stalking her.

"Where are you?" The voice was more demanding now. Male, annoyed, and authoritative.

Before Delight could even think to reply, she heard a shout behind her.

"There she is."

Glancing over her shoulder, she could see them getting closer to her. Her legs were shaking and threatening to collapse, but she forged onward. The cemetery was still too far away, so she ducked behind a building, clinging to the shadows.

She stumbled over something in the darkness and fell to her hands and knees. Biting her lip, she swallowed back her cry of pain and pushed herself to her feet. Ignoring the stinging in her palms and knees, she limped further down the alley.

The hand came out of nowhere, spinning her around and flinging her to the ground. Pain shot through her entire body as she landed hard, skidding across the rocks and dirt. She struggled to breathe as she rolled to her side. A large male shoe planted itself in the middle of her chest and pushed her flat on her back.

"I've got her."

Delight could just make out one of the two large goons who'd held James captive at the restaurant. Gripping his ankle, she tried to push his foot off her chest, but he just laughed and ground his heel deeper, making her cry out in pain.

More cruel laughter echoed in the dark as the other two men joined them. "Well, well. What do we have here?" The man with the cruel face and the banker's clothing moved closer to her, circling her supine body as he taunted her. "Not very pretty, but still, not bad I suppose."

He glanced at his watch and sighed. "I don't have time for you. Pity." Leaning down, he gripped her cheeks between his fingers, squeezing tight. "The boys won't be too rough with you. And if you don't fight, it will all be over soon." Turning, he walked away. "Finish her and meet me back at the Club. I've got a meeting with the boss." He never looked back as he tossed her death sentence casually over his shoulder.

The man with his huge shoe buried in her chest just smiled. Tipping her head back, she tried to scream, but nothing came out of her mouth except a low moan. Between the pressure on her chest and fear, she could barely breathe.

Then the weight was gone. She gasped, desperately trying to drag air into her starving lungs. The strap of her purse was pulled tight across her neck making it harder to breathe. Large, hurtful hands grabbed her shirt, ripping it open. The buttons pinged off the wall next to her as her attacker tore the cloth easily. His fingers dug into her breasts as he grunted. "Not much to her, but her tits are nice and big."

"Just fuck the little cunt so I can have my turn." The other man spoke from the shadows, sounding both impatient and excited.

Delight closed her eyes and gathered her remaining strength. She would fight until there was no breath left in her body. She sent her love to Chase and Miss Nadine, knowing that she would never see them again. Tears seeped from the corners of her eyes as she sprawled in the dirt and waited for an opportunity to fight.

He leaned closer and licked the side of her face. "Fight me." He squeezed her breasts hard. "I like it when they fight."

The air became like a vacuum with all noise absorbed. Menace filled the alley and the man on top of her raised his head to listen. Then he was gone. Plucked from on top of her by an unseen force. Delight heard the cracking of bones and a scream of absolute terror. Then silence.

Just like my dream, she thought, as she drifted in a haze of pain. Then warm, strong arms wrapped themselves around her, lifted her off the hard, dirty ground. Comforting her. Protecting her. "I've got you, little one." His voice enveloped her in its warmth, cocooning her from the pain.

But there was something important she had to tell him. Her forehead wrinkled as she tried to remember. As he carried her away, she glimpsed the bodies of her two tormentors. There was no doubt that they were both dead. After all, no one could live with a broken neck.

Funny how she wasn't afraid with this man. She recognized him from her dreams. Trusted him to keep her safe. There was something she had to tell him. Something important, but the pain kept distracting her.

An image popped in her mind and she closed her eyes and swallowed hard to keep the bile from rising from her stomach. "They killed him." Her voice shook and her teeth began to chatter. She was so cold.

"Don't try and talk." His lips grazed her forehead, soothing her slightly. "Give me your memories."

Delight wasn't quite sure what he meant by that. But she felt a slight push in her mind as if someone were trying to come into her brain. Mentally, she opened the door and felt him drift into her senses. Memories of the evening played in her mind like a motion picture and then it was over.

"Sleep now." His voice washed over her as he cradled her carefully in his arms. "I will take care of everything. You belong to me now."

"But who are you?" It was becoming almost impossible to stay awake. The darkness of unconsciousness loomed in front of her, luring her to its forgetfulness.

She felt the deep rumble in his chest and cuddled closer to his warmth. "I am Lucian Dalakis. And I am your destiny."

Delight was too tired to debate the issue. Her eyes closed, but she fought sleep. "Chase..." She tried to convey her worry about her brother, but talking was becoming way too difficult.

"Trust me, Delight. All will be taken care of." His arms tightened around her even as his voice lulled her.

It was foolish to put all her trust in a man that she didn't even know, but it was as natural to her as breathing. She didn't even question how he knew her name. As if his word was all she needed, she gave herself over to his healing power and slept.

Chapter Five

સ્ઃ

Lucian strode away from the alley without a backwards glance. Delight shivered in his arms and he clutched her tighter. Anger rolled through him. It was like a growing tidal wave that grew with every step he took. He almost wished that the men lying dead in the dirt were alive again, just so he could kill them again. That they would lay their filthy hands on his Delight and harm her was beyond his comprehension. They were lucky he killed them quickly and cleanly when what he'd really wanted to do was rend them limb by limb.

Delight's moan pierced his heart like a knife. He wanted to hear her moan, but in pleasure, not in pain or fear. Quickly, he raced through the Quarter towards his home. Her weight was nothing to him and his speed was faster than the human eye could see. Lucian knew he wouldn't be content until he had her safely locked behind the walls of his home where he could protect her.

The door swung open as he approached. Every muscle in his body clenched, battle-ready. His fangs lengthened and he growled a warning.

Stefan barely glanced at him. His eyes were glued on Delight. Lucian held her even tighter in his embrace, possessive as he'd never been in his life.

"Your room is ready." Stefan ignored Lucian's threatening demeanor. "I drew a hot bath. I didn't know if she'd need it or not."

Drawing a deep breath, Lucian slowly released it. This was his brother, whom he trusted above all others. Still, it was hard to release the fury of his emotions. No one would take Delight from him and live.

As if sensing his unsettled emotions, Stefan stepped back, giving him plenty of room. Lucian felt his brother scanning his mind, silently asking for details. All of it came flooding back to Lucian. The anger and then the fear that he wouldn't be in time to save her from harm. Then the unholy satisfaction when he'd killed her tormentors and fed on their blood.

Stefan took it all in and then headed for the front door. "Take care of your woman, I'll dispose of the bodies."

"Thank you." His words were softly spoken, but he knew that his brother heard him. With one hand on the doorknob, Stefan stopped and turned.

"It is no more or less than you would do for me." Again, Stefan stared at Delight with a deep yearning in his eyes. "Hold her tight and kill all who would threaten her. If you did any less you would not be a Dalakis." Then he was gone, swallowed up into the darkness of the night. The door slammed shut and bolted behind him.

Lucian climbed the stairs and strode down the hall, carrying his precious bundle into the master suite. Carefully, he placed her on the silky coverlet. Was it only a few hours ago that he'd dreamed of having her here with him? Now that she was here in the flesh it was almost too much for him to comprehend. Delight was no longer just a dream, but a flesh and blood woman, and she was his.

Gingerly, he unhooked the purse that was still slung around her neck and tossed it on the floor. Rolling up the sleeves of his shirt, he went to work. Taking care not to disturb her, he stripped her dirty, torn clothing from her body. Bruises marred her pale white flesh, stoking the fire of his anger once again.

With great difficulty, he buried his fury, focusing his total concentration on Delight. Nothing mattered beyond her comfort and well-being.

When she was totally naked, he lifted her into his arms once again and carried her to the master bath where a steaming bath was waiting for them. Silently thanking his brother for his foresight and thoughtfulness, he lowered Delight into the water.

Her eyelids fluttered and then her eyes shot open, large and fearful. Frantically, she pushed against his chest, splashing water everywhere, but he kept one arm wrapped around her shoulders until he was certain she was settled safely in the tub. Slipping his arm away, he sat on the floor and leaned over the smooth marble edge that rimmed the large tub. "You are safe now. Nothing can harm you here." He purposely made his voice soft and non-threatening.

"You saved me." Her panic eased when he released her. She seemed a little dazed and uncertain and her blue eyes looked enormous in her pale face.

"Yes." Lucian soaped a soft sea sponge and began to draw it over her arms and chest, washing away the filth and fear of her ordeal.

Uttering a small cry of distress, Delight crossed her arms over her chest even as she curled her body into a tight little ball. "Go away."

The sight of her like that almost brought him to his knees, but her feisty words assured him that she would be fine in time. Carefully, Lucian cupped her chin with his fingers and tilted her face up to meet his.

Stubbornly, she tried to keep her face averted, but he was just as stubborn as she and kept up a steady pressure until she finally relented. Scowling, she lifted her eyes to his. "Well?"

He tried desperately not to laugh, for she was spitting like a bedraggled kitten. But Lucian was no fool when it came to women and he knew that she wouldn't appreciate the analogy. "There is no need to hide your body from me or to fear me."

"You're a complete stranger, so you'll excuse me if we have a difference of opinion over that." Delight spoke calmly, but he could sense her discomfort and rising fear.

"I am no stranger. I am the other half of you. The part that has been missing your entire life." Lucian released her face, again picked up the sponge, and began to run it gently up and down her legs.

Delight shifted in the tub, but didn't pull away from him. "You know me," his mesmerizing voice cajoled her. "You've dreamed of me. Of the pleasure I can bring you." Dropping the sponge, he allowed his fingers to trace her hipbone. "Of the pleasure we can bring one another."

He could feel her heart pounding in her chest as his hand glided up her side and over her shoulder, until he was cupping her neck. Keeping his large hand wrapped around her fragile neck, he tilted up her chin with his thumb. Capturing her gaze with his, he slowly lowered his mouth to hers.

Lucian didn't kiss her right away. He didn't want to rush her or scare her. He wanted her to want him, so he bent all his considerable skills to the pleasurable task of seducing her.

His tongue traced the contours of her lips, memorizing their shape, reveling in their soft texture. Delight tasted faintly of cherries and he knew it was from the translucent lip gloss that she usually wore. He nibbled at her lips, running his tongue along the seam where they met. Slowly, like a petal opening to the sun, they parted and he slipped just inside. Not far, just enough for him to taste the honey of her mouth.

His patience was rewarded when her tongue darted out to touch his before retreating. The game of advance and retreat was played out over and over until Lucian thought he'd go mad with desire. His own lungs were pumping hard and his entire body was throbbing. The press of his cock against the zipper of his pants was almost painful, urging him to bury himself in her warmth and ride her until they were both sated. Yet, he did nothing more than gently kiss her.

It was Delight who finally deepened their embrace. Her hands, which had been clasped tight over her breasts, gradually slid up over his chest, leaving a damp trail on his shirt. He groaned when her fingers sifted through the long strands of his hair, cupping the back of his head and urging him closer to her.

He wrapped both of his hands around the edges of the tub to keep from touching her. Using only his mouth, Lucian plunged into Delight. Their tongues stroked and dueled as he angled his head so he could get deeper inside. Taking his time, he enjoyed her unique texture and flavor.

Like the clever hunter he was, Lucian withdrew from her mouth, lightly skimming his lips against hers. Luring her to him. Delight followed him. This time it was she who thrust her tongue into his waiting warmth. He allowed her the lead, letting her do as she pleased, waiting until she urged his tongue to play with hers.

Her hands were tightly wrapped in his hair, her fingers massaging his skull. Lucian reveled in the sensual delight she gave him as she touched him with her mouth and her hands.

Unconsciously, she arched her back in the tub, offering her breasts to him even as her legs relaxed in the water and parted slightly. Like a sexy water nymph, she tempted him to take her.

Lucian's blood was pumping through his veins along with all the emotion of the evening. It was a dangerous cocktail of lust, anger, possession, and tenderness, all vying for control of his mind and body. Bloodlust was roaring through him, as he smelled her blood and her arousal. Its seductive scent drifted up to him. His nostrils flared as he took a deep breath and pulled away from Delight.

A cry of disappointment filled the air as she tried to bring his mouth back to hers. But he forced himself to ignore it. "I want you."

"Yes," she murmured as she lolled back against the tub.

He almost grabbed her then, but he had to be sure. "Delight." He knew his voice was harsh, but need was riding him hard and there was no gentleness left in him. The water slopped over the side of the tub as she sat up abruptly. He knew he had her full attention now.

"I want you." His words were raw and unadorned. "I want to bury my cock so deep in your body you won't know where I end and you begin. I want to fuck you so many times you won't remember what it was like before me. I want to touch you, taste you, and take you every way possible. I want to eat your pussy and I want you to suck my cock until I come in your mouth. I want to make you mine in every way possible." He paused for a moment, his eyes burning with desire as he stared at her. "Do you understand?"

Delight opened her mouth to speak, but nothing came out. He could see the fine shivers that racked her entire body. Tipping back his head, he closed his eyes, unwilling to see her denial. It was his fault for pushing her so hard and fast.

But he was fighting his own instincts as well. And they were screaming at him to bind her to him using any methods possible. Right now that meant sexually. His cock was throbbing in rhythm to the blood pumping in his veins. He wanted to pound into her soft, welcoming body until they both came over and over. But time was running out. There was only a few hours left in the night and he wanted to spend them fucking Delight.

So light was her touch that he didn't feel it at first over the raging desire that racked his body. He sensed it more than he felt it. Almost afraid that it wasn't real, he slowly lowered his head and opened his eyes. Her small hand covered his where it gripped the edge of the tub. He absently noted that some of the marble had crumbled under his punishing grip.

Her face was solemn as she nodded at him. It wasn't enough. He needed the words. "Tell me what you want."

She flinched slightly at his order, but never faltered. "You. I want you, Lucian." Giving him a small, hesitant smile, she patted his hand. "I don't know why I trust you, but I do. And I've never wanted a man the way I want you."

"You're sure? Because once you are mine there is no going back." His face was as fierce as his words. "What is mine, I hold." Leaning down, he brought his lips close to hers. "Forever." It was a promise that he sealed with a searing kiss.

Delight threw her arms around his shoulders and he plucked her out of the tub. Water sluiced from her body, soaking him, but he didn't care. She'd dry soon enough and he wouldn't be dressed much longer. His lips never leaving hers, he carried her back to his bedroom and his bed.

Chapter Six

ഔ

Delight hardly recognized herself. She wasn't the type of woman who slept with a man she hardly knew. In fact, she'd only slept with two men in her entire life. Well, really one boy and one man.

The first had been a one-night stand with a male friend a few nights after her mother had died. Delight had been looking for comfort and Brad had been only too happy to oblige. Their friendship hadn't survived as the experience hadn't been that great for either one of them. Delight had been emotionally fragile and a virgin, and Brad had lacked the necessary restraint and finesse to make the experience enjoyable.

Her second attempt at a romantic relationship had been with a man she'd dated for a while in her early twenties. It wasn't easy for a young, single woman who was raising a child on her own to get many dates. Most guys didn't want a woman who was tied down so much, so it had been a surprise when Mason Dean had asked her out. Older and more sophisticated, Mason was a banker. Delight had been flattered by his attention. It was unfortunate that she hadn't found out about his wife until after they'd slept together.

Since that debacle Delight had dated, but very infrequently. She'd been burned twice and wasn't willing to risk her heart or self-respect again. That's why her behavior around Lucian surprised her. She barely knew him, but she trusted him implicitly.

She peeked up at him as he carried her into his bedroom. The man was beautiful in a harsh and wholly masculine way. With his high cheekbones and forehead, and thin lips, his face had no softness. Even his eyes were hard, their green depths as piercing and sharp as emeralds. Yet the man oozed a sensuality that would attract women to him like bees to nectar.

His arms were like steel bands around her, his grip unbreakable. There wasn't an ounce of flab anywhere on the man. There would be no escaping him.

Delight had never felt safer in her life.

A shiver racked her body as the memories of the evening assaulted her mind. She'd watched a man be murdered right in front of her. Then she'd run for her very life and faced the real fear of being raped and murdered.

"Shh," his deep voice washed over her, helping to heal her wounded soul. "Nothing can harm you here."

"I need to call the police." Delight was surprised by the hoarseness of her voice. Raising her fingers, she gently rubbed her throat and winced when the action caused her pain.

"It's all being taken care of," he assured her as he stepped up onto the platform and laid her on the bed. Tugging the covers out from under her, he tucked the duvet around her.

Delight sighed as her aching body hit the soft mattress. The luxurious covering felt soothing against her skin. It was so tempting just to sink back and fall asleep so she wouldn't have to deal with any of this. She thought about doing just that. But just for a second. Deverauxes didn't shirk their responsibilities.

"I'll need to give them a statement." She propped herself up on one arm and scanned the room, searching for her clothing. Deciding that the dirty heap by the bed must be what was left of her clothing, she sighed and began to tug back the covers. As much as she didn't want to put those garments on her body again, she really didn't have any choice. And lying there thinking about it wasn't going to make it any easier.

"What do you think you are doing?" His eyebrows came together as he scowled at her, making him look even more austere. The tone of his voice was clipped and his accent was more pronounced than it had been.

"I told you." Delight eased herself into a sitting position and swung her legs over the side of the bed. It was a king-sized one that sat high off the floor on a platform and her feet dangled in the air. "I have to speak to the police."

His large hand clamped over her shoulder, stopping her. "The bodies are being taken care of and the appropriate authorities are being contacted." Gently, but steadily, he pushed her until she was lying back on the bed with her legs dangling over the side. "Tomorrow is time enough to deal with them."

"But…" her voice trailed off as he loomed over her, large and fierce. She really should be afraid of him, but she found she was not. Instead, she found herself becoming unbearably aroused.

Lucian was a very large man. She figured he had to be at least six-foot-four and all of it was solid, rippling muscle. As she watched him, he casually unbuttoned his shirt, one button at a time. With each button that was undone, the silk fabric of his shirt parted a little more, revealing a wide, thick chest that tapered down to a rippling washboard stomach. Delight licked her lips, her mouth suddenly dry.

He shrugged out of his shirt and tossed it aside. Bending down, he removed his shoes and socks before straightening once again. His green-eyed gaze never left her as his hands went to the opening of his black pants.

Delight shifted her legs restlessly as she watched him. She could feel the moisture seeping from her core. Her sex felt hot, swollen and needy. Her breasts seemed to swell even more as she arched her back against the bed. Her nipples were tight buds and the thought of his mouth on her body made them tighten even more.

In one part of her mind, Delight could feel the aches and bruises from her attack, but they seemed incidental when weighed against her growing need for Lucian. Almost like a background noise. You knew it was there, but it no longer mattered. And it didn't. Right now, the only thing that mattered to Delight was making love with Lucian. And that frightened her almost as much as what had happened early tonight. She made a slight noise of denial, trying to refute her need for him.

Lucian had his pants unzipped, but they were still on as he stepped between her spread legs. She could see the large bulge filling his underwear, straining to escape the confining fabric. "You are so beautiful." His fingers grazed up and down her inner thighs, leaving a trail of fire in their wake.

After what those men had tried to do to her, Lucian should have repulsed her. But instead, she wanted him even more. What would occur between them would wipe away the memory of those other men's hands on her.

He continued to touch her, the strokes of his hands getting firmer as they skimmed up and down her legs. Delight felt flushed, as if she was running a fever. But she knew it was no temperature. It was Lucian and the way he made her feel inside. Her body was on fire with desire for him.

Her hips arched up to meet his fingers as they lingered at the creases at the tops of her legs. She felt like a prisoner to her own desire. Wanting him. Needing him. "Lucian," she moaned as his finger sifted through the soft thatch of her pubic hair.

As she watched him, he stepped back and in one quick motion shucked his pants and underwear. Totally naked, he stood in front of her and let her look at him. Lord, he was gorgeous. His cock jutted out in front of him, large and hard. Delight bit her lip. She wanted his cock buried deep inside her, but she didn't know if she was going to be able to take all of him.

"I'll fit." His words startled her slightly. How had he read her mind?

"Your eyes are so huge and concerned." Grasping his cock in his hand, he skimmed his hand over its length. "But don't worry. We'll keep working until we get it right." His grin was wicked as he moved back between her legs.

Delight tried to scrabble back on the bed, but he gripped a knee in each hand, holding her captive. Slowly, he moved his hands apart, spreading her legs wide, until she was totally exposed to his view. She could feel the heat on her cheeks as he looked at her wet, swollen pussy. Just knowing he was watching her made her sex cream and she could feel her juices trickling down between the cheeks of her behind.

His laugh was low and sexy as he bent over and inhaled deeply. "You belong to me. Every part of you is mine." Leaning forward, he dipped his tongue into her belly button and swirled it around. "That includes your smell. And baby," he paused and nipped at her hipbone. "You smell hot."

She brought her hand to her mouth, trying desperately to swallow back a cry. His hands released her knees and manacled her hands. Dragging them up over her head, he held them easily with one hand. With his other hand, he tilted her chin up and waited until she gave him her full attention.

"Don't try and hold anything back from me, Delight. I want it all." Lucian kissed her lips lightly until they parted of their own accord. But instead of deepening the kiss, he nibbled his way across her cheek and down the curve of her jaw.

She could feel his teeth as they bit lightly on her neck, scraping over the sensitive skin. Delight arched her neck, giving him better access. She didn't know what she wanted from him, but a deep pulsing started deep in her core and grew until it filled her entire body. It felt as if every hair on her body was standing on end and she was poised to explode. Pushing her neck closer to him, she offered herself to him. Instinctively, she knew he needed something from her, but would not take it without her approval.

"Take what you need." Her voice was barely a whisper, but it was enough.

His teeth pierced her flesh, making her arch even harder towards him. There was a burning at her throat that went straight to her breasts and her pussy. Moaning, she arched her head back even further as Lucian continued to suckle.

Her body was on fire with a need that was more than sexual. She could feel his fingers wrapped around her hands, keeping them stretched over her head. His other hand gently cupped her chin, keeping her head tilted. He loomed over her, his mouth firm on her neck. She could feel every inch of her body responding to him.

Suddenly, she came in a rush of pleasure so sweet that it hardly seemed real. Convulsing, she rode the orgasm to the end and then melted into the mattress. Her entire body felt relaxed, as she drifted in a haze. She felt Lucian release her arms, but it was too much trouble to move them, so they stayed raised above her head.

Lucian's tongue lapped over her neck and then she felt him kiss her lips. Gently, he lowered her arms back down by her body and lifted her until her face was against his chest. She nuzzled closer, wanting to get closer to the heat radiating from him. He supported her neck and head as he urged her to drink. Delight tried to make sense of it, but she was so tired and started to drift off.

"Drink." His voice was more insistent now and she started to speak, to tell him to let her sleep.

Then she tasted it.

Warm and rich and slightly salty, her tongue lapped at the liquid as her entire body buzzed with renewed arousal. This was delicious. Like nothing she'd ever tasted before. Wanting more, she opened her mouth and sucked hard. Liquid rushed into her mouth and she swallowed with a satisfied moan.

"Enough." Delight could hear Lucian, but she didn't want to listen to him. How could he give her something this delightful and not let her drink her fill? His laughter was dark and sensual as he pried her mouth from his chest. "Enough for now."

His eyes seemed to pierce her very soul as he watched her. "Close it with your tongue." Not really knowing what she was doing, she ran her tongue over his flesh, whimpering when she got another taste of him.

Lucian gripped her head in his hands and held her gaze with his. "You will not remember this in the morning."

That didn't seem right to her. "Yes, I will."

Her stubbornness seemed to amuse him further. "No, you won't." He shifted so that he was standing back between her legs. "But you will remember this."

Bending down, his tongue stroked the wet folds of her labia, up one side and down the other. Arousal flared hot once again as Delight arched her hips up to his mouth. She felt lethargic and wanton spread out before him. For the first time in her life, she felt powerful and sexy.

Taking her hands, he wrapped them around the backs of her legs, behind her knees. Pushing her legs as wide as they would go, he held his hands over hers for a moment before letting go. "Spread yourself for me."

Delight forced her legs wider. Her earlier aches and pains were gone. She felt wonderful, but she needed more from him. Her eyes went to his throbbing cock. It looked so red and almost raw and the blue veins that ran up and down the sides looked almost painful. She wanted it buried in her pussy. All of it.

His warm breath caressed her swollen flesh before his tongue flicked at her clit. But he left her immediately and moved his head towards her breasts. Her legs started to close around him to keep him where she wanted him.

"If you want me to pleasure you, then you have to keep your legs spread for me." He blew on one of her nipples, making it bead even tighter. "Now, open them wide."

Delight not only spread her legs wide, she arched up and rubbed her wet pussy over his cock, pleasuring herself on his length. His laughter was wicked as he took her nipple deep into his mouth and sucked hard. He propped his hands on either side of her body to keep him balanced as he pleasured both of her breasts. Taking his time, he laved both soft mounds with his tongue before flicking each swollen nub. Delight pushed harder against his cock, rocking hard against it.

Suddenly, Lucian reared back. She dropped her hands from her legs and reached for him. Gripping her under her arms, he moved her up so that she was lying crossways on the bed. Grabbing one of the pillows, he lifted her head and propped it up so that her chin almost touched her chest and she was looking down at her torso. Her breasts were wet and swollen, her nipples red and distended.

Satisfied, he straddled her, supporting his weight on his knees. Picking up her hands, he placed a kiss on each palm before wrapping them around the outside of her breasts and pushing them together. "Keep your breasts pushed together."

Leaning forward, he slipped his cock between her breasts, sandwiching it between them. Slowly, he pulled back and surged forward until the tip of his cock brushed her lips. Automatically, Delight opened her mouth and took it inside.

His skin was velvety soft, but it covered pure steel. She could taste the salty, warm liquid that seeped from the head. He pulled back again and she licked her lips and opened her mouth wider. This time, he thrust back harder and deeper.

"You have such a sexy, sassy mouth, Delight. Just perfect for fucking." He kept thrusting as he spoke. She could feel his testicles, heavy and full against her chest as he moved.

This time when he surged inside her mouth, she ran her tongue along the length of his cock, stroking wherever she could reach. His groan was music to her ears and made her even hotter.

Keeping her breasts pressed together, she used her thumbs to play with her own nipples. The sensation was pleasing, so she did it again, this time pushing a little harder. She moaned and the sound vibrated around his shaft.

Sucking as hard as she could, Delight tried to keep him inside her mouth. She wanted Lucian to come in her mouth. Wanted to taste him, hear him and see him as it happened.

The image sent shivers racing to every nerve ending of her body. She was close to coming again. Her pussy wept with desire and her inner muscles clenched. They were both so close.

Lucian shouted like a man in pain as he pulled his cock from her mouth. His eyes glowed almost eerily in the darkness of the bedroom and his lungs worked like bellows in his chest. She could see the sheen of sweat on his skin as he sat back on his haunches.

He shifted his body until he was kneeling beside her with his large hand resting possessively over her stomach. His face was hard, almost unrecognizable as he struggled with some inner demon. This was the man who had ruthlessly killed two men in a dirty alleyway tonight. Power and danger seeped from every pore in his body until she was surrounded by it, submerged in it.

Still, she was not afraid.

He pinned her with his reddish gaze when she moved restlessly on the bed. His mouth opened on a growl and his elongated teeth shone in the moonlight. "I am a Dalakis and we have always been different. You must choose now."

He seemed to be waiting for some sort of acknowledgement, so she nodded her head and waited.

"If you wish to leave, run now while there is still a choice. If you stay, I will take you and make you mine." Closing his eyes, he tilted back his head. His hands clenched into fists by his sides. "I cannot be gentle this time. I have waited too long. My need is too great."

Delight could hear the apology in his words even as she sensed his anger at himself. She knew he felt he needed to be gentle with her, but she was no hothouse flower. Granted, she looked small and delicate compared to him, but in reality, she was strong and hearty. He could be gentle later. Right now he needed something from her that she could give him. Acceptance and sexual release.

Reaching out, she placed her hand over his heart. The muscles of his chest tightened beneath her touch. He did not look at her, but kept his shuttered gaze on the ceiling. Sitting up, she curled her legs beneath her bottom, and then came up on her knees next to him. She slipped her fingers through his long, black silky hair, tugging on it until he lowered his face to hers. His eyes were dark and fathomless now as he watched her. He was totally still now, like an animal waiting to pounce on its prey.

Delight swallowed hard. Her life had changed tonight. She had almost died. If that had happened she never would have had the chance to explore this attraction to Lucian. She wasn't sure where it was going or where it would lead, but she did know that she would regret it to her dying day if she didn't take a chance and explore it. For better or for worse, she was a different person now and there was no going back to her safe, predictable life.

Gathering all her courage, she looked him straight in the eye. Taking a deep breath, she spoke the words that would change the course of her life. "I want to stay."

Chapter Seven

ဆာ

Lucian stared at Delight, hardly able to believe her words. He had been so certain she would run from him, and not all that sure if he would have let her. Like a wild beast that had scented his mate, all his instincts were beating at him to take her and bind her to him.

He had already taken her blood. The rich, heady taste still tingled on his tongue. Never in his life had he tasted anything as sweet and satisfying as Delight's blood. It made him feel like a god among immortals. He felt alive and powerful as never before.

He had been unable to keep from sharing some of his blood with her. It was not enough to convert her, but it was more than enough to strengthen the mental and physical bonds that they already shared. He could lie and tell himself he only did it because he knew that his blood would help heal her aches and bruises. But in truth, it was because he couldn't resist the opportunity to tie Delight to him with every means at his disposal.

Lucian wanted to be fair to Delight. But he was finding that his primal instincts were much more powerful than the trappings of civility. Looking down at her with her short tousled hair and her pale blue eyes shimmering with desire, Lucian knew he'd never seen a woman look as beautiful as she did at that moment. Her face was lovely, with its heart-shape, high cheekbones and tip-tilted nose. And she was offering herself to him.

It took all his strength not to toss her facedown on the bed and devour her, his body craved her so badly. His hands, which were always rock-steady, now shook with a lust so strong he knew he would stop at nothing to have her. Extending his hand, he cupped one of her lovely, pale breasts. Using his thumb, he stroked around the edges of her turgid nipple.

Delight closed her eyes and tilted her head back, a soft cry escaped her parted lips. Her neck was totally exposed to him as she sat there with her legs slightly spread, panting with desire.

Unable to resist, he sifted his fingers through the soft nest of curls between her legs, letting them stroke her wet flesh and her swollen clit. She sucked in her breath when his finger stroked the small bundle of nerves, her hips rocking towards him.

Lucian could feel the light sheen of sweat covering his body. Every muscle was clenched in anticipation of what was to come. His fangs were extended and aching to sink into her sweet flesh and taste her blood.

The time had come.

His voice was harsh and she flinched slightly when he spoke, her eyes coming to rest upon his face. "Turn around and kneel up on your hands and your knees." She licked her lips, looking uncertain. "I want to fuck you from behind, and I want you to offer yourself to me." He removed his hands from her body. "Do it."

Lucian was a man at war with himself. Every animalistic, primitive instinct in him insisted that he throw her facedown on the bed, mount her, and fuck her. The logical, sane part of him knew that it had to be her choice or it was worth nothing.

For a long moment, Delight didn't move. Then ever so slowly, she came up on her knees and turned her body away from him. Reaching out her hands, she planted them on the mattress for support. Lucian swallowed back a howl of triumph, but could not suppress the exaltation that flooded him.

Taking his time to prolong the pleasure, he caressed the back of one of her legs before tapping the inside of her thigh with one of his fingers. "Bend down a bit, stick your ass in the air, and spread your knees apart." He slipped his finger inside her moist sex and pulled it out again. Delight arched her bottom up and widened her legs.

She was the most enticing creature he'd ever seen. Her smell, taste, and the feel of her supple flesh intoxicated him. He'd have all she had to offer and then some before they were finished tonight.

"Now reach behind and spread the cheeks of your ass and show me all of you." He trailed his damp fingers from her clit to the tight hole of her behind, smiling when her ass pushed towards his fingers, seeking to deepen his touch. "I want to see all of your pretty, pink pussy. I want to see it, touch it, and taste it."

Delight moaned and reached behind her back, gripping the soft curves of her ass with her fingers and spreading the lush mounds as wide as she could. Lucian bent forward and licked his way up the dark line from her pussy to the mouth of her behind. She shivered deliciously, but didn't move.

"Perfect," he whispered, blowing on her damp sex even as he thrust two of his fingers into her eager core. Her inner muscles gripped his fingers tight and he almost came then and there. The sight of her offering herself to him almost sent him over the edge. His testicles were so tight it was almost painful and the head of his cock was wet with his own arousal. Removing his fingers, he knelt up behind her and moistened his cock on her cream.

Delight was panting hard now as she thrust her bottom back towards him. "Now, Lucian."

"Yes," he hissed as he gripped her hips in his hands and buried his cock deep. He closed his eyes and threw back his head, gritting his teeth to keep from coming immediately. She felt so damned good wrapped around him, squeezing him tight.

Leaning forward until his chest covered her back, he nipped at her shoulder. "Move your hands back up so you can support yourself." He waited until she'd complied and then he set to work pleasuring them both.

He kissed a trail down the center of her back while he slipped his hands up her torso until his palms covered both her breasts. Her nipples stabbed the center of his palms as he moved them in a circle, stimulating her to even greater arousal. She was making little whimpering noises that were driving him wild. She sounded so damn sexy.

Withdrawing until only the head of his cock was still inside her, he thrust back, burying himself to the hilt. Tightening his fingers around her breasts, he pulled her back to meet his thrusts as he stroked in and out of her body. His rhythm increased until he was pounding harder and faster into her moist core.

Delight was tightening around him as she pushed her bottom back to meet his forward thrusts. Her inner muscles were quivering as they gripped him. He could feel her juices flowing freely now.

Lucian shifted until one of his hands was buried between her legs, stroking her hard little clit. She was wild now, driving for completion. He could feel his testicles pull up hard and tight to his body even as his cock began to spasm. Pressing on her clit, he drove into her with one last, hard stroke. Delight came apart in his hands, her body clamping down on his cock. As she shivered and shook, her body milking his cock dry, he leaned forward and buried his face in the curve of her neck.

He licked her salty skin once before sinking his fangs into her. Her blood spurted into his mouth and she shrieked as the intensity of her orgasm increased. He could feel her coming again and he reveled in her sexual pleasure. His own orgasm seemed to last forever as he poured himself into her body. Both of them were gasping for breath when he finally felt her slump forward on the bed. Only his grip on her breast kept her from collapsing completely.

Removing his fangs, he closed the small wound on the side of her neck and kissed it before lowering her to the bed. She gave a muffled groan, but didn't move. Carefully, he pulled his cock from her pussy, swearing softly when her inner muscles gripped him even tighter. Beads of sweat trickled down his back as he disengaged from her welcoming body.

She lay there, totally still and unmoving except for the slight rise and fall of her shoulders as her breathing returned to normal. Lucian was filled with a contentment he'd never known before. He could pass many happy hours just watching her sleep. A line of goose bumps appeared on her body and she shivered slightly, so he lifted her until her head was on her pillow at the top of the bed. Tugging the covers out from under her, he tucked them around her naked body. Giving a little sigh of contentment, she snuggled under the sheets.

Whether she knew it or not, she was his now. He would never let her go. Lucian pushed a lock of hair off her forehead before smoothing his fingers down the soft skin of her cheek. Like a contented kitten, she pushed her face closer to his hand. She might seem soft and cuddly now, but he knew that deep inside her beat the heart of a lioness. That fact was never more evident than this evening. She had fought for her life, never giving up her struggle against attackers much larger than herself. Delight had used her intelligence and what physical strength she possessed to fight. She was indeed a worthy mate for a Dalakis.

Watching her now, you would never tell that she had been attacked. Her bruises were almost faded and by the time she awoke they would be totally healed. His blood would see to that. In the meantime, he knew that Stefan would have gathered much information about the men who had attacked her. Lucian would not leave any loose ends. If someone were still after Delight, he would take care of him.

He could feel the anger building inside him once again and forced himself to relax. Whatever the problem, it would be dealt with. Right now, he wanted to enjoy the pleasurable sensations flowing through his body. He had achieved the deepest sexual satisfaction of his life only moments before, but already his body was clamoring for more. His cock stirred once again as he watched Delight sleep.

Sighing, he resigned himself to celibacy for the rest of the night. Delight had already been through too much tonight and he had worn her out with his lovemaking. The last thought made him smile. This was just the beginning for them. There would be many nights where they would make love all night long.

He would have to court her as well. There had been no time to ease into a relationship with her and he knew her natural inclination would be to pull back from the intensity of their first meeting. He could not allow that. Instead, he would offer her space and court her with a determination that would leave her breathless and wanting more. She would think it was all her idea, when she finally came to him. Pleased with his plan, Lucian gave a decisive nod before leaning over and placing a soft kiss on Delight's lips.

Carefully, so as not to disturb her, he rolled out of bed and padded naked to the window. The sun would be coming up within the hour, so he closed all the shutters, making sure they were locked down securely. The room was in total darkness, but Lucian could see perfectly as he padded across the floor. Delight didn't move as he pulled on a bathrobe and eased out of the bedroom.

Stefan was waiting for him downstairs in the library. Sitting back in a leather recliner with his feet propped up, he sipped a glass of brandy that Lucian knew would be laced with blood. Lucian raised one of his eyebrows and waited. Stefan saluted him with his glass before launching into a full report.

"The men that you disposed of in the alley were local thugs in the employ of one Mr. Jethro Prince." Stefan got up from his chair, laid his glass on a side table and wandered over to the decanter that sat on the antique sideboard. Picking it up, he filled another goblet and carried it to where Lucian was sitting and handed it to him.

"Go on." He accepted the glass and took a sip, knowing he wasn't going to like what was coming next.

"Prince is a powerful crime lord. He is into everything—prostitution, drugs and gambling. If there's an illegal way to make a buck, he is involved." Stefan ambled back to his chair and sank back into its comfort. He picked up his glass, warming the goblet in his hands for a moment before taking a large swallow. "He is also rumored to be half insane, as well as being a sadistic little bastard who likes to hurt people. His temper is well-known among his associates as people who cross him tend to turn up missing or dead."

Stefan paused for a moment and took another drink from his glass. "The man who Delight saw murdered tonight was her manager, James Brenner. From what I have been able to find out, he owed Prince money for a gambling debt. Word is that Prince thought that Brenner might have talked to the authorities, so he had to be made an example of. Hence the killing."

Stefan subsided for a moment and Lucian curbed his impatience, knowing his brother would finish in his own good time. His eyes were burning red in anger when he finally met Lucian's gaze. Lucian had never seen his brother this angry before.

"It was only by accident that Delight was even there. The bastard Brenner had her stay late to work on inventory, so she just happened to be in the wrong place at the wrong time. They would have raped and killed her just because she was unlucky enough to be there." Stefan tossed back the remains of his drink. "There was another man there tonight as well."

Lucian was totally alert now as he sat forward in his chair. "Who?" His eyes promised retribution to the unknown man who had hurt his Delight.

"His name is Smith. He is Prince's enforcer. His right-hand man, so to speak. He would have been the one to order Delight's murder. The other two did not have enough brains between them to make a decision, just muscle and meanness."

Lucian carefully placed his glass on the table in front of him before he accidentally crushed the fragile stem in his hands. "I will pay a visit to Mr. Prince." He'd kill the man without a single qualm if it came to that. Nobody would be allowed to hurt Delight again.

Stefan nodded and echoed his thoughts. "Prince and Smith will have to be taken care of."

Lucian knew he could count on Stefan's help in protecting Delight. He had claimed her, and as such, she was under Dalakis protection and all that it entailed.

Stefan's voice broke into his thoughts. "You can let her know that the night janitor was just wounded. He will be fine in a few weeks, but they hit him from behind so he does not know anything. I also visited her brother while he slept and planted the suggestion that Delight was fine and that they did not expect to see her until tomorrow night because she was staying with a friend."

Stefan glanced at the covered windows and Lucian knew that his brother was feeling the same lethargy spreading throughout his own body as he was, heralding the coming sunrise.

"Thank you." Lucian didn't have to say anything more. They were so close, he knew that Stefan understood everything that went unsaid between them.

Stefan rose from his chair and headed towards one of several hidden passageways that connected their two houses. "Keep her close and we will deal with this tomorrow night."

Before Lucian could speak, his brother was gone. He could sense him moving swiftly through the hidden tunnel towards his own home. Lucian did a mental sweep of the house, making sure everything was locked up tight. He knew that Stefan would have already done this, but he wasn't taking any chances with Delight's safety.

As he climbed the stairs towards his bedroom, he could hear the soft sounds of Delight's breathing and the gentle rhythm of her heart. Having her in his bed, waiting for him, filled him with a strange combination of lust and tenderness that was almost overwhelming. In his short time with her, she had managed to make him feel more emotions than he had in several hundred years. Without even trying, she had laid a gentle siege and claimed his heart.

Closing the door to the bedroom, he secured it before removing his bathrobe and slipping under the covers. Delight rolled towards him, seeking his warmth and comfort. Wrapping her in his arms, he eased her head down onto his chest. Her breath tickled his chest hairs and his cock twitched in response to her nearness.

The dawn was just breaking, but he had one last thing to do before he could sleep. Cupping the back of her head, he focused all his mental power on Delight. "You will sleep until I awake tomorrow night."

Satisfied, he settled himself in the comfort of his bed, and with Delight clasped tight in his arms, he awaited sleep. The moment the sun crossed the horizon, he felt a deep lassitude fill him and gave himself over to rest. His body stilled, his breathing stopped, and his body ceased to function. Knowing Delight would be here when he awoke, he allowed himself to sleep deeply.

Chapter Eight

ॐ

Delight fought her way out of sleep. She usually awoke easily, alert and energized to start her day. But for some reason, this morning it felt as if she was trying to swim through quicksand just to scratch the surface of wakefulness. Her limbs were heavy and her eyes felt as if they had lead weights attached to them.

It would be so easy to drift back to sleep, towards the beckoning darkness, but she resisted. In the back of her mind, something was nagging her. There was something she had to do. Something important.

She frowned as she desperately tried to remember what it was that she needed to know. A dull throbbing behind her eyes made it almost impossible to think. That in itself was strange as she rarely ever had a headache.

Taking a deep breath, she forced her eyes to open. Squinting into the darkness she looked around and could just make out the shapes of the furniture. Immediately alarmed, she tried to sit up in bed and found that she couldn't move. This was not her room!

She began to struggle against the covers and the weight that kept her pinned to the bed. It was then she noticed a man's arm wrapped tight around her waist, manacling her to his body.

All at once, memories began to flood back into her brain. Her hand went to her head, as if it could somehow stop the pounding rhythm and the pictures that filled her mind. Sinking back into the pillows, she inhaled deeply, forcing herself to breathe, trying to remain calm.

That was a mistake. With the first breath she took, Delight was filled with the masculine scent of the man lying next to her, a kind of combination of sex, male, and just a hint of brandy. Lucian Dalakis.

How could she have forgotten, even for a moment, the events of last night? The murder, the harrowing race for her life, and then there was Lucian. Delight was appalled at how quickly and easily she'd fallen into bed with a man who was little more than a stranger. She just didn't do things like that. And the things they had done! Delight could feel the heat warm her cheeks at the memory of their sexual encounter.

Right now, she needed to go home. Chase and Miss Nadine would be frantic by now and had probably already called the police. She felt guilty about last night. A man had been killed, her family had to be worried sick about her, and she'd spent the night having the most fantastic sex of her entire life.

She chewed on her bottom lip as she thought about it. The only excuse she could come up with was that she must have been more shaken and muddled by the events of last night than she'd thought. Otherwise, she would have called the authorities immediately and then gone straight home to reassure her family that she was fine.

It took her a while to get her body to cooperate, but Delight finally managed to roll out from under the male arm. Sitting on the side of the bed, she stared down at his sleeping figure. He was so gorgeous. Lucian's long, black hair was pushed back from his face and rested on the plump pillow under his head. Even in sleep, his face looked stern with its severe lines and angles.

Reaching out, she placed a hand in the center of his chest. The sheet had slipped to his waist when she'd moved from his embrace and she couldn't resist touching the hard planes of his torso. The man was hard everywhere. She kept her touch light so as not to wake him. The last thing she wanted was to have to deal with what they had done last night. Moving her hand, she placed it over his heart, wanting to feel its steady beating once more before she left him.

Frowning, she shifted her hand a little to the left. Nothing. Leaning down, she placed her ear on his chest, no longer worried about waking him. Nothing.

"Lucian." She shook him slightly and got no reaction. He didn't seem to be breathing. "Lucian!" Her voice was louder now and had a slight hysterical edge to it. He couldn't be dead. She'd seen three dead men last night and that was more than enough for her to have to deal with.

As she opened his mouth and tilted back his head, she glanced around the room, frantically searching for a telephone. Reaching across Lucian, she clicked on the bedside lamp and flinched when the light hit her eyes. Her worried gazed went back to him and she froze. Lying on his back in the bed, he looked dead. There was no sign of life in him at all.

There was no phone and she didn't have time to try and find one. Trying to remember everything she'd learned about first aid, she began to give him CPR. As she blew into his mouth, she felt his lungs rise. When her lips touched his, an elusive memory floated to the surface.

She could hear Lucian's voice telling her that she wouldn't remember what had happened. Her own reply echoed in her brain. She would remember. She started chest compressions. "Come on. Breathe!"

It hit her suddenly. Pulling back so quickly she almost fell off the bed, visions of herself totally naked, offering herself to Lucian, flooded her. She'd not only offered her body, but her blood. And he had taken both.

Shaking now, she concentrated on the growing memory. Two of his teeth had grown into fangs, and he'd sucked the blood from her body. Her tongue tingled as she remembered drinking his blood in return.

Clapping her hand over her mouth to keep from screaming, she launched herself from the bed, stumbling down off the platform. Slowly, she backed away from the still body lying there. *Vampire.* The word was loud and clear in her head. This was no dream, but a living nightmare. She had escaped being murdered by local killers just to end up with a vampire.

Clutching her chest, she realized that she was beginning to hyperventilate and forced herself to control her breathing. Everything was okay. If Lucian had meant her any harm, she'd already be dead. As strange as it all seemed, she still wasn't really afraid of him. She was more afraid of what he was. Deep inside, she felt she knew Lucian and trusted him. Which was crazy and showed her just how precarious her mental state was at the moment. This was all just too much for her to take in.

Needing to be home among everything and everyone that was familiar to her, Delight groped around the room until she found her soiled clothing from the night before. Wrinkling her nose in distaste, she pulled on her underwear before tugging on the ruined pants and blouse. Most of the buttons were gone from the blouse, so she tied the tails together as tight as she could. Slipping on her shoes, she sent up a prayer of gratitude before bending down and scooping up her purse, which had been lying next to them.

As much as she wanted to be gone from here, a part of her didn't want to leave Lucian. Just the thought of leaving made her break out into a cold sweat. No matter what he was, Lucian had saved her and given her the best sexual experience of her life. Just watching him lie there made her breasts swell and she could feel moisture pooling between her thighs. *That* only confused her more.

Padding silently back to the bed, she stepped up onto the platform, bent down and kissed his lips softly. "Goodbye and thank you." As she pulled back, she thought she saw his eye twitch, but when a minute passed and he didn't move, she convinced herself that she'd been mistaken.

Walking to the bedroom door was one of the hardest things she'd ever done. The farther away she got from Lucian, the worse she felt. It was as if his soul was calling to hers, pleading with her to stay. Tears filled her eyes and she dashed them angrily away. She'd only met him last night. There was no way she could be this attached to him.

But she was. Her heart was pounding and she rubbed at the pain in her chest as she moved one step at a time to the doorway. Placing her hand on the doorknob, she turned it quietly. She could hear his voice in her head, commanding her to stay. She hesitated, but pushed onward, determined to find the space she needed to try and understand what had happened to her.

Pulling it open, she slipped through the opening and carefully closed the door behind her. She felt like a thief and a traitor as she crept down the stairs to the front door. She expected the bedroom door to slam open at any minute and have Lucian stop her from leaving. But that didn't happen.

Her hands were shaking so badly that it took her a few tries to open all the locks on the front door. When the door closed and she heard the lock click behind her, she almost cried out in distress. She had to fight the urge to turn around and pound on the door until Lucian let her back into his home and into his life.

Gritting her teeth against the grief that threatened to swamp her, Delight looked around the neighborhood. She had no idea where she was. From the position of the sun, she could tell that it was late afternoon. Appalled that she'd slept the day away, she hurried down the front steps and started up the sidewalk. At the corner she glanced at the street sign and was relieved when she recognized it immediately. She was only a few blocks from home. That gave her the small boost of energy she needed to get her moving again.

Home was close now, so she kept putting one foot in front of the other and ignoring the part of her that felt as if she was really moving further from home with every step she took away from Lucian.

As she trudged up the steps to The Grande, Delight finally breathed a sigh of relief. Right now, she wanted a long, hot shower, clean clothing, and food. She knew she was putting off the inevitable. The police would have to be called and she would have to give her statement. She'd already decided not to tell the police about Lucian. She would say that a stranger saved her and that she remembered nothing. They might not believe her, but that was their problem. Delight would protect Lucian at all costs. That he was a vampire didn't seem to matter and that was something else she really had to think about. But not now.

The door opened just as she reached for the handle. "Child, you look like something the cat dragged home."

Delight took one look at the concern on Miss Nadine's face and burst into tears. Saying nothing, the older woman just wrapped her arm around Delight and led her into the parlor. Sinking down into the sofa, Miss Nadine held her in her comforting embrace and rocked her back and forth, crooning a soft lullaby.

When she had no tears left, Delight lifted her head. "I don't know where to begin."

"At the beginning, child." Sitting back, she quietly waited as the story came pouring out of Delight. She didn't interrupt as Delight told her about the murder and about Lucian.

As much as she loved and trusted Miss Nadine, she couldn't bring herself to tell her about the steamy lovemaking she and Lucian had shared or the fact that he was a vampire.

Now that she was away from him, Delight could hardly believe it herself. It wouldn't be too hard to convince herself that she was wrong about Lucian and it had all been brought on by the stress of what had happened to her, except for one thing. Delight wasn't a weak-willed woman, nor was she prone to hysterics or exaggerations. She'd always been strong and dealt with life's problems head on. And this would be no different.

Delight sighed, knowing that Miss Nadine was smart enough to fill in many of the blanks in her story, but she wouldn't ask many questions. For that, she was very grateful.

"I didn't believe that story that your brother spun this morning." Reaching out, she clasped Delight's hand in hers.

"What story?"

"That you were staying with a friend last night after work and that you wouldn't be home until late today." Miss Nadine shook her head. "I asked him how he knew that, but he couldn't tell me. It seemed to come out of thin air, but Chase was adamant that it was the truth." She watched Delight, waiting for her reaction.

Delight's head was spinning with the implications. Were Lucian's powers so great that he could plant a suggestion in someone's mind? The answer was, of course, a resounding yes. She'd seen for herself last night just how powerful and dangerous a man he was.

The other woman was still waiting for an explanation. Giving her a half smile, she shrugged. "Chase wouldn't lie. Maybe he just got mixed up." It was a lame excuse, but it was all she had.

"Uh-huh." From the tone of her voice, she could tell that Miss Nadine didn't believe her, but would let it go for now. "No matter." Briskly, she rose from the sofa. "First thing is to get you a shower and some hot food. I'll call the police and then we'll see what's to be done."

Nodding gratefully, she rose and followed Miss Nadine back to the kitchen. "I'll be back down in twenty minutes."

"Take your time, child. I'll have some hot chicken soup and warm fresh, sourdough rolls for you when you're ready. That and a hot cup of tea will help put you to rights."

Delight trudged up the stairs. She let her mind go blank and concentrated totally on her physical needs. Pulling off her clothing, she stuffed it all in the garbage. Turning, she headed towards the bathroom and suddenly stopped. Her head fell to her chest and she sighed deeply. As much as she wanted to toss all the clothing, she knew she couldn't. Turning, she went back to the pail and pulled every soiled item of clothing out again and laid it carefully aside just in case the police wanted it for evidence.

Leaving it behind, she padded into the bathroom and turned on the shower. Stepping under the hot spray, she allowed it to clean her body and wipe the cobwebs from her mind. The hot beads of water pummeled her skin and it was only then that she realized that something was very wrong.

There were no bruises anywhere on her body. Shutting off the water, she grabbed a towel and wrapped it around her before stepping out onto the bathmat. Wiping the steam off the mirror with the palm of her hand, she stared at her reflection. The pale face staring back at her was filled with disbelief.

Delight turned her head one way and then another. Checking her throat and her neck, she found nothing. Not a blemish or a bruise. Lowering the towel to her waist, she examined her breasts. The milky white globes were not marked at all, but her nipples were slightly redder than usual. At that thought, a rosy blush began to cover her breasts and move up her chest and neck to her face.

The mirror reflected a woman who had been well pleased by her lover the night before. The only minor soreness she felt was between her legs and given the activity of the night before she wasn't surprised. Lucian had been a demanding lover. Delight moaned aloud as her inner muscles clenched and her sex moistened in anticipation. Shivering, she turned from the mirror and finished drying herself.

Hurrying into her bedroom, she pulled on a fresh pair of panties and bra. Riffling through her closet, she found her most comfortable pair of faded jeans and slipped into them, topping them with a soft cottony blue sweater with long sleeves. Even though it was warm, Delight still felt cold. Tugging open a dresser drawer, she dug out a pair of white sweat socks and pulled them over her chilly feet before stuffing them into old brown leather loafers.

Running a brush through her hair, she was finished. She didn't even bother with any makeup as she longed for the comfort of Miss Nadine's company. Hurrying down the back stairs she came to a sudden halt as voices drifted up to her. She shivered in pleasure as the male voice washed over her.

Glancing out the small window at the bottom of the stairs, she noticed what she had missed before. While she'd been showering and changing, the clock had ticked onward. The sun had gone down and now there would be a reckoning.

Chapter Nine

ഇ

"Why don't you join us, Delight?" Lucian's voice enveloped her like a warm hug, even as she heard the bite of anger running beneath it.

Closing her eyes for a moment, she wrapped her arms around her waist and hugged herself tight. He had come. As much as she wanted time away from him to think, Delight realized that a part of her had been waiting for him. Her stomach jumped and her nerves jangled. She had no idea what he wanted from her. Placing her hand on the rail for support, she eased her way down the last few remaining stairs and stepped into the kitchen.

Her lips curved up in a slight smile at the sight of Lucian sitting at Miss Nadine's kitchen table, sipping a cup of tea from a china cup. It should have looked ludicrous for a man as large as Lucian to be holding delicate china in his enormous hands. Instead it was almost sensual. It announced that this was a man who knew his own strength and knew how to protect something that was precious and weaker than him.

Delight shivered as she watched his fingers stroke the side of the pale white cup. She could easily imagine those fingers stroking the sides of her breasts in just the same manner. Forcing herself to look away from the mesmerizing display, she glanced at his face and froze at the knowing look in his eyes. The corner of his lips quirked up in a half-smile that made him appear both sexy and dangerous at the same time.

This was a man who would not be ignored or denied. He would take whatever he wanted and woe to the person who stood in his way. Her hand went to her throat and she retreated a step. Immediately, his expression changed and became softer.

Rising from the table, he pulled out the chair next to his and arched his eyebrow, daring her to sit next to him. Raising her chin, she dropped her hands to her sides and marched over to the chair.

She could feel his warm breath on the back of her neck as he bent down to whisper in her ear. "I did not like waking up and finding you gone."

His words were softly spoken, but they were like a lash on her skin. She had hurt him, and that was something she hadn't meant to do. In spite of her intention to be strong and self-contained, she flinched slightly, but recovered quickly and sank down into her seat. "It couldn't be helped." Picking up her own cup, she took a large swallow of the strong, sweet tea that Miss Nadine had poured for her, desperately needing its strength.

Miss Nadine had been watching them both, her eyes shrewd and watchful. "Mr. Dalakis came looking for you when you were in the shower. Claimed he was worried about you and wouldn't leave until he saw for himself that you were fine." She continued to putter around her kitchen, ladling up a large bowl of chicken soup for Delight and placing it in front of her.

Delight cleared her throat, but Lucian spoke before she could get her mouth open. "Please, call me Lucian. You have been very kind to allow me into your home." The charm practically oozed from every pore of his body as he spoke and Miss Nadine was not immune.

Delight could only stare as yet another facet of his personality was revealed to her. Right now, he was the epitome of suave masculine charm, you'd hardly say he was the type of man who could kill two men in an alleyway without hesitation and walk away as if nothing had happened.

"Lucian is a little too used to getting his own way, if you ask me." Suddenly hungry, Delight picked up her spoon and began to eat.

"I'm wounded by your words." He gave her a quick, fleeting grin.

"But not fatally, I imagine." Reaching across the table, she helped herself to a warm, yeasty roll. Tearing it apart with her fingers, she buttered it before taking a bite.

"Then you do not know your own power, my Delight." The tone of his voice made her look his way. His face was stern and his eyes grim. "Do not underestimate yourself."

She swallowed hard, the bread a lump in her throat. He was dead serious. Her hand went to her stomach that was filled with butterflies. Lucian was telling her that she was important to him. She wasn't quite sure how she felt about that at the moment.

"I expect the police will be by soon." Miss Nadine's words broke the tension between her and Lucian, but filled her with dread of another kind.

Lucian jerked his head away from her and pinned Miss Nadine in his laser green-eyed gaze. "What's this all about?"

The older woman paled as he spoke. Although his voice never rose a notch, his anger radiated with every word. "Delight asked me to call them while she was taking a shower."

Both women felt the full brunt of his displeasure. "You should not have done that."

Recovering herself, Miss Nadine sat forward in her chair and glared at Lucian. "I don't rightly care what you think. Delight is my main concern and what she wants takes precedence over any ideas you might have about how things ought to have been done."

Lucian seemed almost dumbfounded for a moment, then his face softened and he reached over and picked up her hand. Holding it carefully, he brought it to his lips and kissed it. "Delight is most fortunate to have one such as you watching over her."

"Well, yes…" Miss Nadine trailed off, obviously flustered by Lucian's attention.

"If you're both finished deciding what's best for me, can you tell me what the police said when you called?" Delight knew her voice was sharp, but really, this was beyond ridiculous. She was an adult and would handle this situation how she saw fit.

Miss Nadine tugged her hand from Lucian's grip and placed it in her lap. "They said that the detectives in charge of the case would be by as soon as possible and that you should stay here and wait for them."

"I hadn't planned on going anywhere." Picking up her spoon, she began to eat again.

"I had other plans, but they will have to be adjusted." Lucian leaned back in his chair, stretched his legs out in front of him, and watched her eat.

She couldn't help but notice that the black pants he wore accentuated the length and muscularity of his legs. He'd crossed his arms across his chest, making the muscles of his arms bulge against the material of his black shirt. His long hair was tied in a queue at the back of his neck, and his sensual lips were pushed together with displeasure at the thought of having to rearrange his plans.

Her fingers itched to touch his chest, to shape every contour and tease the soft hair that grew in a straight line from between his male nipples down to his groin. She wanted to lick a path down his torso to his groin and taste the hard length of his cock. Her own nipples were hard nubs against the cups of her bra. She squirmed in her chair, trying to get comfortable, but there was no relief. Her panties were already soaked and her sex was clenching hungrily, craving his hardness.

As she watched him, the front of his pants twitched. Before her very eyes, his cock swelled until it was straining against the front of his pants. The muscles of his thighs grew tight and his hands clenched into fists. Startled, she looked up at his face, but no sign of his growing desire showed there. He looked mildly perturbed, but otherwise relaxed.

Delight bit her lip to keep from moaning aloud as her pussy continued to throb with growing desire. She looked down at her half-eaten food. Anything to take her mind off Lucian and his gorgeous body sitting right next to her. They were so close together, she could even feel the heat from his body.

Miss Nadine said nothing, but Delight knew that she could sense the tension. It was time to get things back on track. "Don't let us keep you from your plans. You're free to leave at any time."

The temperature in the room dropped and the air seemed to thicken. The room swirled with a male anger so potent Delight was surprised that something didn't burst into flames. She held her breath, not sure what to do to soothe the savage beast that she had aroused.

Lucian straightened in his chair before slowly rising to his feet. His movements were precise and unhurried. Like a large predator gathering its strength before it struck. His voice was so soft Delight had to strain to hear it, but every word was spoken in a precise, cool manner. "Would you care to rephrase that last statement?"

Delight thought about it for a moment. "No." Lucian shook his head as if he couldn't believe her words, and truthfully, neither could she. "Listen to me, Lucian." Pushing back her chair, she stood so he wouldn't be towering over her and came face-to-face with his chest. The man was incredibly tall.

Tipping back her head, she propped her hands on her hips and continued. "You saved my life last night and for that I'll always be grateful. But the truth of the matter is that you don't have to get further involved in this situation. In fact, maybe it would be best if you were gone before the police got here."

The more she thought about it, the more Delight knew she was right. The last thing Lucian needed was the authorities looking into his life. And then there was the small matter of the two dead bodies in the alleyway. The man was a vampire, for heaven's sake, didn't he have any sense of self-preservation?

From the stubborn look on his face, Delight knew he would say no. It was up to her to make him leave and quickly. The police would be here any minute now, and she wanted Lucian safely gone by then. "I'm asking you to leave."

Lucian snaked a hand out and gripped her chin. His thumb grazed the side of her cheek as he continued to study her, his eyes deep and unreadable. Delight could feel her legs tremble under his scrutiny, but she forced her muscles to keep her steady.

It continued to surprise her that she really wasn't afraid of Lucian. Even knowing what he was, her first instinct was to protect him. Her stomach did back-flips as she pondered what that really meant. Even though she'd only known him a matter of hours, he was already a very important part of her life. And Delight feared that he would only grow more important with each passing hour they spent together.

Her breathing grew deeper as she forced herself to relax. Nothing had to be decided at this very moment. She wasn't quite ready to admit that she was falling in love with the man.

Falling. That was an understatement. She was ready to lie to the police to protect him, and it took all her willpower not to lead him upstairs and have mind-blowing sex with him. She was afraid she was well past falling and had already landed in love with Lucian.

And that was just crazy.

"What the hell is going on here?" At the first sound of the angry male voice, Delight found herself staring at Lucian's back. She clutched his waist for support. He'd moved so quickly when he'd thrust her behind him that he'd made her dizzy.

She scooted around Lucian, but he grabbed her upper arm before she could cross the room. "Lucian, this is my brother, Chase." Turning, she gave her brother a reassuring smile. "Chase, this is a friend of mine, Lucian Dalakis."

Chase continued to stare at Lucian's hand where it gripped her arm. "You want to unhand my sister."

Delight didn't know whether to laugh of cry, caught in the middle of a war of male wills. She heaved a sigh of relief when

Lucian slowly released her arm. His glance warned her to stay close, but she ignored it and hurried over to her brother.

Chase was as stiff as a board when she hugged him, but he relaxed after a moment and returned her embrace. "Lucian saved my life."

Chase immediately stiffened once again, his arms tightening around her. "What happened?"

Delight patted his chest to reassure him. "I'll explain everything in just a minute, but I want you to meet Lucian."

He gave her a squeeze before releasing her. His gaze went to Lucian, whom he was still regarding with suspicion. Chase offered his hand to Lucian, and Delight held her breath as she waited to see what he would do.

Lucian shook Chase's hand with a grave sense of ceremony. "It is a pleasure to meet Delight's family."

Nodding, Chase stepped back. "If you did save Delight's life, then I'm glad to meet you too."

One corner of Lucian's mouth quirked up as her brother continued to study him. Delight cleared her throat. "Why don't you sit down?" She motioned Chase towards a chair. "I'll explain everything to you."

Turning back to Lucian, she gave him an expectant look. "You were just leaving, weren't you?"

He shook his head solemnly. "I believe I can spare more time to spend with you and your family."

She smiled through her gritted teeth. The man was being purposely obtuse. "I'm just as certain you need to be going."

"Ah, Delight, you are indeed mistaken."

Miss Nadine's laughter made them both start. "Listen to the two of you. You sound like an old married couple arguing like that."

Delight stared at her friend in horror and then turned back to Lucian. As she watched, a huge grin split his face, making him look so handsome she almost forgot to breathe.

"I believe you are correct, Miss Nadine." His eyes seared Delight as he spoke.

He bent towards her and she rose on her toes to meet him. She needed to kiss him and didn't care who was in the room with them. Miss Nadine was chuckling softly in the background, but Chase was strangely silent. Then Delight ceased to think about their audience at all. His lips were almost on hers. So close.

The pounding on the back door made her jump. Her head banged into Lucian's and she lost her balance and started to fall. His strong arms captured her, keeping her safe as they turned to face this newest threat.

Through the glass in the door, Delight could see two men peering into the kitchen. As she watched, one of them held up a wallet that held an ID and a shiny badge. "Police. We'd like to speak with a Miss Delight Deveraux."

Miss Nadine patted her lips with her napkin and laid it by her plate before rising from her seat. Walking gracefully to the door, she pulled it open and motioned them inside. "Come in. We've been expecting you."

Chapter Ten

ဢ

Lucian kept Delight tucked under his arm as the two police detectives entered the room. He'd hoped to avoid this. If Delight had only stayed put, they would be meeting the detectives in his home with his lawyers present. It was always advantageous to be in a position of power when dealing with the authorities. Not that he expected to have any problems, but it was always better to minimize any complications before they arose. He would just have to adjust.

Keeping silent, Lucian watched the men and took their measure. They introduced themselves as Detectives Jean Gagnon and Sam Cassidy of the New Orleans Police Department. Gagnon was the picture of urban sophistication with his styled dark hair, Italian suit, and fine leather shoes. Cassidy was the exact opposite. He wore jeans, boots, and a sports coat. His blond hair was cut short. However, both men had one thing in common. Cop's eyes. Two pairs of deceptively shrewd eyes had already catalogued everything and everyone in the room.

Lucian smiled inwardly, already sensing their suspicion towards him. He decided to make the first move. Seating Delight once again, he sat back in his own chair and laid one arm over the back of Delight's in a blatant show of possession. Both detectives showed an immediate male understanding of the action. They now knew that Delight was his and he would protect her.

"And you are?" Detective Gagnon's question and tone were polite, but there was an edge to both.

Lucian slowly came to his feet, allowing his large frame to unfold from the chair until he was standing at his full height. At six-foot-four, all of it solid muscle, he knew he was an intimidating sight. Keeping his own voice low and pleasant, he addressed both detectives. "I am Lucian Dalakis." Nodding to both men, he then resumed his seat and replaced his arm around Delight.

Detective Cassidy's eyebrows rose in surprise at his obvious recognition of the name. He glanced at Delight, giving her a second, slightly more appraising look as if suddenly realizing that there was more to her than he'd noticed at first glance. Lucian's entire body grew tense and it took all his discipline not to rip Cassidy's throat out for staring at Delight with masculine interest.

Gagnon cleared his throat, obviously trying to break the tension. "Let's get down to business, shall we?" Taking a notebook and pen out of his pocket, he flipped it open until he found the page he was looking for. "If you'll give us a few moments alone with Miss Deveraux to question her."

"Absolutely not." Lucian's voice was almost drowned out by similar denials by Chase and Miss Nadine.

Gagnon held up his hand. "We only want to talk to her. We understand that she's the victim here, but Miss Deveraux is also a witness to a murder."

"We stay or you can talk to my lawyers about making an appointment with Miss Deveraux. She is being very cooperative, but she does have rights." Lucian leaned forward threateningly in his seat. "And I am here to make sure that she and her rights are protected."

Anger was pumping so hard through his veins, he was surprised that he didn't explode. It was bad enough that Delight had to witness a murder and then be threatened and attacked herself, but now she had to recount it all over again. It made him furious at himself for not protecting her better. That he hadn't really known she existed until the night before it happened didn't matter to Lucian. Delight was his and he had failed to protect her.

He felt her small hand on his arm. It was such a light, gentle touch, but it immediately soothed some of the fury swirling around inside him, allowing him to gain control once again. It was amazing to him, a man who had always prided himself on his ironclad control, that any threat to Delight churned up the most primitive of emotions within him. It would take some adjusting.

Lucian respected the fact that the police had to do their job, but in the end, it was he who would decide how best to protect Delight. When she tugged on his arm, he allowed her to pull him back next to her.

Leaning close, she whispered in his ear so that only he could hear her. "It's all right, Lucian. I'll talk to them." Her tone became more pleading. "Don't make any trouble. I don't want them looking into your life."

For the first time in his over five hundred years of living, Lucian was stunned. Other than his parents and brothers, no one had ever tried to protect him. He was the monster of people's dreams, the one the hero in the movies slew. He was a vampire. His power and abilities were beyond the comprehension of most people.

Delight's earlier insistence that he leave now made sense to him even if he was having a hard time processing the information. She was protecting him. Even knowing what he was, Delight was trying to keep his secret from others.

His heart pounded and he had to force himself not to rub the ache in his chest. Pride welled up inside him at his chosen one. Surely, no other man had a woman as wonderful as Delight. Love and lust washed over him and all he wanted to do was drag her onto the table and bury his hard, throbbing cock in her waiting warmth. His fangs ached to sink into her luscious flesh and taste her blood.

Lucian shook his head. She was doing it again. Distracting him from the moment at hand. Detective Cassidy was speaking, so Lucian focused on what he was saying.

"Look, Mr. Dalakis. I know who you are." Cassidy gave them a boyish grin and struck a good ol' boy pose. Lucian was not deceived by the action, recognizing it as the ploy it was to get them to relax and talk to him.

"Really." Lucian scrutinized Cassidy until his easy grin faded. "I do not recall meeting you."

Cassidy gave Lucian a nod, as if conceding him the point in their match of wits. "Let's just say, I know you by reputation."

Delight's fingernails were digging into his arm. She was very tense and growing more upset by the moment. It was time to end this charade. "This is upsetting to Delight. You will do nothing to distress her further. Ask your questions."

His voice was filled with compulsion as he spoke. Detective Cassidy eyed him even more suspiciously as if he suspected Lucian had done something, but he couldn't quite figure out what it was. However, Detective Gagnon, who was the more susceptible of the two, began to ask his questions immediately.

"Start from the moment you were asked to work late, Miss Deveraux, and tell us what happened."

As Delight recounted her horrific tale, Lucian watched the other occupants of the room. He could feel Miss Nadine's love reaching out to Delight as she spoke. Lucian knew the older woman was a permanent part of Delight's life, and truthfully, he liked her. Her energy was invigorating, and her devotion to both Delight and Chase was unquestionable. For the rest of her life, Miss Nadine would now be under the care of the Dalakis family. Lucian or one of his brothers would make sure she was well taken care of.

Then there was Chase. He was young, but he showed all the signs of becoming a formidable man. Chase had immediately jumped to Delight's protection against Lucian, who was obviously a bigger and more powerful opponent. But he hadn't flinched from Lucian, instead he had become more aggressive. Lucian was impressed by Delight's younger brother and looked forward to getting to know him better.

Lucian made a mental note to contact his lawyer immediately. He had to make provisions for his little family in the event that something did happen to him. The detectives' frustration reached out to him, so he turned his entire focus back to the conversation, which had been up to now nothing more than a recounting of events.

"How can you not know what happened to the men in the alleyway?" Detective Cassidy's voice was laced with suspicion.

"All I know is that one minute they were hitting me and tearing at my clothing." Delight's voice broke on a sob and she took a deep breath, trying to regain her composure. "Then they were gone. I didn't stop to question it. I only wanted to get away."

Delight's entire body started to shake and she began to cry. Lucian turned and lifted her off her chair and cradled her in his arms. "Enough." His soft voice cracked like a whip in the small area, making everyone jump. Delight snuggled closer and he tucked her tighter to his chest.

"You have blood in the alleyway, but no bodies. Until you find the bodies, you have no crime. She has told you everything she can about the murder she witnessed. You have upset Delight. I suggest you leave." Detective Gagnon opened his mouth to speak, but quickly closed it when Lucian pinned him with a glare. "Now."

Both of the detectives stood, knowing that this interview was at an end. Cassidy reached into his pocket and took out a card, laying it on the table next to Delight. "If you think of anything else, please call me, day or night. In the meantime, we'd like to take the clothing you were wearing last night back to the lab for analysis. Maybe we'll get lucky and get a DNA sample that will match someone already in our database. It's a long shot, but it's worth a try."

"They're upstairs. I'll go get them." Delight started to rise from the table, but Miss Nadine stopped her.

"You sit right there, Delight. I'll take the detectives upstairs to get what they need." Nobody said anything else as Miss Nadine jumped up from the table and directed both of the men up the back stairs. A few minutes later they all came back down and Miss Nadine saw both men out the door.

The second the door was closed behind the detectives, Chase turned towards his sister. "Tell us what you didn't tell them."

Lucian could feel Delight shifting in his arms. She had lied to the police to protect him, but he didn't know what she would say to her family.

"There's really nothing else to tell."

"That's bullshit!" Delight flinched from the accusation in Chase's voice.

Lucian could not allow this to harm her relationship with her brother. "She is protecting me."

Chase stood quickly, knocking his chair to the floor. "Who the hell are you anyway? And why would she protect you? I thought Delight was supposed to be with a friend last night. Instead, all this crazy stuff happened to her and then she was attacked." Stalking around the side of the table, he plucked his sister out of Lucian's arms and thrust her behind him. Crossing his arms across his chest, he glared down at Lucian. "But I get the feeling she was with you last night. Just who the hell are you?"

Lucian felt a deep pride in the young man as he defended his sister once again. Delight had done an amazing job raising her brother on her own. But right now, he had to diffuse the situation. He needed to take Delight somewhere quiet so they could talk.

"I am Lucian Dalakis. And I am the man who is going to marry your sister."

Chapter Eleven

** හ**

Delight looked around the fancy restaurant, feeling slightly dazed. Absolute chaos had erupted the second Lucian had dropped his little bombshell on her and her family. Chase was both hurt and angry, but strangely enough, Miss Nadine seemed quite pleased by the turn of events. Lucian had sat calmly in his chair, looking so pleased with himself that she'd wanted to smack him.

Marry him. The man had completely lost his mind. Her life was totally out of control and his life certainly couldn't bear scrutiny by the police. She kept trying to distance herself and her problems from him and Lucian kept pulling her closer. It was enough to make any sane woman want to beat her head repeatedly against a wall.

Instead, she had taken the time to calmly assure her family that this was the first she'd heard of this proposal. That appeased her brother somewhat, but Delight had felt Miss Nadine's obvious disappointment.

When Lucian had suggested that he take her out to dinner so that they could discuss the matter further, she'd readily agreed. She wanted to give the man a piece of her mind and she didn't want to do it where Miss Nadine or Chase might overhear.

Delight had managed to put Chase off by promising to tell him everything. Soon. He was still mad with her, but he'd grudgingly agreed to give her a little more time. She ached to tell Chase everything, but she would have to clear it with Lucian first. After all, it was a very big secret she was asking the man to share with her family.

It hadn't taken her long to run upstairs, slap some cold water on her face and haul on a dress. It was made of a black, stretchy material that clung to her curves and ended just above her knees. She paired it with a pair of black sandals and decided that it was good enough to go anywhere. It would have to be, as she didn't own another fancy dress. A swipe of the brush through her hair and a quick slick of lipstick and then she was hurrying back downstairs. Delight hadn't wanted to chance leaving Chase and Lucian alone together for too long.

So here she was, with Lucian's large hand on her back, being ushered across the floor of a very exclusive restaurant. They hadn't had reservations, but the moment the maitre d' had seen Lucian, he had welcomed them effusively, assuring Lucian that his usual table was ready for him. Delight had felt the stares of envy from several people who were still waiting for a table. If she wasn't mistaken, one of them was a famous movie star.

In spite of her determination not to be impressed, she couldn't resist a discrete peek around the place. It was harder to get a table at Black Velvet than any other restaurant in the city. Only the rich and famous got to dine here and even they sometimes had to wait for a table. But Lucian had been immediately whisked away from the reception area.

Her feet sank into the plush carpet as she walked across the floor. Everything about Black Velvet screamed good taste and money from the cream-colored walls to the lush greenery that gave the impression that one was seated in a rooftop garden. Balcony doors were wide open and Delight glimpsed some patrons dining outside.

The clink and clatter of people dining followed them across the room. All the tables were covered with floor-length, snowy white linen tablecloths and were set with the finest china and crystal. Everything gleamed. She managed to catch a quick glimpse of some of the meals people were eating. Everything looked and smelled delicious, and her stomach growled.

Embarrassed, she placed her hand on her stomach, hoping no one had heard. Lucian dispelled that myth when he leaned down and whispered in her ear. "Not much longer. We must keep your strength up." She didn't even acknowledge his words, but she could hear the wicked, teasing undertone and could feel the heat creeping up her cheeks.

Keeping her head down, she followed the man in starched white shirt and black tuxedo as he led them to an isolated corner. The table was round and had a curved bench seat instead of chairs. With lush greenery surrounding it, it was almost like entering a private bower. Delight forgot her embarrassment and just enjoyed herself by taking in the splendid sight.

"This is beautiful." She hadn't meant to speak aloud. Now she felt totally gauche, but the headwaiter just smiled at her.

"Thank you, madam." Extending his arm with a flourish, he motioned her to take her seat.

Delight sat down and scooted around the bench. Lucian was right behind her, his large body taking up much of the space. There was room for only two people at the table and the small size of the seat assured that they would indeed be close. It was a table for lovers, cloaked in shadows and lit only by two white pillar candles that sat in silver holders.

Lucian immediately ordered a bottle of wine. Delight's eyes widened as she recognized the exclusive label. Their waiter beamed his approval before hurrying off to fetch their wine. "That's too expensive." She kept her voice to a whisper, not wanting to be accidentally overheard.

He shook his head at the scolding tone in her voice. She could tell he wasn't taking her seriously at all. Fine. Let him waste all his money on a stupid bottle of wine. What did she care? Her hands shook as she clasped her small purse in her lap. She knew she was being unreasonable about the wine, but it gave her something to focus on other than the much larger problems facing her.

Sighing, Lucian placed his finger beneath her chin and raised her face up. "I did not bring you here to distress you." Bending forward, he nipped at her lips and then soothed them with his tongue. "You do not seem to comprehend that money is of no concern to me. I have more than I can ever spend and it is easy to make more."

Delight licked her lips, wanting to capture Lucian's taste on her tongue. It took her a moment for his words to register in her mind and when they did, she spoke without thinking. "That doesn't mean you have to waste it."

Lucian threw back his head and laughed. It wasn't a light chuckle, but a straight from the bottom of the stomach belly laugh. The sight of him mesmerized her. With his head thrown back, his long black hair trailed down over his shoulders and disappeared behind his back. His normally austere features relaxed, making him look younger and more carefree.

There was no way she could stay mad at him. Delight smiled even though his laughter was at her expense. When he looked back at her, his eyes were twinkling with delight. She just shook her head at him and shushed him. Unfortunately, that set his laughter off once again.

"My sweet," Lucian said as he regained control of himself. "I'll never have to worry about you wanting me for my money. You object so strongly when I try to spend some of it on you."

"Money isn't important to me."

Lucian sobered at her words and she regretted them immediately. Once again, he was the strong, silent man she'd come to know. She already missed his laughter and his smile.

He clasped one of her hands in his and brought it to his lips, kissing each knuckle individually. "I know you do not care if I have money. But the fact is that I have it." She shivered as his tongue snaked out to taste between her fingers. "I want only to bring you pleasure and if spending a few dollars can do that, then please allow me the privilege."

"All right," she murmured. When he put it that way, she felt slightly silly for having objected. After all, it was his money.

Just then, the wine steward materialized by the table and began the ritual of opening and presenting the wine to Lucian for approval. Delight sat back against the plush cushions and watched Lucian. Sophisticated and cultured were the two words that came to her mind. When both wineglasses had been filled, Lucian handed one to her and waited for her to taste. The golden liquid tingled in her mouth and slid easily down her throat. She'd never tasted anything quite like it. "It's wonderful."

The wine steward was replaced by their waiter who handed them both gilded menus as he listed the evening specials. Delight was pleasantly amused when she opened the heavy vellum pages and realized there were no prices listed. She guessed that if you had to ask, then you shouldn't be here. Determined to enjoy herself, she scanned the menu and then ordered the poached salmon in dill sauce with baby potatoes and glazed carrots. Lucian ordered a steak, rare.

It occurred to her that in the short time she'd known him, Lucian had become the most important person in her life next to her brother and Miss Nadine. It was crazy and impossible to fall for a man so hard and so fast, but Delight was very afraid that was exactly what she had done. The thought of not seeing him again made her heart ache and her soul weep.

Physically, he appealed to her in every way. She seemed to be in a low-level state of arousal every time she was near him. Just sitting next to him was turning her on. His large body radiated a strength and warmth that made her want to just crawl right inside him and never come out.

The thought of his hands on her skin made her breasts swell and ache and her nipples bead into hard nubs that pushed against front of the dress. She wasn't wearing a bra, as the dress had one built into its construction because it had spaghetti straps. The rasp of the material against her sensitive nipples made her want to moan.

She shifted on the seat, trying to ease the throbbing between her thighs. Her panties were already soaked in her juices and her pussy clenched in need. What was it about Lucian that made her want and need him so? She didn't know and for tonight, she didn't want to question it.

Her problems were still very real and had to be dealt with, but for once in her life, she wanted to throw her responsibilities aside for an evening and just immerse herself in her sensual side.

A need to please Lucian grew deep inside her. Last night, he'd brought her to sensual heights that she'd never even dreamed of. Tonight, she wanted to return the favor. A wicked idea formed in her mind. She licked her lips, wondering if she was daring enough to do it. Taking one last look around, she confirmed their absolute seclusion from the rest of the restaurant. Only the muted sounds of people talking and eating permeated their privacy.

When the waiter gathered their menus and left them, Delight made her move. Casually dropping her linen napkin on the floor. She feigned surprise and then reached down beneath the table. "Oops. I'll just get that."

"Leave it. The waiter will bring you another."

"No, I've just about got it." Not giving herself time to think about what she was about to do, Delight allowed herself to slip from her seat until she was on her hands and knees under the table. Ignoring the napkin, she scooted over until she was kneeling in front of Lucian.

"Delight." Lucian sounded slightly perplexed. She felt him shift as he lifted the edge of the tablecloth.

Acting quickly so she didn't lose her nerve, Delight placed her hands on the front of Lucian's legs and slid them up over his knees until they were on top of his thighs. The muscles shifted and clenched beneath her palms.

She pushed his legs apart and scooted between his spread thighs. Her face was directly in front of the crotch of his pants. The material bulged forward as his cock grew and thickened. Delight licked her lips in anticipation as she reached for the fastener on his pants.

The button was hard to undo because the material was pulled so tight, but she persevered and was rewarded when it finally slipped through the hole. Lucian muffled a groan as she eased the zipper over his swollen cock. Pushing back the material, she was slightly startled when warm flesh leapt out to meet her hand. He wasn't wearing any underwear.

His musky scent filled her senses, making her squirm with need. She wanted that cock thrusting hard against her sensitive flesh. But that would come later. This was for him.

The table moved slightly, making her jump. Her startled gaze flew to Lucian who was now staring down at her. He'd only moved the table a few inches, but by doing that and tugging up the ends of the tablecloth, he could see her kneeling between his legs waiting to service him.

His eyes scorched her entire body as he stared at her. "Pull down your top so I can see your breasts."

Delight felt wicked as more liquid seeped from her core at his heated command. Taking her time, she shimmied the straps down over her shoulders before peeling the clingy dress down her torso and letting the material pool at her waist. Skimming her hands back over her stomach, she palmed her breasts, rubbing the sensitive tips until she moaned.

Lucian's strong fingers tangled in her short hair and guided her mouth towards his straining cock. She laughed wickedly as she swirled her tongue around the bulbous tip, taking pleasure in licking the liquid seeping from its slit. Using her fingers, she cupped his sac gently and massaged his balls as she continued to flick her tongue around the top of his cock.

With her other hand, she gripped the bottom of his shaft, squeezing it tight. Then she began to move it up to the very top before sliding it back down to the base. Up and down, she pumped her hand in a slow rhythm. His cock pulsed in her hand and she felt an answering call from her pussy.

Shifting slightly, she straddled one of his legs, rubbing her aching sex as hard as she could. Lucian thrust his leg harder against her pussy and Delight moaned with pleasure. His cock jumped in her mouth as the vibration went through him.

She thought she heard him swear softly and then her head was caught in the vise of his hands. "Deeper."

Not waiting for her to comply, he arched his hips and drove his length into her warm mouth. Delight parted her lips, eager to take him as deep as she could. Using her tongue, she stroked the length of his cock as he pulled it to the edge of her lips before forging his way back in again.

Delight could feel his tension as she continued to suck and lick his thrusting cock. She could feel his sac moving closer to his body and knew he was close to coming. Feeling her own desire growing, she arched her lower body against his leg.

Reaching down, she tugged the skirt of her dress higher until she could rub her damp panties against him. Her inner muscles were clenching tight now, needy and desperate.

Lucian's fingers grew almost painful as he clutched at her hair. Pumping his hips hard, he drove his cock deep into her throat one final time. His release was fast and furious and brought on her own. The moment she felt his cum spurt inside her mouth, she pressed her sex as hard as she could against his leg and came immediately. She swallowed as her lower body jerked and heaved.

When Lucian finally finished and sank back into the plush seat, Delight continued to suck on his length, unwilling to let him go just yet. She was just about to move when the tablecloth was jerked back in place.

Delight blinked at the darkness and then froze when she heard the waiter's slightly perplexed voice. "Mademoiselle has left?"

"The lady is powdering her nose. Leave her dinner and do not disturb us." Lucian's deep commanding voice made her shiver and to her surprise, she felt desire welling up inside her again. She lazily sucked on his semi-erect cock and was annoyed when one of his hands reached beneath the table and tugged her head back until he popped out of her mouth. Sighing softly, she rested her head on his thigh and waited.

The waiter's quick "Yes sir" was followed by the clink of dinnerware being place upon the table.

Delight didn't move, even when she heard the retreating footsteps of the waiter. She was content to stay where she was so she wouldn't have to face Lucian. Now that the pleasure was fading from her orgasm, she could hear the sounds of the restaurant around her, and common sense was beginning to reassert itself. She couldn't believe that she'd just given a blowjob in a public place.

"You can't stay down there all night long." Lucian's amused voice drifted down to her.

"Yes I can."

The tablecloth was flicked back and she blinked as his face came into focus. "Where has the temptress gone?"

Delight buried her face against the fabric of Lucian's pants, ignoring him as he zipped and buttoned them. Before she could figure out what to say or do, he reached down and eased her from under the table.

His hands slid from her shoulders and came to rest over her bare breasts. Using his thumbs, he teased the still hard nubs before leaning down and sucking one right into his mouth. Delight shifted on the bench, pushing her breast closer to Lucian's mouth. She suddenly no longer cared that they were in a public place, she wanted his mouth everywhere.

As if he'd read her mind, he raised his head and smiled a wicked smile. "Soon, my love." He lapped at her nipple one last time before sitting back. "But first you must pay for your teasing."

"What do you mean?" She could feel her pussy clench as Lucian spoke and more of her cream seeped from inside her.

"First, we will enjoy our dinner." Delight was confused by his change of subject and started to tug her dress back up to cover herself. Lucian's hand shot out and grabbed her wrist, stopping her. "Leave it. I want to look at you while we eat."

"I can't." She cast a worried gaze to the small secluded opening that led to their private corner.

"But you will. There is no need to be concerned." It was a command. But Delight felt as if it was a test as well. A test of trust.

She trusted him with her life. She could give him this. Her sense of humor reasserted itself and she felt the corners of her mouth turn up slightly. The worst thing that could happen was that the waiter would see her and they would be asked to leave.

Picking up her fork, she tasted her salmon. Chewing carefully, she savored the flavor before swallowing. Pointing her fork at Lucian, she made her final plea. "Remember, if we get thrown out of here it's all your fault."

Lucian chuckled as he picked up his cutlery and sliced off a thin piece of the bloody rare steak. His teeth gleamed in the candlelight as he forked a piece into his mouth. She trembled slightly as she watched him chew and swallow. His every movement was one of sensual pleasure. He never took his eyes off her breasts as he ate.

"I will remember." Delight felt goose bumps cover her torso and she knew he was referring not to what she had said, but rather, to what she had just done.

Chapter Twelve

ഇ

Delight hadn't realized there was such a thing as sensual torture until this evening. Because that's exactly what supper had been. She felt edgy and her skin felt like it was too tight on her body, she was so aroused.

Lucian had finally allowed her to dress when he'd finished eating his steak. Or rather, he'd dressed her. Enjoying every moment of her discomfort, Lucian had once again fondled and kissed her breasts until she was ready to throw him on the table and have her way with him. Then, the devil had calmly tugged the straps over her arms and fixed them into place seconds before the waiter had returned to find out if they'd wanted coffee. Both of them had declined.

Lucian was close behind her as they walked up the steps of his home. Neither of them had spoken on the short ride back to his house. Both of them were lost in their own thoughts. Now that the time had come to talk, Delight wasn't sure she was ready. It was easier just to live in the moment and to enjoy the sexual pleasures they shared.

When the door closed behind her with a solid thud, Delight tossed her small purse on the table that sat just inside the foyer as she turned to face Lucian. All thoughts of talk fled the moment she laid eyes on his face. His green eyes blazed with lust and the hard planes of his face were even more chiseled in appearance. He had the look of a man who had reached the end of his limits.

Every muscle in his huge body seemed to be pulled tight, making him seem even larger than usual. The front zipper of his pants bulged. Lucian was very aroused again and making no secret of the fact. His blatant desire fanned the embers of her own and her body responded immediately.

She licked her lips as she felt the moisture between her legs coat her already damp panties. The ache between her thighs began to throb once again and her hips swayed towards him.

Lucian stalked towards her, his intent clearly stamped on his face. He wanted her. Now. Delight took a step back, partly aroused and partly afraid of his overwhelming passion. He didn't stop, but kept coming towards her. Delight kept backing up until she felt the wall at her back. There was nowhere left to go.

He loomed over her, his eyes running down over her body from her head to her toes and back up again. His eyes lingered on her breasts and the juncture between her legs, pure possession blazing from their depths.

She felt all the air leave her body in a rush. It was if he was physically touching her with his hands instead of just with his eyes. Her skin sizzled wherever his eyes landed until she felt as if her entire body was ablaze.

"Breathe." She felt his breath on her cheek as his softly spoken word seemed to drift towards her. Air filled her lungs as she took a deep breath and then another.

Crowding closer to her, he inserted himself between her legs, forcing her to spread her feet wider to accommodate him. His hard erection poked against her stomach, making it flutter with nervousness.

She glanced up at him and froze as he smiled at her. In the dim light of the foyer, she could see two long fangs gleaming. Her hands clutched the front of his shirt, whether to push him away or pull him closer, she wasn't sure. With her entire world turned upside down, he offered her stability and she clung to it.

With her lower body pinned to the wall by his, she was at the mercy of his superior strength. Yet, she still had no fear of him. One hand rose slowly to caress her cheek. His fingers were so gentle, she nuzzled her face closer, wanting more. He groaned and his fingers slid down to cup her chin, tilting it up so she was caught in his burning gaze.

"You know what I am."

"Yes."

If anything, her single word seemed to drive the tension in him even higher. The grip on her face tightened as if he wanted to make sure she could not escape him.

"I am a vampire." He spoke each word carefully, making sure she did not misunderstand him.

She tried to nod, but his fingers made it impossible for her to do more than tilt her head slightly. He thrust his lower body harder against her. She arched her hips in response, wanting him closer. Longing to have him buried inside her.

"I am immortal. I need blood to sustain me. Prolonged exposure to sunlight, a stake through the heart, and beheading will kill me. Nothing else." He gave a short bark of laughter. "Except perhaps you."

"I would never hurt you." The promise poured from her lips before she had time to think. Just the mere thought of hurting him was abhorrent to her.

A grim smile crossed his lips, making his face look cruel in the meager light. "Dalakis men love only once in their lifetime. It is their gift and their curse." His hand curved down her chin until it was wrapped loosely around her throat. "Many have given up in despair and faced the killing sunlight rather than live any longer without finding their true love. Others have done the same after being rejected. And a few have joined their love in death after a human lifetime is lived and their mate dies."

Leaning down, he rested his forehead against hers. "It is your choice to make."

Delight sagged against the wall for support when he stepped back from her, releasing her totally. Her knees felt weak and she felt empty inside at the thought of never seeing him again.

"But know this," he continued, drawing himself up to his full height. "If you stay now, I will never let you go."

The force of his words rocked her to her core. In a flash, the urban, sophisticated man disappeared to be replaced by the barbarian warrior of old. Cold ruthlessness and power emanated from him. This was not a man to be crossed or thwarted by anyone.

It would be so easy just to give in to him, lured by the sensual promise he offered. But Delight wanted more. Needed more than just a sexual relationship. She licked her dry lips, and locked her knees to steady herself as she pushed away from the wall. He had to say the words. She needed to be sure before committing herself to what was sure to be an impossibly difficult relationship. "Does that mean that you love me?" She'd meant her words to be forceful, but they'd come out more as a plea for reassurance.

Lucian stared at her as if she was mad. Giving an exasperated huff, he stepped towards her and then stopped. He raised his hands and then dropped them back to his sides, clenching them into fists that shook slightly. The expression on his face softened slightly as he shook his head at her.

Delight felt as if she'd disappointed him. That she'd somehow missed something important in what he had said. "I've got to be sure."

"Choose." His face was set like stone once again, totally unreadable. Crossing his arms across his chest, he waited for her decision.

She knew that whatever choice she made, her life would never be the same again. Lucian was such a strong, forceful man it would be easy to be overwhelmed and dominated totally by him. She had the feeling that it would be natural for him to try and control every aspect of her life if she let him. A small smile grew on her face as she imagined the arguments they would have in the future if that was the case. She might not be very large, but she had a will of iron and a backbone of steel. She would be an equal in their relationship.

Her forceful thoughts startled her. It seemed that there was really no decision to be made. She knew she loved Lucian and wanted to be with him for whatever time they had. He completed her in some way she couldn't really explain. It was as if she had found a part of herself she hadn't known was missing until she'd found it.

Reaching down, she gripped the bottom of her dress and in one motion pulled it up and over her head before tossing it to the floor beside her. Lucian's chest rose and fell as his breathing deepened. His cock was straining against the front of his pants and she reached out a hand to stroke the hardness hidden beneath the cloth.

Lucian's hand shot out and gripped her wrist in a gentle, but unbreakable, vise. "Is this your answer?" His voice was guttural and strained and Delight longed to break his rigid control.

"Yes," she purred as she flexed her fingers around him.

He lifted her hand from the front of his pants and brought it to his lips, kissing each of her fingers before placing it on his chest. "Remove my shirt."

Eagerly, Delight unbuttoned his shirt to uncover the hard muscles beneath. Tugging the shirt from his pants, she pushed the edges open to reveal the perfect male chest. A six-pack of abs rippled as her fingers grazed his sides. A thin line of hair ran from between his flat, brown male nipples and disappeared into his pants.

Excitement filled her at having this man as her own. Placing her hands on his stomach, she stroked her way up his torso to his shoulders, pushing the shirt down his arms until it dropped to the floor. Moving closer, she nuzzled the crisp chest hair on his chest as she kissed her way towards one of his nipples. Flicking the flat, brown disk with her tongue, she reveled in the way it pebbled into a hard nub.

Her breasts felt swollen and heavy and she pressed them against his hard, muscular chest. Little sounds of contentment escaped from her lips as she rubbed her tight nipples against him.

Lucian's fingers tangled into her hair, holding her tight to his chest. She laughed as sensual excitement flooded her veins and she sucked his nipple into her mouth. His finger tightened in her hair, and she gave a moan of dismay when he pulled her away from him.

"Strip for me."

Delight shivered as she watched him. Large, powerful and totally aroused, he waited for her to comply. She slipped her feet out of her sandals and kicked them to one side. Wearing only thigh-high stockings and her black lace panties, she stood in front of him.

"Finish it." He looked totally in control of himself once again, so Delight set out to unleash his passions.

Turning sideways, she bent forward and began to unroll the first stocking. Her breasts hung in front of her, swaying as she worked. Glancing towards him, she was pleased to note that the front of his pants twitched as she rolled the stocking down to her ankle and whisked it off her foot. The floor was warm and hard against her bare sole and her toes curled slightly. Then she repeated the maneuver with the other stocking.

Facing him fully now, Delight hooked her fingers in the waistband of her panties and shimmied her hips as she pushed them down her legs and kicked them aside. Totally naked now, she skimmed her hands up her stomach and cupped her breasts in her hands, pinching the hard buds between her thumbs and forefingers. She could feel the dampness on her thighs and smell her arousal in the air and she knew Lucian could too.

While Lucian watched her fondle her breasts, he kicked off his own shoes and removed his pants. His legs were long and strong, muscles bulging as he spread his thighs and braced his feet on the floor. Totally aroused, his cock thrust out in front of him, bobbing slightly as he watched her pleasure herself.

He looked feral and wild, a man in his prime, powerful and strong and hers. Delight wanted all of him. She wanted him to let down his guard and give her all that he was. Giving her nipples one final pinch, she skimmed her hands down her body until they were on her thighs.

Lucian's mouth tightened and his chest expanded. "Spread your legs." His hoarse whisper trickled down her spine like a caress and her hips undulated towards him. "Show me."

Her feet moved of their own accord and her hands spread the lips of her sex wide. Flexing her hips towards him, she offered the wet, pink lips to him for his perusal. Knowing that he watched her, she sinuously moved her hips back and forth in a parody of the sex act. She could feel her inner muscles clenching tight as her arousal grew almost painful.

She held her breath as Lucian took a step towards her.

"Don't stop."

His words seduced her further and her hips kept up their seductive motion as his hand slipped between her legs. This time when her hips swung forward, two of his fingers slipped along her wet flesh and buried themselves inside her.

Delight moaned as her hips swung backwards and his fingers eased almost out of her, thrusting deep as she shoved her hips forward once again. It felt so good, but it was not enough. She was on the edge, needing very little to send her spiraling out of control.

"Lucian." She arched towards him, almost sobbing his name as his fingers continued to tease her.

"Tell me what you want."

"You, Lucian," she panted.

"Then turn around and brace your hands on the wall. Spread your legs wide and offer yourself to me." Lucian pulled his fingers from her body and raised them to his nose, smelling her desire. As she watched, he stuck his fingers in his mouth and sucked her cream from them.

Delight had never seen anything so blatantly erotic in her entire life. Taking one last look at Lucian, she turned and spread her arms and legs wide and bent forward, bracing herself against the wall. Her bottom was thrust back towards him and she was totally open and exposed to him. A single shiver racked her body from head to toe.

"Take me, Lucian. Make me yours." Her words seemed to echo in the entryway as she waited to see what he would do next.

Chapter Thirteen

&

Lucian could barely believe his eyes. Delight knew what he was and still she offered herself willingly to him. He wasn't sure she truly understood the implications of giving herself to him so totally, but he wasn't about to argue with fate. She was his, now and forever. Whatever the future held, their lives were intertwined for as long as they lived.

The smell of sex wafted on the air, thick and potent. The most erotic perfume in existence. Lucian battled his baser instincts, which were screaming at him to mount her and fuck her until she screamed for mercy. And he might do just that. But later. Delight had offered herself willingly to him and he would not abuse her trust.

Just looking at her with her hands braced against the cream-colored wood of the wall with her legs spread was almost enough to make him come. He could feel the liquid seeping from the tip of his cock as his body reacted strongly to her. A sheen of sweat clung to his body and he shoved his long hair over his shoulder to get it out of his way.

Stepping up behind her, he reached out and placed his hands over hers even as he spread his legs so they were directly behind hers. His body covered hers easily and he felt a savage pleasure rise up within him as he physically dominated her smaller frame.

Bending down, he took the lobe of her ear between his teeth and nibbled carefully. Delight gave a small cry and tilted her head to allow him easier access. Lucian almost howled with primal satisfaction. He felt all-powerful. King and conqueror. She was his for the taking.

Then Delight moved.

It was a subtle motion, but it shot through his entire body like an electric shock. Moving her bottom, she nestled his cock between the plump folds and gave a sigh of contentment. That small sound almost brought him to his knees. It would never do for her to know how much power she wielded over him.

Lucian shook his head as he straightened and took a deep breath to center himself. In truth, there was nothing he wouldn't do to make Delight happy or to protect her. She belonged to him.

The air in the room seemed to come alive and crackle with his rising anger. The need to seek out and punish the ones responsible for Delight's ordeal was almost overwhelming. The only thing that was more powerful than that thirst for vengeance was the necessity of claiming Delight as his own. Once he had done that, then he would be free to exact his vengeance.

"Lucian." Delight's voice was like music to his ears and helped calm his growing rage. She had sensed his aggravation and was seeking to soothe him.

His heart pounded as he took in her tousled hair, the curvy line of her spine, her slender hip, and her plump bottom. Physically, he'd never reacted to any woman this strongly before. Delight was perfect for him in every way. It was as if she had been fashioned specifically for him, and in a way, he supposed that she had been. There was no other woman in the world who would ever suit him as well as Delight.

But it wasn't just physical attraction. It went beyond that, as powerful as the physical connection was. He admired her loyalty to her family, her intelligence, her work ethic, and her strength. Her heart, once given, would remain true and that was the greatest gift of all.

With that in mind, he set out to seduce her, to bind her to him. He pushed his swollen shaft tighter into the dark cleft of her behind. Tilting back his head, he reveled in the feel of his cock being squeezed by her bottom.

Wrapping his fingers around her wrists, he was shocked by the smallness and fragility of them. She had such a large, strong personality, it was easy to forget how much weaker she was compared to him. Although, he knew she wouldn't appreciate the comparison. He knew she thought of herself as strong and competent. And she was, in her own way, but the fact remained that he was physically stronger and she was rather delicate.

Lucian ran his fingers down the underside of her arms. "Your skin is so soft." He kissed the nape of her neck as he spoke and smiled when he saw the goose bumps his words had raised on her arms and neck.

Continuing his exploration, he slipped his hands around her torso and wrapped his fingers over her plump breasts. The mounds fit his large hands perfectly, the taut nipples stabbing his palm. His cock jerked and he pushed it harder against her ass as he began to rotate his hands. Delight moaned and sinuously moved her bottom.

Lucian hissed as he struggled not to lose control. While he began to tease her tight nipple with one hand, he slipped the other down over her flat stomach and right between her legs. His fingers sifted through her pubic hair, but he didn't stop. Her cream coated the sensitive layers of her skin, allowing him to skim his fingers right over them and straight into her opening.

She cried out as two of his large fingers slipped into her heated depths. He could feel her inner muscles clenching his fingers tight and realized that she was very close to coming. Carefully, he stretched his fingers apart as far as they would go and withdrew them to the edge of her opening. Frantically, she tried to move her hips to keep his fingers inside her. Lucian drove his fingers deep as he gently pinched her swollen nipple. Delight bucked against his hand.

"Come for me." He scrapped his teeth against the back of her neck, but did not allow himself a taste of her rich blood. Not yet. He would lose all control then and he wanted her pleasure first.

Her head jerked back and she moaned as he nipped her shoulder, her body racked with shudders of desire. Lucian worked his fingers in and out of her body, feeling her muscles contract as she came. The gush of her release washed over his fingers. He bit his lip to keep from roaring his satisfaction out loud.

When she was finished, he withdrew his hands and wrapped them around her waist while she regained her composure. "What about you?" Her words were little more than a whisper, making Lucian smile.

"We have only just begun." A shudder racked her body, but she didn't pull away from him or move from her position against the wall. "Remain as you are." It was almost painful to pull away from Delight, but he did so. His cock protested, throbbing almost violently and his testicles felt swollen and heavy. He ignored his discomfort and trailed hot kisses down her spine.

Dropping to his knees behind her, he nipped and licked at her soft, plump behind. He was so tempted to sink his teeth into her ass and sample her blood, but he didn't think she was ready for that just yet. Instead, he cupped both mounds and spread them wide, opening her ass to him. He licked the dark cleft, ignoring her shriek as he continued downward, past the slick folds of her sex until his tongue slipped inside her. He withdrew almost immediately and sat back of his heels, licking his lips, enjoying the taste of her on his tongue.

"Spread your legs wider and bend over more. I want to see more of your pretty behind." He sensed her hesitation and reached out and ran one finger between her legs, finding her swollen clitoris and massaging it lightly. Her hips jerked and she moaned. "Wider, Delight. I want to see all of you."

Slowly, Delight moved her feet until her legs were further apart. Lucian placed his free hand on her stomach and urged her bottom back further even as he whispered encouragement to her. "You can spread your legs a little wider for me, Delight."

Her feet inched apart, leaving her wide open to him. "Beautiful," he muttered as he kissed her bottom.

Bringing both hands between her legs, he traced the damp folds of her sex until his fingers were coated in her cream. Her clit was swollen and needy, so he teased it ever so gently before dipping his fingers into her opening once again. Over and over, he stroked the bud of her pleasure before plunging his fingers into her waiting warmth.

With his other hand, he traced the dark cleft of her behind to her other tight little opening. He stroked his fingers over it until it was wet with her own cream, then ever so carefully, he inserted the wet tip of one of his fingers into her ass.

"Lucian," she squealed. He could sense her discomfort.

"I won't hurt you," he reassured her. "But this is something that can bring you pleasure as well, my love. Someday, I want to be able to love you in all ways, so we must start to prepare your body." He kept inserting his finger as he spoke, pushing it deeper and deeper, past the tight resistance of her bottom. "Your ass is so tight. The pleasure will be incredible for both of us when I can finally get inside you."

Delight shivered as the pleasure-pain racked her body. He knew it was a bit of both as his finger was long and thick and her small hole was tight. He used his other hand to his advantage, stroking her clit and the folds of her sex as he pushed his finger as far as it would go in her behind. The sensations were too much for her and he could feel her body tightening as he slipped his fingers into her wet pussy. Her muscles clamped down hard, squeezing the fingers he had inserted in both openings.

Leaning forward, he blew on her heated flesh. Delight cried out and came in a rush, her entire body shaking as she convulsed around him. It was incredible to watch her give herself over to the pleasure he gave, knowing she trusted him in a way she'd trusted no other man. Her body was racked with shivers and Lucian carefully removed his fingers from her body, ignoring the slight flinch of her body as he pulled his long finger out of her behind.

Sitting on his knees on the floor, he pulled her into his lap. She collapsed in a heap against him and he wrapped his arms around her to keep her from toppling over. His cock was like steel against her back and Lucian knew he could wait no longer. He was in real pain now. His cock and his balls were so heavy they were about to burst and his teeth ached to sink into her skin and taste her blood. The craving was upon him and could no longer be denied.

Lifting her easily, he laid her on her stomach on the soft Persian carpet that covered the center of the foyer. He knew he should take her upstairs to his soft bed, but he had waited too long. Past the point of no return, he had to have her now.

She shifted and turned her head to look at him. Her eyes were drowsy and her smile was sultry. When she got a good look at his face, her eyes widened and she licked her lips nervously. Lucian could well imagine the picture she saw. He knew that his normally green eyes were probably glowing an eerie reddish color and that his fangs were extended over his bottom lip. His face, austere at best, would look harsh and unforgiving in the dim light cast by the lone lamp.

Delight glanced at his cock and gasped when she saw how swollen and red it was. A growl vibrated in his chest as he felt her gaze like it was a caress. His cock jumped and more liquid seeped from the slit. He was so close to coming, he'd soon come on the carpet if he didn't get inside her.

But now that the moment was at hand, and the final act of claiming was upon him, he found that he was waiting for her decision. It had to be her choice. While every instinct was screaming at him to just drive into her and take her, he could not.

He'd always laughed at his ancestors and the stories they'd passed down throughout the ages of a love so great a man would deny his very salvation rather than take what was not freely given. Now the cruel joke was on him. He finally understood what it meant to find his one true love, the woman who would complete him and be his for eternity. Lucian knew he would rather face his own death than to take what she would not offer. He waited, his life in her hands.

"What's wrong?" She sounded confused, but Lucian couldn't answer her. Speaking was beyond him now. It was taking all of his strength to keep his passions under his control. "Lucian?"

He shook his head and clenched his fists. The pain in his body was almost overwhelming and he could feel a bead of sweat roll down his back. Delight moved in one motion. Coming up on her hands and knees, she glanced over her shoulder and captured his fiery gaze. "Take me, Lucian. Make me yours." She hesitated and swallowed hard. "Love me forever."

Before she'd spoken her final word, he was between her spread thighs, driving himself home. He felt her shudder as he surged past her swollen, delicate flesh and into her body. Unable to stop, he seated himself to the hilt in one thrust.

Dropping his head to her shoulder, he gasped for breath. "I'm sorry if I hurt you."

"I'm fine, Lucian." Her words were gentle and giving even though they did not deny the hurt.

He nodded and licked the slick flesh of her nape, tasting the mixture of salt and desire. "I have no control left," he gritted out between clenched teeth. His cock was pulsing hard and the urge to thrust was enormous.

Delight pulled her hips forward and then slammed them backwards, giving him all the permission he needed. Wrapping one arm around her waist, he slammed his cock into her from behind, driving it as hard and as far as it would go. Her body shivered, but accepted him. A wild pleasure grew in him as he repeated the motion, over and over.

He palmed one of her breasts, gripping the soft mound in his hand as he continued to pound into her willing flesh. Her moans quickly became ones of pleasure that made him thrust even harder. He couldn't get far enough inside her to please him. Harder and faster, he ground his cock into her wet pussy. This was his, now and forever.

They were both so close to coming, but another need, a far more powerful one, needed to be assuaged first. The words welled up deep in his soul and spewed forth, both a promise and a vow. "You are my heart and my soul. I will protect you with my entire being for as long as you shall live and beyond if you some day choose to join me."

Now that the words had been said, Lucian finally relaxed and let go. His testicles drew up tight to his body as he shoved his cock hard within her one last time. As he started to come, he leaned over her and bit the back of her neck, burying his teeth to the hilt. Delight's body jerked as she came, her inner muscles clutching his cock even as he drank her blood. The sensation was incredible.

Lucian emptied himself into Delight even as he fed from her. It was only when she slumped forward that he realized he'd lost all sense of time. Retracting his teeth, he licked the wound, closing it and healing it instantly. He withdrew his semi-aroused cock from her warmth and slowly lowered her to the floor. She shivered even though she wasn't cold.

Lucian slumped next to her, pulling her into his arms. He felt totally drained, yet fully alive at the same time. As her blood seeped through his veins, he flicked his tongue over his teeth, capturing the last taste of her. Delight sighed and shivered once again.

Heaving himself up off the floor, Lucian bent down, easily scooping Delight up into his arms. Ignoring the clothing strewn all over the floor, he padded up the stairs with his treasure clasped tight in his arms. They had much to sort out, but that was for later. Right now, she needed to sleep and regain her strength. There would be time to talk tomorrow.

Locking all the doors carefully behind him, he deposited Delight onto his bed. She immediately rolled to her side and snuggled under the covers he pulled over her. Taking his time, he checked to make sure all the windows were barred tight and locked down. After doing a mental sweep of the house and assuring himself that everything was as it should be, he climbed into bed and pulled Delight into his arms. Although she had already drifted off to sleep, Lucian planted the suggestion in her mind that she would sleep until the next sunset.

The dawn would be breaking soon, but Lucian didn't wait for the sun to rise. Instead, with Delight tucked tight against his chest, he relaxed and drifted off to sleep.

Chapter Fourteen

ဆ

Just like the last time she was here, Delight awoke with great difficulty. She really had to have a talk with Lucian about his tendency to want her to sleep while he slept and be awake only when he was. She had an entire life and a family to take care of and she couldn't do that if she was in bed all day.

She had no idea what time it was, but sensed that it was once again late afternoon. Stretching gingerly, she smothered a gasp when some of her muscles protested. Her poor body wasn't used to all the vigorous sexual activity. She hurt in places she hadn't even known existed until she met Lucian.

Even in sleep, his arm was locked tight around her waist. Carefully, she pried his fingers open and slipped from his grasp. He didn't move, but continued to lie there as still as death. Delight bit her lip nervously as she placed her open palm on his chest. Nothing.

Tugging her hand away, she brought it to her own chest and felt the comforting thump of her heart. Intellectually, she knew that Lucian was a vampire. As farfetched as that sounded, it was indeed a reality. What that actually entailed, she wasn't really sure. She had so many questions to ask him, but they always seemed to get sidetracked when they were together.

Delight shivered as memories from last night flashed in her brain. Everything that she'd done in the restaurant and the downstairs hallway both astonished and delighted her. She seemed to have no control where Lucian was concerned and that would have bothered her, except that he seemed to have very little control himself when they were together.

When he'd finally taken her on the floor last night, it was if something inside her had changed. As he'd recited what sounded like a vow before allowing himself to finally make love to her, she'd felt as if she'd finally come home. There was a sense of belonging and almost of destiny with Lucian. It sounded silly when she thought about it, but it was true nonetheless.

That was all fine and good, but she still had responsibilities and one of those would be waiting at home to talk to her. She and Lucian hadn't had time to talk, but she'd already decided to tell Chase the truth. He was her brother and if Lucian was going to be a huge part of her life, then he had to know that Lucian was a vampire.

"He'll think I'm nuts," she muttered as she made herself roll out of bed and pad to the bathroom. The woman in the mirror looked a fright with her hair sticking up on end and her pale face staring back. Delight stuck out her tongue at herself before stepping into the large shower stall and turning the water on full blast.

She didn't linger, but quickly washed and rinsed herself. Turning off the water, she climbed out of the shower, grabbed a towel off the rack and quickly dried herself off. There wasn't much she could do with her hair, so she finger-combed it before wrapping the towel around herself and padding back to the bedroom.

Lucian hadn't moved. Delight walked over to the bed, stepped up onto the platform, bent down and kissed his warm lips. "I'll talk to you later." She continued to watch him for a moment, unable to pull her gaze away from his beloved face.

Finally, she made herself step down from the bed. "You've put off leaving long enough." Delight continued to talk to herself as she unlocked the bedroom door, being careful to close it tight behind her when she stepped out into the hallway.

"Now, where are my clothes?" She crept down the stairs, nervous for some unknown reason. She felt more like an intruder than a guest, and she really didn't like the feeling that she was sneaking out on Lucian. Again.

"I'm not really," she assured herself as she picked her black lace panties off the floor, shook them out and stepped into them.

Her dress was a black clump on the floor. It would have a few wrinkles, but that couldn't be helped. Bending over, she plucked it off the floor and straightened the fabric. "I'll be back. I promise." Dropping the towel, she raised the dress to pull it over her head.

"I'm glad to hear that."

Delight shrieked as a rough male voice startled her. Pulling the dress back in front of her like a shield, she backed away from the unfamiliar voice. Clad only in her underwear, she confronted the intruder. "Who are you?"

He continued to advance on her, his every movement filled with a masculine grace that reminded her of Lucian. The more she stared at him, the more convinced she was that he had to be related to Lucian somehow. This man was even larger than Lucian, which made him absolutely huge, but he had the same green eyes and they shared the same basic facial structure. The stranger also had long black hair that was pulled back in a ponytail.

"You're Lucian's brother." She was both thrilled and dismayed by this turn of events. Delight was pleased to meet Lucian's family, just not in her underwear. Trying to ignore the fact that only a small black piece of fabric covered her, she thrust her hand towards him. "I'm Delight."

"You certainly are." His words charmed her as he took her hand in his much larger one and held it for a moment before bringing it to his lips. "I am Stefan Dalakis." After placing a soft kiss on the back of her hand, he kept possession of it, ignoring her attempts to pull her hand from his grasp. "But where are you going? Lucian would not be pleased that you are leaving on your own."

Delight stopped trying to pull her fingers from his grasp. What was it with these Dalakis men that made them think she had to do whatever they told her? Frowning, she glared up at

Stefan. "Well, he'll just have to get over it now, won't he? I've got things to do." Her scowl got even deeper as another thought occurred to her. "Why are you awake and Lucian isn't?" She glanced out the window and noted that the sun was just sinking.

"Because I have learned to test my limits, while my brothers have not bothered. There is much to be learned if one is willing to reach for the knowledge."

It occurred to Delight that just because he was Lucian's brother didn't mean that Stefan wasn't dangerous. Her heart was pounding in her chest as she gave her hand one last tug. He released her so suddenly she would have fallen if he hadn't steadied her.

Stefan's face was impassive, but his eyes swirled with myriad conflicting emotions. She feared that he might even be more dangerous than Lucian. Lucian might be a force of nature, wild and powerful, but this self-contained man was terrifying.

Delight screamed, loud and shrill, when a pair of arms locked around her from behind. Her terror was so great that it took a moment for the voice to penetrate her fear.

"Shh, my love. Everything is fine." Lucian rocked her in his arms as he whispered in her ear.

She calmed immediately, slightly ashamed at her outburst, but excusing it as a result of the crazy few days she'd endured. "I'm okay. I was already freaked out and you startled me, is all."

It was definitely the wrong thing to say. Delight found herself thrust behind Lucian's back as he confronted his brother. "What did you do to frighten Delight?" The words were practically growled and she could see that his fists were clenched by his sides. Stefan on the other hand, looked mildly amused and extremely sad. It was that sadness that reached out to her and touched her heart.

Scooting around Lucian, she tapped her hand on his chest until he looked down at her. "I hardly expected to meet someone in your home. You didn't tell me you had a brother, so it's your fault he frightened me, not his."

"Is that so?" He sounded more amused than angry.

"Yes it is. And how is it that he can be up around in the daylight and you can't? If I'm going to be a part of your life, we've got to talk about these things."

Stefan snickered under his breath so she turned on him as well. "And just because you're Lucian's brother doesn't mean you can boss me around."

The look of surprise on Stefan's face was priceless. He looked at her as if she was some strange creature he didn't quite know what to do with. Delight risked a quick glance at Lucian and noted that he looked none too pleased either. This wasn't good. Not only had Lucian caught her sneaking out of his house, now she was telling off his brother. Deciding it was better to stay on the offensive than the defensive, she shifted her attention back to Lucian. "Any other family I should know about?"

"Yes. An older brother and a new sister-in-law." Before she could even think of a response, he cupped the back of her head, leaned down and kissed her.

It wasn't a soft, gentle kiss, but a stamp of possession. He claimed her mouth with his, thrusting his tongue inside and stroking hers, challenging it to duel with his. Delight forgot everything as his mouth continued to devour hers.

Her fingers released the death grip she had on her dress and it dropped to the floor. Coming up on her toes, she flung her arms around Lucian's neck. She wanted the kiss to last forever. She could feel Lucian's arousal growing and she nestled her hips tight to his to help ease the growing ache between her own thighs.

"Don't mind me. I'll just leave." The amused masculine voice was as effective as a dousing with a cold bucket of water.

Delight pulled away from Lucian and buried her face against his naked chest. "Now look what you made me do," she wailed.

"Me," he replied incredulously.

"Yes," she nodded her head against his chest. "It's all your fault for being so damned sexy. I never had these kinds of problems until I met you."

Stefan gave a bark of laughter and when she turned her head and peeked at him, he was smiling at her. It was only the slightest upturn at the corner of his lips, but it was a smile. He gave her a small bow that was oddly formal and looked right even though he was wearing a pair of faded blue jeans and a black T-shirt.

"Welcome to the family." All traces of humor fled from his face as he continued. "Know that I will protect you and yours with my very life. You are a Dalakis now."

"Thank you." Stefan's words touched Delight, but she didn't quite know what to say to his second proclamation. "But I'm a Deveraux, not a Dalakis."

Stefan immediately looked to Lucian and seemed relieved when he nodded. "No, you are a Dalakis now, for better or worse." Stefan's eyes began to twinkle as he ran them down along the curves of her body. "And from what I can see, it is definitely for the better."

"Omigod." It was only then that she realized that Stefan had the perfect view of her almost naked body. Even though her back was to him, with her dress on the floor and wearing only her underwear, he'd gotten quite the eyeful for the last while.

Keeping her arms locked around Lucian's waist, she scooted around until she stood behind him. Lucian had his hands on his hips as he shook his head at his brother. "Now you've embarrassed her."

Stefan snagged the towel off the floor and held it out to her. "She has nothing to be embarrassed about."

Grabbing the towel from his outstretched hand, she wrapped it around her body, thankful for its meager protection. She started to thank Stefan but got sidetracked when she noted the bulge in the front of his jeans. The man was seriously aroused. Her mouth went dry, so she licked her lips before she tried to speak. "Thanks," she managed to croak out.

"My pleasure." There was a warmth in Stefan's voice that caused Lucian to stiffen. Sighing, Stefan turned to leave. He got as far as the door, but stopped before he opened it. "I cannot help but want what you have, my brother, but I would never take that which was yours. She is now family and under my protection."

"Thank you, my brother." Stefan relaxed the moment Lucian spoke, his shoulders dropping from their tight, slightly hunched position. Delight found the tension seeping out of her own body as well. It was only then that she realized how uptight she'd been. The sun had finished setting while they'd been talking and they both watched Stefan as he walked out the front door and into the gloom of early evening.

"Now." Lucian turned to her. His chest was bare and it was obvious he'd only taken time to haul on his pants before coming after her, as they were zipped but not buttoned.

Facing him, she was determined to ignore the faint stirring of guilt welling up inside her. She had every right to do whatever she wanted to. She still had a life and responsibilities. She opened her mouth to tell Lucian just that and closed it abruptly. There was more than just concern in his eyes. There was hurt as well. She'd hurt him with her actions and hadn't meant to.

Sighing, she went to him and wrapped her arms around his waist, hugging him tight. "I'm sorry. I guess it's going to take me a while to get used to having someone worry about me."

His sigh of exasperation ruffled her hair. "It is more than just worry, Delight. You are my very heart. My whole purpose in life is to keep you happy and protected."

"That's not very fair to you." She wasn't sure she wanted to be that important to anybody.

"Fair," he muttered as he buried his face in her hair. "What is fair? I have lived hundreds of years without you. Maybe that was fair, maybe not. All I know is that I have you now and I will not lose you." He kissed her forehead, her nose and her lips as his fingers traced her cheeks. "Come live with me. Share my life with me." He punctuated each sentence with a kiss on her lips. "Will you?"

"Yes." There was no other answer she could give. Even though she knew that he was immortal and she was not, she wanted whatever time they could spend together.

Lucian held her so close she could barely breathe, but she didn't care. She'd made him happy and his happiness had become very important to her. But there were still problems to be worked out. "We still have to talk. I need to know how the whole vampire thing works. What can you do? How does it affect our life together?" Delight's head almost hurt, she had so many questions. "I also want to know all about your brothers and your sister-in-law."

He let her go, but Lucian was smiling when he scooped her up into his arms. "I will tell you everything, but first I want to celebrate." He carried her up the staircase and into his bedroom, kicking the door closed behind them.

Chapter Fifteen

ഇ

When Delight awoke, she was alone in the large bed. She smiled as she rolled over and buried her face in Lucian's pillow, breathing in his scent. The man was insatiable.

As his smell filled her nostrils, her breasts began to ache and she could feel her juices start to flow between her thighs. If she could bottle Lucian's unique essence, she could make a fortune. The man smelled good enough to eat. She licked her lips at the prospect.

Laughing, she flung the covers off and sat up on the side of the bed. She was becoming as insatiable as he was. Raising her arms overhead, she stretched, working the kinks out of her muscles. She was unused to the demands of Lucian's voracious lovemaking and her body ached, but it was a pleasant feeling.

She eased off the bed, onto the platform and down over the step. Ignoring her own dress, which was nothing more than a crumpled heap on the floor, she padded to Lucian's closet and tugged it open. Not surprisingly, his closet was huge and filled with the best quality clothing. Delight glanced at a couple of labels and shook her head in disbelief at the sheer extravagance of it all. Lucian certainly liked to dress well.

Forcing herself to ignore the fact that one of his shirts probably cost as much as the sum of half of her wardrobe, she tugged one of them from its hanger and slipped it on. The fabric was soft and luxurious against her skin and she wrapped her arms around herself, reveling in the feel of it.

Buttoning the shirt as she went, she left the bedroom in search of Lucian. A clock struck the hour as she walked down the dimly lit hall and she was surprised to realize that it was one o'clock in the morning. She must have dozed for an hour or so after they'd made love.

Pausing at the top of the stairs, she turned towards the end of the hall as a faint noise caught her ear. The long hallway was cast in shadows, but a faint light shone from a doorway at the end. Curious, Delight crept down the hall and peeked inside.

It was Lucian, but a Lucian she'd never seen before. This was the medieval warlord in the flesh. Clad only in a pair of fitted black pants with his feet and chest bare, his torso gleamed with sweat and every muscle in his body bulged as he swung a huge ornate sword in a series of intricate maneuvers. He moved with a grace and speed that was surprising in a man of his size.

The room was empty of furniture and one entire wall was covered with a floor-to-ceiling mirror that reflected Lucian's fierce image as he trained with his sword. The far wall was filled with a collection of swords and other instruments of war that Delight did not recognize. There was no doubt that this was a workout room and from the skill with which Lucian wielded the massive weapon, it was apparent that he used it frequently.

She couldn't tear her eyes from him as the sword dipped and his body moved in a lethal dance of advance and retreat. His long hair hung over his shoulders and his face was a mask of concentration as he glided and thrust effortlessly, swinging the heavy sword as if it were nothing more than a toy. The steel of the blade was reflected in the light and mirrors—a deadly yet beautiful weapon, much like the man who wielded it.

Her mouth went dry and she licked her lips as she leaned against the doorjamb for support. She made a small sound of disbelief as he executed a series of movements so fast he was little more than a blur. He whirled towards the doorway, his stance battle-ready as the sword swung loose and ready to strike.

His cold, hard gaze changed in an instant, becoming molten hot in the blink of an eye. He smiled a small, knowing smile that was filled with sensual promise as he looked his fill of her.

Delight could feel her nipples poking at the front of the shirt and clamped her thighs together to try and stop the ache that had begun to throb at her very core. Lucian's smile grew as he stared at her chest.

Lowering the four-foot blade, he propped it carefully against the wall before turning back to her. Her eyes widened at the huge bulge in the front of his pants. There was no mistaking that he wanted her. Again.

"Come." His deep voice vibrating through every cell in her body, and before she could even think, her feet were carrying her towards him.

She stopped just out of his reach, determined to have a sensible conversation for once. "That was amazing."

"Thank you." Lucian didn't move, but she felt as if he was crowding closer to her, his large body taking up most of the space between them. It was hard to concentrate when her fingers itched to caress every inch of his huge chest. The man was turning her into a sex fiend. She shook her head to clear it, forcing herself to pay attention to what he was saying.

"Skill with the sword was once a way of life." He shrugged. "Not useful now, but Stefan and I enjoy it and practice often to keep us sharp."

She sensed that it meant more to him than he let on. "It's a link to your past."

"It was a simpler way of life then." Reaching out, he slipped his finger inside the open collar of the shirt and ran it lightly over her collarbone. "Might was right and if you wanted something you took it."

He loomed over her now and she had an image of being thrown over his shoulder and dragged back to his big stone castle where he'd keep her naked and locked in a tower room. A sexual slave awaiting his pleasure.

His hand skimmed down over the front of the shirt she was wearing, cupping and shaping one of her breasts in his palm. She leaned into his caress, but he had already moved on, the heat from his large hand almost scorching her stomach as it continued to move lower.

Bending down, he traced the outside of her ear with his tongue. "You'd be a much prized sex slave, my love. A man would kill to keep one such as you."

Delight's breath hitched in her throat as she realized that he'd read her thoughts. His words set her skin on fire and she whimpered as his tongue stroked behind her ear and nipped her sensitive earlobe.

She swayed towards him, but he pulled back before she could touch him. The sound of fabric rending filled the air as he ripped the shirt open. Buttons popped and scattered across the floor as he pulled the garment from her body. "A sex slave should always be naked for her lord and master."

Delight was secretly appalled by how turned on his words were making her. Visions of her naked and kneeling at his feet, awaiting his pleasure, filled her mind.

"Kneel." Her entire body shook at his command. She had no doubt now that he was reading her every thought. Her every desire.

Slowly, she lowered herself to her knees. His erection was huge and straining against the front of his pants and she couldn't resist reaching out and wrapping one hand over it and squeezing it through the fabric.

Lucian hissed in a breath before he moved away and quickly shucked his pants. His cock was huge, the tip was large and red and bobbed almost angrily in front of him, demanding her attention.

She reached for him, wanting to touch his hard length, but he caught her hand in his. "Put your hands behind your head and spread your knees."

Her breasts bobbed and thrust forward when she clasped both hands behind her neck. Her pussy throbbed and ached. She could feel her juices flowing down her thighs as she spread her knees wide. She wanted to close her legs so badly over the empty need within her, but did as he asked. Unconsciously, her hips undulated as she waited to see what he would do next.

"Open your mouth."

Delight opened her mouth immediately and he laughed. It was a low, sexy and very satisfied male laugh. "Such an obedient little sex slave you are."

Leaning forward, she licked at the tip of his cock and his laughter quickly turned to a groan of pleasure. Gripping her hair in his hands, he guided his cock into her eager mouth. Delight licked at his length as it filled her.

She could see their reflection in the mirror. The sight of her naked and kneeling on the floor in front of him was enthralling. Her nipples were hard and red and her breasts bobbed with every move she made. Her blood sizzled as her excitement grew with each passing second.

As she watched, his cock slid past the opening of her mouth and deep to the back of her throat before withdrawing again. His butt flexed and tightened with every thrust of his hips.

A movement in the mirror startled her. Delight continued to suck Lucian's cock as she fixed her attention on the mirror. She could see the outline of a man in the doorway. The harsh desire and raw need stamped on his face was frightening. Her cry was swallowed as Lucian thrust deep in her mouth.

"Shh." He pulled his erection from her mouth and came down on his own knees in front of her. His lips captured hers in a searing kiss, his tongue thrusting inside and dueling with hers.

Delight no longer cared that Stefan was watching them from the shadows. Wrapping her hands around Lucian's shoulders, she leaned close and rubbed her swollen breasts against the hard planes of his chest, seeking relief.

Lucian broke away from their kiss and turned her so that she was facing away from him and towards the doorway. Lifting her, he pulled her onto his lap so that her legs were draped over his and spread wide. Both his hands came around her sides, cupping her breasts. As his fingers stroked and teased her nipples, she pushed her bottom back against his erection.

The sharp sting of his teeth on the nape of her neck jolted a moan of pleasure from her. He lightly pinched her nipples between his thumb and forefinger as she bucked her hips against the air. Giving in to her silent plea, he buried one of his hands between her legs and stroked her clit.

Moaning, she opened her legs wider. Her gaze was drawn back to the doorway as she sensed Stefan's growing excitement. His eyes gleamed in the darkness as he watched her. With Lucian's hands arousing her and Stefan's eyes devouring her, Delight thought she would explode with desire. It felt wicked and wanton, but she didn't care. Being watched by one man while being sexually engaged with another was an incredible turn-on.

She licked her lips and stared into the darkness. As she watched, Stefan unzipped his jeans and his large erection sprung from the opening. He never took his eyes off her and Lucian as he wrapped his hand around his cock and began to pump it up and down.

Delight couldn't take it any longer. "Take me, Lucian. Now." Breaking free of his grip, she tried to lever herself up to draw him inside her.

Lucian swore softly and he gripped her waist in his hands, lifting her up easily. The head of his cock was sucked eagerly into her hungry pussy. Not pausing, he pulled her down hard, impaling her on his hard length.

As he filled her, Delight closed her eyes and tipped her head back to rest on his shoulder. Squirming on his lap, she tried to pull him deeper inside her. Lucian came up on his knees and bent her over until her hands and knees were planted on the floor in front of him. She barely had time to catch her balance before he pulled back and began to hammer into her.

As Lucian fucked her hard from behind, she raised her head and watched Stefan watching them. His face was filled with carnal pleasure as he watched them mating on the floor in front of him. His hand continued to pump up and down at a frantic pace as Lucian continued to pound into her pulsing sex.

The pleasure was almost painful. For a moment, she was suspended on the edge and then Stefan groaned and pulled his T-shirt over the top of his cock as he came. As Stefan continued to pump out his release, Lucian drove into her one final time and her orgasm hit her so hard and so fast, she screamed.

Her entire body shuddered as Lucian jerked and emptied himself inside her. He knelt back up with her still locked in his arms and sank his teeth in her nape. Each sucking motion was like a mini-orgasm and it went on and on until her head was spinning and her vision blurred. She cried out when Lucian withdrew his fangs and closed the small pinpricks with his tongue, not wanting him to leave her yet.

As Lucian withdrew from her body, her muscles gripped his cock tight, sending off another round of pleasure. Delight shivered as he cradled her tight in his arms. She looked up at him, but his attention was on the door. Following his gaze, she saw Stefan still watching from the doorway. Now that the moment was past, she felt embarrassment taking the place of desire and turned into Lucian, seeking his protection.

Stefan nodded slowly and withdrew from them, leaving a feeling of sadness behind in the spot where he'd stood. "Did you know he was there?" She hadn't meant to ask, but needed to know.

"Yes." Lucian sighed and stood with her still locked in his arms. "He envies what we have and I could not refuse him a glimpse of the pleasure denied him. He will not seek to do so again as I think he feels the void in him even more keenly now." Lucian strode towards the open door.

"It was strange to know that someone was watching us." She didn't quite know how to explain her conflicting feelings.

"You found it exciting and that bothers you." As usual, Lucian went to the heart of the matter. "It is natural to be aroused by another man watching you, but I will not share you." His arms tightened around her threateningly. "Ever."

"I don't want anyone but you." Wrapping her arms around his neck, she leaned into his chest.

As they'd talked, Lucian had carried her down the hallway and back to the bedroom. She could feel his erection poking her in the bottom with every step he took. She stared up at him with disbelief in her eyes. "Again?" She couldn't hide the hint of amazement in her voice. The man had an amazing recovery time.

Laying her down on the top of the bed, he stood over her fully aroused. "Again." He came down on top of her and left no doubt that he was more than capable of loving her again.

It was just after sunset the next evening and Delight was dressed and ready to go home to talk to Chase. She'd had her day reprieve, but now it was time to deal with the problems at hand. She'd already called the owner of Etienne's and quit her job, knowing there was no way that she could go back to work there after what had happened. He had been very understanding, offering to mail her last pay check to her and assuring her that he would certainly give her a good reference. She was pleased to have at least one thing taken care of.

She felt refreshed and invigorated after sleeping all day and had been surprised, but pleased to find a fresh change of clothing waiting for her when she awoke. She hadn't been looking forward to pulling on her black dress to wear home.

Since Lucian had been with her the entire time, she knew that it was Stefan who had slipped into her home and brought some of her own clothing to her. She appreciated his thoughtfulness, but didn't know if she'd ever be able to look the man in the face again without blushing.

She hurried down the stairs eager to see Lucian before heading home. He emerged from the living room and had taken one step towards the stairs when there was a pounding on the front door.

He scowled and turned towards the intrusion. "Stay here," he barked over his shoulder as he strode to the door and flung it open.

Miss Nadine practically fell through the doorway. She was sobbing so hard it was almost impossible to make out what she was saying. When she did, Delight almost wished she hadn't. "They took him," she cried over and over. "They took our boy."

Delight's blood ran cold and she lost all feeling in her body as she sank to the stairs. She was only dimly aware of Lucian carrying Miss Nadine into another room.

"I've got to save him," she whispered. Delight needed Lucian's strength in that moment more than she'd ever needed anything in her life.

Returning for her, he wrapped his arm around her shoulders and pulled her to her feet. "We'll get him back," he promised her. "Then I'll end this once and for all."

She nodded, feeling stronger and more sure. If Lucian said they'd get Chase back, then they would. Delight couldn't bring herself to face the other possibility.

Chapter Sixteen

ഇ

It wasn't that hard to find where they were holding Chase. The kidnappers had been quite explicit in their instructions. Delight was to come to them herself, or they would start sending her brother back to her. One piece at a time. Chase's knapsack with the note pinned on it had been dropped at the back door of The Grande just before dusk. Miss Nadine had found it shortly after and had rushed to Lucian's home.

When Lucian had given Miss Nadine his phone number and address, he'd never dreamed she would be using it so quickly or for such a reason. It hadn't occurred to him that the murderers would be desperate enough to attack Delight through her family. He'd assumed that they would come directly for her and he would be there to protect her. Instead, they'd hit her where she was most vulnerable. Her family.

Inwardly, he was furious at himself for not anticipating such an action. He'd grown soft and lax in the last century. In the old days, such treachery was commonplace and to be expected. He watched helplessly as the two women sat side by side on the sofa, consoling one another.

Stefan had returned to the house the moment that Lucian had sent out the mental call for help. Now his brother waited patiently for him to decide their course of action.

"It's not your fault." Lucian knew that Stefan meant well, but right now the words didn't help.

"Then whose fault is it?" Turning, he faced his brother, his face a grim mask. "Delight and her family are my responsibility."

Stefan nodded his understanding. "What will you do?"

Lucian glanced at the ornate sword that was hanging over the fireplace. "It is time to pay Mr. Prince a visit."

"In days of old, you could have just lopped off his head. But nowadays, we must hide and act with stealth." Stefan sighed in obvious disappointment. "I will go with you." He crossed his arms over his chest, a stubborn gleam in his eye.

"No." Lucian shook his head. "You must stay here and protect Delight. I am leaving my greatest treasure in your care. My life is in your hands."

Stefan straightened and nodded once. "As you wish."

Lucian knew that he understood the importance of the task. If anything happened to Delight, Lucian knew he would not survive. His life was now linked to her and by protecting Delight, Stefan was protecting Lucian's life as well. Decision made, he strode towards Delight. A quick goodbye and he'd be on his way.

Delight sprang from the sofa. "When do we leave?"

He could only stare at her, awed by her bravery and her willingness to sacrifice for her brother. Of course, he could not allow her to do such a thing, but he was pleased by her strength. "You will stay here with Stefan. I will go and bring Chase back home."

Scowling, she fisted her hands on her hips. "Chase is my brother. Besides, it's me they want."

"Precisely." Lucian cupped her face in his hands, willing her to understand his position. "That is why you cannot go. Once they have you, they have no reason to keep him alive."

Delight chewed her lip with uncertainty. "But what if they hurt him?"

"What is done, is done." As much as he wanted to spare her, he knew she needed the truth. "But I promise you, I will bring him home to you."

Lucian glanced at his brother and knew his face was a mirror image of Stefan's. Controlled anger, power, and the promise of retribution shone from his brother's eyes, echoing his own feelings.

Bending down, he kissed Delight lightly on the lips, savoring her sweet flavor. "I will be back soon." Releasing her, he turned and stalked out of the room. He heard her calling his name, but did not look back. The front door opened before he reached it and he stepped out into the darkness. It slammed shut behind him and he waited until he heard the bolts being driven home before he sped off into the night.

With his unnatural speed, he was outside Prince's club in a matter of minutes. Aptly named The Club, it was the current hotspot in the city. The rich, famous, and beautiful all vied for entry. Lucian smiled coldly as he walked towards the entrance. This time tomorrow, they would be looking for a new place to go. The Club was about to be shut down.

Ignoring the hulking bouncer, he continued past the long line of people hoping to gain entry. The bouncer stepped in front of Lucian with his massive arms folded across his chest. He glared at the man, his fangs flashing as he issued his mental command. The bouncer paled and immediately stepped back, opening the door for Lucian.

The music assaulted Lucian as he stepped inside. Loud and obnoxious, the band screamed into the microphones as couples crammed the dance floor. Lights of all colors flashed through the darkened room. The smell of sex, sweat, drugs and alcohol permeated the air.

Scanning the interior, he found what he was looking for and walked directly across the club's jam-packed dance floor. The crowd parted in front of him and closed behind him as he made a straight line towards a door near the back of the club.

Several hulking men in dark suits with weapons bulging under their arms stood in front of the doors that led to the office area. Stopping in front of the men, he stared at them and smiled. "Tell Prince that Lucian Dalakis is here to see him."

Their eyes widened at the name. Delight might not be impressed by his money, but Lucian was very rich and powerful and there were those who were easily swayed by such things. Prince was a man who placed a very high value on both, craving them with equal greed.

One of the men slipped through the door, while the other stood and waited nervously. Lucian could feel the man's heart pounding in his chest and did nothing to lessen his discomfort. The door suddenly swung open and Lucian was ushered forward. "Mr. Prince will see you."

Lucian didn't bother to answer, but walked down the hallway and up a set of stairs. Another man was waiting at the top of the stairs for him and from the cruel look on his face and the immaculate banker's suit, he knew that this must be Mr. Smith.

Smith stared at him in a manner meant to intimidate, but only served to amuse Lucian. "I'll have to search you if you want to see Mr. Prince."

He spread his arms wide. "By all means." He could tell he'd surprised Smith with his easy capitulation. The other man now regarded him with slight disdain. In his eyes, Lucian was now just another rich, but weak man, looking for some vice or another from his boss. That suited Lucian just fine. For now.

Smith led him to another door that opened into a large, opulent room. It was obviously an office as it contained a huge mahogany desk and a wall of computer screens filled with images from the club below. However, there was also a sitting area with a leather sofa and chairs. Priceless oriental rugs were scattered across the gleaming hardwood floor and artwork adorned the walls. It was a room that screamed money and seated at the very center, behind the desk, was Mr. Jethro Prince.

As he walked across the room, Lucian sized up his opponent. Prince was whipcord lean, with dark, empty eyes and a scar on his right cheek. He leaned back in his chair, rested his elbows on the arms of the chair, and tapped his fingers together. Prince made no move to rise or to offer him a seat. It was a definite power play, meant to put Lucian on the defensive. His face impassive, Lucian walked up to the desk, keeping his body loose and fluid, and waited.

Prince scowled when he didn't get the response he'd obviously been expecting. "What can I do for you, Dalakis?"

Having already done a mental scan of the room, he knew Chase was there, slumped in a chair that was facing away from them all with his hands tied. "You have something that belongs to me." He waited, giving his words time to sink in. "I want it back."

Prince lunged forward in his chair and slammed his hands on the desk. "How dare you come into my office with demands."

Lucian could feel Smith moving up behind him, but didn't move from his position. "This can be easy or hard. That is entirely your choice."

The scar on Prince's face turned white as his anger grew. "I don't like your accusations, Dalakis. You're either very brave or very stupid." His pointed look left no doubt in Lucian's mind that Prince thought he was the latter.

Lucian shrugged, his massive shoulders rising and falling easily. "What you think of me is of no consequence. It doesn't change the fact that you have something of mine."

Prince's eyes grew colder as he studied Lucian. "Do you think your money will protect you? You're on my turf now, not yours." Making an effort, Prince relaxed his stance and allowed a slightly amused and sardonic smile cross his face. "I wonder if anyone even knows that you're here? People go missing every day in a city like New Orleans."

The menace underlying his words was very real, but Lucian just inclined his head slightly in recognition of Prince's threat. "Yes, they do, don't they. I understand that you've recently lost some men of your own. Such a shame." He allowed the corners of his mouth to turn up in a dangerous smile. "But then a man like you doesn't care much about human life. The inconvenience of it all was probably nothing more than a minor nuisance to you."

Prince reached under his desk, pulled out a handgun and leveled it at Lucian. "You seem to have quite a knowledge and interest about my business, Dalakis. That kind of curiosity can be dangerous to a man's health."

Lucian ignored the gun and shrugged unconcerned. "You still have something that belongs to me. And I will have it back."

Prince's eyes widened and he vibrated with fury even though his gun hand never wavered. "I could kill you now, but I'm curious. What do you think I have that belongs to you?"

"Chase Deveraux."

The other man's demeanor changed in a flash, becoming more cunning and sly. "It seems I may have underestimated the value of my new young friend. His continued safety and good health would be worth quite a bit to you?"

"I don't pay for what is already mine. But if you let him go and leave the Deveraux family alone, I will let you live." He inwardly sighed even as he made the offer, knowing that the only reason he did so was that he could assure Delight that he'd done all he could before killing Prince and Smith. He knew they had to be dealt with, but women could be funny about these kinds of things.

Prince started to laugh as he strolled out from behind his desk and ambled across the room to a large wingback chair that was facing a dark corner of the room. Reaching around, he hauled a battered Chase to his feet and yanked the gag out of the boy's mouth. Chase stumbled as he was dragged towards Lucian, but managed to stay on his feet. From the bruises and swelling on his face, it was obvious that they had beaten the boy badly, but he still managed to glare at his captor.

"You shouldn't have come." Chase spit the words at Lucian.

Lucian ignored Chase, knowing he feared for his sister's life. Prince smiled cruelly as he backhanded Chase's already battered face. Chase bit back a cry as he fell sideways, striking his head on the floor as he landed. He lay there moaning, his eyes closed and his body still.

"Enough." Lucian's softly spoken command cracked like a whip, causing all of them to freeze. The time had come to end this. He turned his attention to Prince, focusing all his energy on him. "Come to me."

Prince looked surprised, then shocked before his face went lax and his gun hand dropped to his side. As if pulled by some unseen hand, he stumbled towards Lucian. Lucian could sense Smith's surprise and sent him a mental command to freeze.

Everything was under control until the door to the office slammed open, causing him to lose concentration for a split second.

"Chase!" Delight cried as she raced across the room.

Lucian took it all in at a glance. Stefan burst through the door behind Delight, followed by a disheveled Detective Cassidy. Smith broke free of Lucian's thrall, raised his own weapon and turned it on Delight.

Not wasting any time, Lucian grabbed Prince by the neck and gave it a violent twist, breaking it in one easy motion. He let the body drop to the floor, even as he was moving towards Smith. He knew he wouldn't make it.

The gun went off just as Stefan reached Smith, wrapped one heavily muscled arm around his neck and snapped it like a twig.

Lucian howled in anguish as he caught Delight's falling form in his arms, lowering her to the carpet. Her lifeblood was spilling through his finger and soaking his clothing. Stefan was by his side in a flash, shoving him aside and applying pressure to the wound.

He could hear Cassidy in the background checking the bodies and untying Chase, but nothing mattered to Lucian but Delight. He could feel her slipping away from him and knew that his life was over.

Chase scrambled to his side, his battered face white as he stared at Delight's still form. "Do something. She can't die. She can't." Grabbing the front of Lucian's shirt, he shook him hard. "Do something."

Stefan continued to lean hard on the wound, but blood was still seeping from under his fingers. "You only have one choice, Lucian."

Cassidy was on the phone calling for backup and requesting an ambulance, but they all knew that they'd never make it in time to save Delight.

Lucian stared down at the woman he loved more than life itself and willed her to open her eyes. They fluttered and then finally opened. Pain and anguish shone from their pure depths and he could sense that most of her pain came from the thought of leaving him and her family behind.

"I'm sorry, Lucian…" Her voice trailed off as a wave of pain racked her body.

"Don't talk. Listen to me." He leaned down until his nose was almost touching hers. "There is one chance. I can try to change you so you become as I am. You would be vampire, but your life would be linked with mine. If I die, then you too will die. You would be susceptible to other dangers as well. But I would be by your side for eternity, and no man living or yet to be born will love you as I will. Your happiness and protection are my life's work and my life's joy."

Ignoring the startled gasps from behind him, he focused all his concentration on Delight. "Choose."

Her hand slowly raised and grazed his face before falling limply back to the floor. "You," she gasped. "Choose you." Lucian was moving as Delight's eyes fluttered shut.

"I'm losing her." Stefan's voice seemed to come from far away, but Lucian heeded the warning.

Kneeling on the floor amidst her spilled blood, Lucian pulled Delight into his arms. Bending his head, he sank his fangs into her neck and began to drink from her. She unconsciously arched her neck towards him.

"What the hell is he doing?" He felt Cassidy's hand on his shoulder, but kept his concentration on Delight. He had to stay linked with her or he could lose her.

"Leave him alone." Chase ripped Cassidy's hand away from Lucian. "I don't know what the hell he is, but he's her only chance."

"But he's killing her."

"No." Stefan stepped between Chase and Cassidy, momentarily taking his attention off his brother. "He is offering her a chance at life."

Lucian felt the last of Delight's life start to slip away. Bringing his wrist to his mouth, he bit down hard. His fangs ripped through his skin and opened a vein. Cradling her head against his chest, he held his wrist to her mouth as his own blood seeped from his body and flowed over her parted lips. "Drink, my love. Stay with me."

She lay totally unresponsive in his arms. Lucian looked up at his brother, anguish in his eyes. Stefan dropped to his knees, grabbed Delight's lifeless fingers in his own and began to chafe them. "Come, little sister. You must try."

Lucian could feel his brother's energy combine with his and was shocked at the extent of Stefan's power. It was enormous and gave him renewed hope. Focusing all his love on Delight, he begged, pleaded, scolded, and commanded her to live. Rubbing his wrist over her lips and coating them in his blood, he silently urged her to drink.

"This is sick," Cassidy muttered in the background, but he made no move to stop them. The scent of blood and power was strong in the air as they all waited and hoped.

"Come on, Delight," Chase encouraged as he reached out and stroked the back of her head, pushing it closer to Lucian.

She jerked slightly in his arms and her lips moved ever so slightly. "Drink. I'm ordering you to drink, damn it." Lucian's voice rose with every word he spoke until he was screaming at her.

Delight stiffened and then her mouth latched onto his wrist and she began to suck. Lucian could feel the tears welling in his eyes as he closed them and tipped back his head. "Thank you." His words were like a whispered prayer in the silence of the room.

As Delight drank, her wound began to close and the bleeding slowed until it finally stopped. Lucian knew that after several days' rest, there wouldn't even be a mark left on her skin. When he felt she'd had enough, he eased her mouth away from him. She gazed up at him and smiled before closing her eyes and falling into a deep sleep.

Raising his wrist to his mouth, he traced the open wound with his tongue. The skin closed over and the bleeding stopped. Bending down he licked the traces of blood that still clung to her lips.

"How the hell am I gonna explain this?" Cassidy's outburst shattered the silence.

"You're not." Stefan stood and walked towards the detective, pure menace in every step. "We were never here. No one ever saw us. This is obviously a falling out among criminals."

Cassidy smirked at Stefan. "That's going to be a little difficult to pull off."

Stefan's eyes were blazing as they locked on Cassidy. "No, it isn't. Lucian and I will take Chase and Delight to our home. By the time I finish with the guards, none of them will remember seeing us. One of the guards will say he asked you to come up and investigate when he found the two dead bodies."

"Is that right?" The detective crossed his arms over his chest and glared back at Stefan. "And how are you going to explain the blood on the carpet?"

"I will take care of that."

"Enough, you two." Lucian stood with Delight cradled in his arms and motioned to Chase who had passed out and was lying unconscious on the floor. He faced Cassidy, noting the lack of fear in the man's eyes. This man could be a powerful ally and right now they needed help. "I will give you all the answers you seek later, but for now you must believe what Stefan has said will happen."

Cassidy's gaze went to Delight's limp form and his face softened. "I don't know what the hell I believe anymore." He raised his eyes to meet Lucian's straight on. "But I do know that she was as good as dead a few minutes ago and now she isn't."

As the sounds of sirens filled the air, Stefan bent down and deftly rolled the thick blood-stained carpet into a bundle, making sure that not a drop of blood remained behind on the floor. Tossing it over his shoulder as if it weighed nothing, he scooped up Chase and strode from the room without a backwards glance. Lucian waited to see what Cassidy would do. He knew he could alter the other man's memories, but he was loath to do so. There was something about the man he liked.

"Go on." Cassidy motioned him towards the door. "I'll clean up the mess here."

Lucian was almost out the door when Cassidy's parting words reached his ears. "But you can bet your ass, I'll be coming to get some answers when this is all over."

Joining Stefan at a back door, they stepped out into the night just as the police were racing through the club and up the stairs to the office. Lucian knew that his brother had already taken care of the guards, planting the appropriate memories in their minds. None of them would remember seeing anyone but the police detective. For now, they were all safe.

He could hear Cassidy identifying himself as a police detective and taking over the investigation. Stefan shifted beside him, adjusting the large carpet that was still draped over his shoulder, while easily retaining his hold on Chase. They would dispose of the carpet later. Satisfied that everything was under control, they started for home, each of them carrying a precious burden in their arms.

"Race you." Stefan's words were barely out of his mouth before he disappeared. Laughing, Lucian tightened his grip around Delight and raced after his brother.

Chapter Seventeen

&

Delight's head was pounding when she awoke. She'd swear she had a hangover except she wasn't much of a drinker. The sound of someone moaning made her head hurt even more and she wished they'd shut up. Ever so carefully, she moved her hands to her ears to shut out the sound, but she could still hear it. She felt pity for whoever was in such pain, but she still wished they'd shut up.

"Shh," a voice whispered near her. "I know it hurts, but this will help." Her hands were pushed away from her face and a cool cloth was placed upon her forehead. Delight sighed with relief and was surprised to discover that the moaning had stopped. It took her befuddled mind a few seconds to realize that it had been her who was making the ungodly noise.

She tried to focus her thoughts. There was something important that she was supposed to remember, but she just couldn't think what it was. Her brother's face suddenly popped into her mind and the memories and fear came flooding back.

"Chase?" Even though it hurt, she tried to sit up in bed. A strong hand steadied her and lowered her back to the pillows.

"Don't try and move, love." The covers were tucked around her shoulders. "Chase is fine and sleeping comfortably in another room. The doctor has been here and gone." A large hand cupped the side of her face and Delight snuggled closer to its warmth. "I won't lie. He was beaten badly, but surprisingly nothing is broken. He's got a few cracked ribs, a sprained wrist, some minor cuts, and a hell of a lot of bruises. It'll take a while, but he'll be fine."

She licked her dry lips and tried to speak, but it came out more of a croak. "What happened?"

"Drink this." A straw was placed near her mouth and she sipped a small amount of water, easing some of the dryness in her mouth.

"What's wrong with me?"

Delight sensed Lucian's reluctance to talk to her. That surprised her as he hadn't flinched from the raw truth since their first meeting. A huge knot formed in her stomach and she could feel her palms get sweaty. His silence was scaring her.

Pushing the damp cloth off her face, she cautiously opened her eyes, sighing in relief at the darkness of the room. Only a dim lamp was lit in the far corner of the bedroom. Delight immediately recognized Lucian's room and a soothing comfort enveloped her.

Blinking several times to steady her vision, she turned her head towards Lucian, but most of him was lost in the shadows. "Lucian?" Her voice shook and her hand trembled as she reached out to him. He seemed further away from her than he'd ever been, even though he was sitting right next to her.

Lucian heaved a deep sigh, gently clasped her hand in his and moved closer to her. The moment the light hit him, Delight almost cried out in pain again. He looked ravaged. His skin was pulled taut against his face, his green eyes were cold and his thin lips were clamped together. He looked hard and unforgiving as he stared down at her. She felt very small and fragile in that moment. There was a remoteness to Lucian that made her feel incredibly cold inside. It was if he was distancing himself from her.

"What have I done?" The question was torn from her lips before she could stop it. She pulled her hand away from him and slapped it over her mouth, but it was too late to stop the words from spilling out. As a strong, independent woman, Delight was appalled at her question, but as a woman in love, she needed to understand what had come between her and Lucian.

A look of horror and pain flickered on his face before the hard, cold mask descended once again. "You have done nothing wrong. What do you remember?"

Delight thought hard. The memories were a jumble in her head. "I tricked Stefan and snuck out of the house." Lucian's scowl deepened. "Chase is my brother and I had every right to try and help him. Besides," she mumbled. "I did call Detective Cassidy."

"You did not trust me." Pain echoed in each word he spoke.

"I did trust you. I do trust you." Reaching out, she grabbed his hand and tugged him closer. Although his expression didn't change, he allowed her to tug him down onto the bed until he was seated next to her.

She had to find a way to make him understand. "I didn't trust Prince and his men. I couldn't bear it if anything happened to you or Chase. I thought if I was there that I could help you in some way." She watched his face, searching for any reaction at all, even a flicker that he understood and could forgive her for interfering. "I couldn't let you face them alone."

The reaction she got almost made her wish that his cool mask was back in place. Fury radiated from every pore of his body. Every muscle in his body tensed, his hands clenched into fists as he pulled away from her, his eyes blazed pure fire, and his lips curved up into a cruel smile. His fangs gleamed a pearly white in the faint light as he gave a bark of laughter.

"Do you have any idea what you have done?" His words fell on her like hot coals. There was no mistaking the fact that she had angered him and she didn't think he would get over it any time soon.

Delight felt an icy cloak envelop her from the inside out. She welcomed the numbness as it helped block out the pain of his withdrawal from her. Her actions seemed to be unforgivable to him and she could stay here no longer.

Home. She needed to go home where she could be alone and nurse her broken heart as well as her brother. Right now, she didn't know how she'd survive it, but she would.

Turning away from Lucian was the hardest thing she'd ever done in her life. Throwing back the covers, she edged to the end of the bed and carefully stood.

"Where in the hell do you think you're going?"

Delight could no longer feel his anger. In fact, she could feel nothing. It was if she no longer inhabited her own body. Not bothering to look back, she began to make her way towards the door. It really wasn't that far from the bed, but the way she felt physically, mentally and emotionally, it looked as if it was miles away. Each step was excruciating as it took her further away from Lucian. Ripping out her own heart would hurt less.

"Delight?" His guttural tone stopped in her tracks, but she didn't turn to face him. She just didn't have the strength. It was easier just to let him have his say and then leave.

Swaying on her feet, she waited for him to speak. Time had no meaning and she waited with a detached patience.

"Don't leave me."

She frowned and felt the first crack in the ice that surrounded her. That couldn't happen. She needed it to protect her, but the pain in his voice was more than she could bear.

"I had no choice. You left me none." His voice was angry now, almost accusing.

Knowing she shouldn't, she slowly turned around and faced Lucian. He had moved silently from the side of the bed and stood right behind her. Startled, she took an involuntary step backwards, away from him.

He flinched as if she had struck him. She felt confused and off-kilter, as if she was missing an important piece of the puzzle. "I don't understand what you want. Obviously, you find my actions unforgivable, so I'm leaving." She rubbed the pain in her temples, wishing it would go away. "I thought that's what you wanted."

"Oh, Delight. What have I done to you?" Falling to his knees in front of her, Lucian hung his head. "It is not you who have done the unforgivable. Do you remember nothing?"

Delight sorted through the images in her head and one by one, they clicked into place. "I got shot." She looked down at herself, only then realizing she was clad in one of Lucian's soft linen shirts. Plucking the fabric away, she searched her naked flesh beneath, but could find nothing but a pale white scar.

"You were dying." Throwing back his shoulders, he met her bewildered gaze with a defiant one. "I did what I had to do."

"You took my blood." Everything was becoming clearer now. "And gave me yours." She remembered sucking at his wrist and swallowing his blood. It should have been repugnant and appalling to her, but it hadn't been. His blood had tasted better than the finest wine, warming her, feeding her hunger. She'd wanted to keep on drinking from him for forever, never letting him go.

"Yes." He made no move towards her, but she could feel him willing her to come to him.

"Am I like you now?" She couldn't quite bring herself to say the word.

"Vampire." Lucian had obviously read her thoughts and had no trouble spelling it out in black and white for her. "Yes."

This was something she really needed time to think about. But later. Right now she wasn't feeling very well. Her head was pounding and her stomach was roiling, but Lucian wasn't finished.

"I understand if you cannot forgive me for what I have done. But know that whatever you choose, I will honor your wishes."

"What choices?" It was becoming increasingly difficult to follow his train of thought. She was getting sicker and sicker by the second.

"You can live alone and I will support you for eternity. You can choose to embrace death and I will gladly die with you. Or," he paused for a moment. "You can choose to stay with me, knowing I will love you for all time. No man living or yet to be born will love you as I will. Your happiness and protection will be my life's work and my life's joy."

The familiarity of his words shook her. "You've said this to me before."

"When I changed you."

Delight didn't quite know what to say or do. She wanted to reassure Lucian that everything would be fine, but her stomach was rebelling. Covering her mouth, she turned from his penetrating gaze.

The howl of pain brought her to her knees. At first, she thought it must be from her. The pain inside her was growing like a living beast, devouring everything in its path. Rolling to her side, she watched in shock as Lucian howled in anguish again. His head was tipped back and he looked like a man consumed with pain.

The need to comfort him overwhelmed her and she swallowed down the bile in her throat and started to crawl towards him. The pain made it almost impossible, but she pulled herself along the floor, inch by inch.

As if he sensed her movement, his head swung towards her. She reached her hand out to him, but it fell to the floor. Silently, she pleaded for his help as speech was beyond her capabilities.

Lucian moved so fast that he was a blur. He scooped her into his arms and carried her to the bathroom just in time. Lowering her head, she was violently ill. Just when she thought she was finished, her stomach would rebel again. Over and over, she emptied her stomach until she swore there was nothing left in her body. Through it all, Lucian held her and soothed her with comforting words. When she was finished, he carefully laid her on the floor.

The tile was cool against her flushed cheek and she sighed when she heard the sound of running water. She felt sweaty and sticky and longed for a nice warm bath. The smell of lavender filled the air, relaxing her and making her feel calmer. She decided that she'd move in a minute, but right now she was content to just lie here on the floor. It was such a relief after being so violently ill.

Lucian's strong arms wrapped around her and plucked her from the floor. Before she could gather the energy to speak, he'd stripped off the shirt she was wearing and lowered her into the steaming bath. A huge sigh of relief escaped her.

"It will get better now." He dragged a washcloth over her arms and torso, cleaning her thoroughly.

"I don't know what's wrong with me." She'd meant to sound strong and sure, but instead sounded weak and shaky.

Lucian's lips tightened. "It is part of the change as your body is purging itself of your human wastes."

Shivers began to rack her body so all she could do was nod. Lucian pulled her out of the tub, quickly dried her with a huge, fluffy towel, and carried her back into the bedroom. Tucking her naked under the covers, he yanked off his clothes and crawled in next to her, pulling her into his arms.

His heat surrounded her and she snuggled closer to his chest, nuzzling the crisp hair there. She couldn't seem to stop shaking and that worried her. "Is this part of changing?" she managed to get out between her chattering teeth.

"Yes." He ran his arms up and down her back and over her shoulders, warming her and comforting her. "You will feel better when you awake tomorrow evening. Then you can make your decision."

She felt sleep pulling at her and longed to give herself up to its healing powers, but there was something she had to do first. "Chase?"

He placed a gentle kiss on her forehead. "I'll make sure Chase and Miss Nadine are looked after."

Delight sighed in relief, but she still had one final thing to do before she succumbed to sleep. "You."

"Me what?" He leaned down so his ear was near her lips. "What do you want, Delight? I'll do anything for you. Give you anything. All you have to do is ask."

"Choose you. Not leaving." Totally exhausted now, she slumped on his chest. Lucian stiffened beneath her, but her body was crying out for rest, so she gave into it.

"Delight?"

She managed to whisper two final words as her world went dark. "Love you." Her body drifted into a state that was deeper than sleep and more like death. Her heart ceased to beat and her body went lax. She didn't feel the lone tear that drifted down Lucian's cheek and onto hers.

Chapter Eighteen

ഇ

The first thing Delight noticed when she next awoke was that she felt surprisingly good for someone who had been shot. Lying in Lucian's large bed, she took stock of her entire body. Wiggling her toes and fingers, she was pleased to note that everything seemed to be in working order. Her stomach was calm and she actually felt energized.

A low pounding sound reached her ears. Cocking her head to one side, she listened intently, trying to figure out where it was coming from. A blast of noise struck her with such force, she actually flung her head back to try and avoid it. Slapping her hands over her ears, she tried to shut out the racket assaulting her poor eardrums.

"Imagine a button in your mind and turn down the volume." She didn't know how she heard Lucian over the din, but she focused all her attention on following his instructions. Surprisingly, it worked and the jumble of sounds became a low hum in the background.

Carefully, she removed her hands from her ears. When the noise remained muted, she smiled up at Lucian who had propped himself up on one arm in the bed and was leaning over her with a frown on his face. "What was that all about?"

He brushed back a lock of hair from her face with his fingers. "You will find that things are different now that you have changed. All your senses are sharper now, but you can easily learn how to control them."

She nodded her understanding. "What else?"

"As I told you before, you need blood to survive. But we're civilized now and no longer need to drink from humans, unless we choose to. We purchase blood through many sources and always have a large supply on hand." Lucian watched her like a hawk, gauging her every reaction. "You can easily drink wine or water and after a time you can tolerate a small amount of food if you choose, but it is no longer necessary for you to eat to live."

Licking her lips, she asked herself how she really felt about these things. She'd miss food, but if she could occasionally enjoy her favorite ones, maybe it wouldn't be so bad.

"Once your body has had time to adjust, you may be able to enjoy the early morning or late afternoon, but I'm afraid that sunlight is now lost to you forever." Bending over, he brushed her lips with his. "For that, I am truly sorry."

She nodded, sensing he was holding something else back from her. "Tell me the rest."

"With time and practice, you may be able to shapeshift. Not all Dalakis brides are able to do so as their minds cannot accept the possibility and they block their natural ability to change." At first she thought that he was joking with her, but the look on his face was deadly serious.

"Into what?"

"The wolf is the most common, although Cristofor can shift into an owl as well." Lucian paused as if searching for the right words to explain it to her. "You let your mind go and think of the wolf and you become the wolf. It is very freeing to roam the woods at night in that form. I admit that I do not do it much here in New Orleans, but when I return home to the mountains of Transylvania, I cannot resist."

She couldn't believe she was lying here calmly discussing the fact that the man she loved could change into a wolf. But she figured if she could accept that fact that he was a vampire and that she was now a vampire, then she certain wasn't going to let a little matter of shapeshifting bother her. The more she thought about it, the more she was intrigued by the idea even if she wasn't sure she'd ever be ready to try it.

Her mind was whirling at the thought of being able to do such a thing. It was almost too much to handle on top of everything else. She'd have to figure out a way to deal with all the changes in her life. All that truly mattered was that she and Lucian were together. Well, that was almost all that mattered. "I won't sleep in a coffin or underground." Just the thought made her shudder in horror.

Lucian threw back his head, his laughter echoing throughout the bedroom. Delight hadn't thought her demand had been funny at all. In fact, she was quite adamant about it. She opened her mouth to scold Lucian, but got sidetracked by the strong column of his neck.

Her nipples tightened and she felt the familiar flood of liquid between her thighs that was common whenever she was with Lucian. Now that she was no longer totally focused on her new reality, she was noticing other things. Like that fact that they were both totally naked and lying in a nice big bed.

She could feel Lucian's shaft twitch and grow as she snuggled closer to his side. A pulsing began deep inside her that radiated outward until she felt as if her entire body was vibrating with need. Her teeth ached and she was filled with a longing to lick and suck at his neck. Lucian was right about all her senses being sharper. Her skin felt totally sensitized and alive.

Still chuckling, he leaned back down and kissed the tip of her nose. "My love, I would never ask you to sleep in a coffin. We will sleep here in this room. It has many protective features built into it. But there are secret rooms underground for safety's sake, but they look no different from this one."

Delight slid her hands over the hard planes of his chest, loving the play of muscles underneath her fingers. Everything about Lucian was strong and masculine and called to everything feminine within her. She longed to belong to him, just as she longed to claim him for her own.

Brushing her fingertips over his nipples, she was rewarded with a rumble of male approval. Desire flared in his eyes as she bent forward and licked the hard nub before lightly scraping her teeth over it.

Lucian rolled suddenly and she found herself flat on her back with him looming over her. Clasping her hands in one of his, he raised her arms over her head and pinned them to the pillow. With his free hand, he lazily stroked her breast, feathering his fingers over the aching tip. Moaning, she arched towards his hand. He smiled down at her as he rolled the nub between his thumb and forefinger.

She could feel his hardness between her thighs and spread her legs to accommodate him. His cock slipped between the wet folds of her sex and she undulated her hips, rubbing her throbbing clit against his cock.

Lucian bit the lobe of her ear before tracing the delicate whorls. "You feel everything more deeply now. Every part of your body is more sensitive than before." Plunging his tongue into her ear, he stroked it in and out before nipping at her lobe again.

Fire shot through Delight's body. Every stroke his tongue made at her ear, she felt between her legs. She'd never felt need this strong before. It was almost frightening just how badly she wanted Lucian. There wasn't anything she wouldn't do for him or with him if it meant she would eventually have his cock buried in her pussy and his teeth sunk into her neck.

"Don't think." Lucian licked the curve of her neck, raising goose bumps on her skin. "Feel."

Heat. That was all she could feel. Heat and need. She felt wild and free and elemental. She could smell her own desire wafting on the air and it made her even hotter. Bucking her hips, she tried to fit Lucian's hard length into her body.

He just gave a small, sexy laugh and pinned her to the bed with his lower body. "Not yet. Soon," he promised as he ground his hips into hers.

Delight was panting for breath as she tried to tug her hands free from his, but it was no use. His grip didn't hurt, but it was like a steel band, totally unbreakable. She was totally at his mercy and that turned her on even more.

He slipped his hand between her thighs, coating his fingers in her cream. Stroking her heated flesh, he touched her everywhere but where she longed to be touched. Around and around her swollen clit his fingers circled, but never touching where she needed it the most. Crying out, she desperately tried to move her hips so his fingers would make contact with her where she needed them the most.

But he was ruthless and moved his hand away from her clit. Stroking downward, he trailed his fingers through the cleft of her behind. She tensed, but then relaxed as he rhythmically rubbed the tight little mouth of her ass. Slowly, he inserted the tip of one large finger inside. She could feel the muscles tightening around it at the unfamiliar invasion.

But he didn't stop. Moving steadily, Lucian pushed his finger until it was all the way inside her. Her ass burned with pain even as pleasure pulsed within her. She tried to move, not sure if she was trying to pull away from Lucian's finger or to get closer. Conflicting sensations were warring within her. But Lucian had her trapped with his body and hands and she couldn't move. All she could do was lie there and let the waves of pleasure and pain wash over her.

"This time I want to take you from behind." He flexed his finger and pulled it out a short ways before pushing it back again. The pleasure-pain sensation washed over her again. "I want to bury my cock in your ass and know that you belong to me totally, in every way I want to take you."

"Yes," she hissed. It might kill her, but she wanted that too. She wanted to feel his cock deep inside her behind as his fingers filled her pussy and stroked her breasts. Her chest was heaving now as she struggled for breath.

The muscles of her behind clamped down hard on his finger as he pulled it free. She bit her lip to keep from crying out in dismay. She wanted him inside her so badly.

He released her hands and rolled off her. His eyes were burning with desire and his fangs were fully extended as he sat up next to her in the bed. The hard muscles of his chest gleamed with a thin layer of sweat and his cock jutted out proudly from his body, long and thick.

As she watched, a pearly bead of liquid seeped from the tip. Without thought, she knelt beside him, lowered her head and licked the head of his cock. His essence was intoxicating and she buried her face in the hair of his groin and breathed deep. Lucian's fingers tangled in her hair, guiding her mouth back to the bulbous tip. Opening her mouth, she lowered it over his length, taking him deep.

Lucian murmured his encouragement as she wrapped her hand around the base of his shaft and pumped. Her tongue traced the pulsing vein as she pulled her mouth back to the tip and then plunged down once again. His testicles were hard and heavy in her hand as she rolled them between her fingers. More liquid seeped into her throat as she continued to suck and lick his length.

His pleasure was hers. Her nipples were harder than they'd ever been before and her pussy burned with need, but she wanted Lucian's pleasure more than her own. His sac moved closer to his body and she knew he was close to coming.

It shocked her when he pulled away from her, pulling his cock from her mouth and holding her away from him. "Not this time. This time, I want your beautiful, tight ass." She could barely make out his guttural words. But when she did, she immediately rolled over on her hands and knees, spreading her legs wide to accommodate him.

He swore softly and fluently and she heard the sound of a drawer opening and closing. Then she felt a cool jellylike substance being rubbed on her behind. This time, Lucian's finger easily slipped past the tight muscles of her behind and she felt only pleasure. Then it was gone, leaving her wanting more.

"Put your hands on your ass and spread your cheeks wide." She felt his lips as he feathered kisses across both mounds before blowing softly on her heated cleft. The sensation had her moaning once again and she laid her forehead on the mattress. Reaching her hands around, she grabbed each mound and pulled them apart, exposing herself totally to him.

"Perfect." Lucian's finger probed her tight opening once again and its cool gel coating allowed his finger to slide in easily. She shivered as his thick finger filled her.

Swearing under his breath, he withdrew his finger and gripped her waist with his hands. Delight felt the tip of his penis at her tight opening. He pushed his way past the resistance of her flexing muscles and stopped.

Pain and pleasure rocked her body. Part of her wanted to pull away from the pain, but a larger part of her wanted the pleasure she knew she could have. Making her decision, she pushed her bottom towards Lucian, driving him deeper.

"Fuck, yes." Surging forward, he didn't stop until he was buried to the hilt. Delight panted hard, breathing into the pain. Lucian held himself still as her body adjusted. She could feel his cock throbbing deep inside her bottom. It set off an ache inside her pussy as her inner muscles clenched around air.

She didn't know how much time passed, but finally the worst of the burning pain was gone and the pleasure began to grow once again. When Lucian finally began to move, he rocked gently within her, barely moving. Bolts of desire shot through her until it was no longer enough.

As if he'd read her mind, Lucian slid one of his hands around to her stomach. His warm fingers combed through her pubic hair, stroking her swollen clit, before surging into her pussy. She arched into his fingers, and as she did so, his cock slid almost out of her behind. He drove into her ass at the same time he thrust his fingers into her pussy. Every part of her was crammed so full of Lucian, she didn't think she could take anymore. Then he thrust again. Harder and faster, going even deeper.

Delight adjusted to the driving rhythm he set. Her ass burned, but the pleasure was overwhelming. He bent over her, plunging deeper as he cupped her breast with his free hand.

Pinching the swollen nipples, he sent her over the edge into oblivion. Her body convulsed as she came hard. The muscles of her pussy and her ass contacted hard around him.

Lucian yelled his release. Delight could feel the hot flood of liquid in her behind as she continued to come. He pounded into her bottom one last time before arching up. She felt herself melting into the mattress as her hands fell away from her behind and dropped to the bed.

Lucian was still coming when he bent over her. She could feel his hot breath on the back of her neck. "Mine." He buried his teeth in the curve of her shoulder and drew hard.

Shockingly, she felt her body convulse again. Desire and pure fire shot through her blood, flooding her body. She could feel every sucking motion at her neck between her legs. The pleasure went on and on, until he finally retracted his teeth from her neck. She shivered as his rough tongue lapped over the small wound, closing and healing it.

Then she shuddered as Lucian pulled out of her behind. It was still painful, but Delight didn't care. She'd never felt so sexually satisfied in her life. Dropping to the mattress beside her, he pulled her into his arms, pushing her mouth towards his chest. "Drink."

Spurred on by his command, Delight licked at his salty skin before sinking her teeth into his chest. What once would have been appalling to her was now beautiful. It was a sharing and giving between them just as their lovemaking was.

As she drank her fill, she could sense his deep pleasure at providing her with what she needed. His hand cupped the back of her head, caressing her hair, as she took his life-giving blood into her starving body. "Drink, my love. I will always provide what you need."

When she sensed she'd drunk enough, she retracted her fangs just by thought and then, as he had done to her, she carefully licked the wound to heal it. The tang of his blood was still on her tongue and she savored it. It surprised her just how quickly she'd accepted the need to drink blood to survive, but she supposed that it was much better than being appalled and afraid. She suspected it was her practical nature that allowed her this easy acceptance.

As much as she longed to stay in the cocoon of their love nest, she knew the time had come to face Chase and Miss Nadine.

"And Detective Cassidy." Lucian's chest rumbled beneath her cheek.

"You can read my mind?" The thought didn't upset her as much as it would have a few days ago.

"Yes. And you can read mine." Shifting, Lucian rolled over and came up to sit on the side of the bed with her still clasped in his arms. His easy strength continued to amaze her. He smiled at her. "You will find that you are much stronger as well." Giving her one final kiss, he stood and lowered her feet until she was standing next to him with his arms still wrapped around her.

"They're all here, aren't they?" She wasn't usually a coward, but she was loath to lose this moment with Lucian.

"They have been waiting for over an hour for us to appear." A wicked grin crossed his harsh face, making him look younger and more carefree. "I must thank Stefan for keeping them occupied."

She could feel the heat in her cheeks, as she buried her face against his chest. "Oh, God. They'll take one look at that satisfied smirk on your face and know what we were doing."

Lucian shrugged, totally unconcerned. "It is to be expected. We are now bound together by the customs of my people."

She froze as his words penetrated her embarrassment. "Does that mean that we're married?"

"Yes."

"But I don't feel married." She could feel him tense, the muscles of his chest tightening beneath her cheek.

His fingers flexed in her hair as he gently pulled, tipping her face to meet his solemn gaze. "What we share is deeper than a human marriage. It is unbreakable."

Delight shrugged, burying her regrets. She'd always imagined a wedding with flowers, a pretty dress and a nice reception. Nothing fancy or expensive, but something special.

His face softened and his fingers relaxed their grip. "Ah, Delight. I cannot bear to see you so sad." He stroked her cheeks with his fingers. "You shall have your wedding. Cris and Johanna will want to come, and of course, Stefan, but other than that, it will be as you desire."

Her heart clenched in her chest. He was looking at her with such love, she felt like the luckiest woman in the world. They would have their share of problems, but they would deal with them together.

"Thank you, Lucian."

He nodded and stepped away from her. "First, we must deal with the problems at hand. Then we will make plans."

Chapter Nineteen

80

When she and Lucian entered the room, Chase was wearing a hole in the expensive Oriental carpet that lay on the living room floor. His movements were slow and stiff, and he cradled his left hand against his chest as he walked. His head snapped towards the door at the muted sound of their footsteps. Frozen in place, he stared at her, his eyes examining her from head to foot.

She hurried towards him, but he met her halfway, moving as quickly as his injuries would allow. Wrapping his good arm around her, he held her tight against his chest. Hugging him now, it shook her to her core to remember just how close she'd come to losing him.

"Are you all right?" His grip tightened briefly before he released her. "It's been two nights since you were shot." He scraped his fingers through his hair, making it stand upright. "I've been so damned worried."

"Let's sit down." She let him lead her to the sofa on the pretext that she needed to sit, but really it was for her brother. He looked ready to fall down. His face was pale and drawn, and his eyes were bleak and bruised. As he sat next to her on the sofa, she got a good look at him. Delight knew then that this ordeal had changed him as well, and not for the better. Gone was the openness and easy humor of youth. Instead, it had been replaced by a general guardedness and an air of mistrust.

"He wouldn't tell me anything." Chase scowled at Stefan, who was leaning unconcernedly against a beautiful oak fireplace.

"There was nothing to tell." Pushing away from the mantel, Stefan crossed his arms over his massive chest. "She was with

Lucian. She was safe." He shrugged as if that was all that any of them needed.

"I wanted to see for myself." Chase turned his back on Stefan, ignoring him totally. Delight caught the quick grin that crossed Stefan's face before it returned to its normal somber lines.

"Sorry to break up the family reunion, but I need answers." Sam Cassidy pushed out of the plush wing-backed chair where he'd been sitting. "We've long suspected Prince of a list of crimes including several murders, but have never been able to gather enough evidence to make any of the charges stick. The man was brilliant, violent, half-mad, and inspired a loyalty among his men that was downright scary. The case is officially closed. With the lack of evidence to suggest anything else, it's assumed that a rival crime boss had Prince and his right-hand man killed inside Prince's own club. A simple territorial take-over. A falling-out among criminals."

He shot Stefan a sardonic grin before continuing. "I'd push it," he paused for effect and Stefan took a menacing step towards him. "But it was a clear-cut case of self-defense."

"Sit down." Lucian's voice was low and pleasant, but everyone could hear the underlying thread of anger beneath it. When the detective continued to stand, Lucian heaved a disgusted sigh and motioned to the chair. "Please."

Stefan snorted, but Cassidy lowered himself into the chair, spread his long jeans-clad legs in front of him, propped his elbows on the arms of the chair and steepled his fingers together. He said nothing, but waited patiently.

The testosterone was so thick in the room that Delight feared she'd choke on it. Deciding that being female and, therefore, the only sensible person in the room, it was up to her to break the silence.

"I want to thank you for all your help in this matter, Detective Cassidy."

His face softened and he smiled at her. "It's my pleasure, ma'am. And please, call me Cassidy. I think we've been through too much together to stick to formalities."

From what Delight had seen, everyone referred to him as Cassidy. She sensed that it was rare for him to allow anyone to refer to him by his first name.

Lucian walked up behind her where she was seated on the sofa and placed a possessive hand on her shoulder. Cassidy's gaze dropped from her face to Lucian's hand and back up again. There was a look of male understanding on his face that annoyed her. Honestly, she felt like a prized possession on display.

"Mine." The word echoed silently in her brain and she knew that it was Lucian's way of telling her she was already his. She didn't mind that they belonged to one another, but she was hardly ready to be claimed in such a blatant fashion.

Ignoring Lucian's rather large presence behind her, she picked up the conversation. "Only if you'll call me Delight." She smiled warmly at the detective, knowing it would annoy Lucian. "As I was saying, I appreciate everything you've done for me and my family. You came so quickly after I called you."

The smile faded from his face and he became all cop, his icy-blue eyes flat and watchful. "You should have called me before attempting your own rescue scheme, Dalakis."

"I am used to giving orders, not taking them." Delight could feel Lucian's anger, but only she knew that he was angrier at himself than at anyone else. Lucian would be a long time getting over the fact that she'd gotten hurt.

"That's all fine and good, except you asked me to cover for you. And you've already got some people in the department very interested in you." Pausing, he rubbed the side of his jaw that was dark with stubble. "You know a guy named Zane York?"

Lucian glanced at Stefan and then shook his head. "Should I know him?"

Cassidy shrugged. "He was very curious about the incident in the alleyway and asked me point-blank if you had some involvement in it. York is a good cop with good instincts and he's very interested in you." He shot Stefan and Lucian an angry look. "I'm just glad that I didn't know about you when he asked me. I wasn't lying to him when I told him no." He glared at Lucian. "You put me in the rather awkward position of having to keep certain information to myself."

"I'm sure we can find a way to compensate you for your trouble." It was the wrong thing to say. Delight knew that as soon as the words left Lucian's mouth.

Cassidy jumped from his chair, his anger a living, breathing thing. "I won't dignify that with an answer, but only because there's a lady present." His stance was like a fighter's, loose and limber, ready to go at a moment's notice. "Hell, all I know is one minute Delight is bleeding to death, then you're sucking the blood out of her, then she's sucking the blood out of you, and then she's miraculously healed. Damned if I don't feel ready for the shrink's chair."

He ambled towards her, picked up her hand and kissed the back of it. His old-fashioned manner charmed her and his forthrightness pleased her. "If you need anything, don't hesitate to call me." He shot a defiant look at Lucian and Stefan, nodded at Chase and then strode towards the door.

"Cassidy." He stopped, but didn't turn around. Lucian swore and sighed. "Will you tell anyone?"

"I should let you wonder about that." A low growl came from deep within Lucian, but the other man ignored it. "But who the hell would I tell? Zane York? And really, what would I tell him? That you're all vampires?" He swore under his breath, shook his head as if he was arguing with himself, and finally turned back around. "Your secret is safe with me."

Lucian gave her shoulder a squeeze before walking towards Cassidy and holding out his hand. Lucian waited patiently and was rewarded when the other man reluctantly shook the proffered hand. "I did not mean to insult you. I owe you more than I can ever repay."

"Just doing my job," he shrugged.

"Few know our secret and only those that we call friend," Lucian paused, letting his words sink in before he continued. "If you are ever in need of anything, you have only to ask. You are welcome in my home." Lucian bowed formally.

A slow grin broke across Cassidy's face. "I'll bet that hurt."

Lucian laughed at the other man's easy humor. Delight shook her head at the changeable nature of the male species. At each other's throats one minute, best friends the next. Not that she minded. She liked Sam Cassidy. He had an easygoing manner that hid a sharp intellect and a keen sense of humor.

"I'd like you to come to our wedding." Lucian looked almost as surprised as everyone else as he uttered the words, but he did not retract them. "Please."

This time it was Cassidy who offered his hand to Lucian. "Congratulations." He rocked back on his heels for a moment as a wistful smile played at the corners of his mouth. "I wouldn't miss it for the world." He nodded once more and then he was gone, the heels of his boots striking the hardwood floor in the hallway. A door opened and closed in the distance, and they collectively let out a sigh of relief.

"Wedding?" Delight scooted closer to her brother as she caught the thread of hurt underlying his question. She should have told him first but there had been no time.

"Lucian saved my life. But beyond that, I love him." She felt the tears welling in her eyes but blinked them back. "What he did changed me." Pausing, she searched for the right words. "We're linked somehow and it feels right. I know I'm different now, but I'm still your sister." She hadn't realized she'd been feeling vulnerable until that moment. There was no way to know how Chase would handle the fact that his sister was now a bloodsucking vampire.

"I love you, you know." Chase banished all her fears with those few simple words. "You're my sister and I only want what's best for you." Reaching out, he drew her into his arms and hugged her tight. He laughed and then groaned as he grabbed his ribs. "Damn, that hurts."

Delight immediately began to fuss over him. "You should still be in bed," she scolded.

Grabbing her hand, he held it tight. "It'll be hard to grow old and die and leave you behind some day."

A single tear slid down her face and she dashed it angrily away. "That won't happen for many years yet. We'll deal with it."

Chase let it drop for now. There was a wisdom and acceptance about him that belied his years. Somehow Delight knew that the changes would be harder on her than on him. Her younger brother had already accepted what she hadn't even begun to think about.

Knowing it was cowardly, she changed the subject anyway. "Where's Miss Nadine?"

"Stefan took her home. She knows that you were hurt, but not what really happened. It's probably better that way."

Delight's heart hurt. This was another big change in her life. She'd already quit her bartending job at Etienne's, unable to return to work there after the murder. But now, it would no longer be possible for her to live and work at The Grande. Lucian had sensed her turmoil and came to sit on the sofa beside her. Scooping her into his lap, he pulled her close to his heart.

"I have already found someone who can take your place at Miss Nadine's. A young college student who needs the room and board and small salary while she works her way towards her degree." The fact that Lucian had already thought of this problem and had moved to fix it didn't surprise her.

Delight twisted her hands in her lap. She wanted what was best for Miss Nadine, but change was hard. This was the only life she'd known for years. It was her stability. "I guess that's for the best."

Tipping her chin up, he kissed her softly, not caring that they had an audience. "Just because you do not live there, does not mean that you are no longer part of her life."

"I know you're right." She squared her shoulders and sat up straight. "I'm just feeling sorry for myself."

"I offered to give her enough money to retire, but she turned me down." Lucian gave a sharp bark of laughter. "She has as much use for my money as you do."

"Well, I should be going." Chase pulled himself off the sofa. Leaning over, he kissed her cheek.

"Where are you going?" She grabbed his hand to keep him from leaving.

"Home. You've got a lot of plans to make." He tugged on his hand, but Delight wouldn't let go.

Lucian frowned at both of them. "I thought you understood that this is your home now, Chase."

"I think you two need your space, and to tell you the truth, so do I." As hard as she tried not to let it, she felt hurt. He tried to give her a smile, but it fell short. "Besides, you'll be newlyweds and you'll need to be alone. I understand that."

She couldn't bear to think of losing Chase and Miss Nadine at the same time. It was too much.

"I think we can reach a compromise of sorts." Lucian glanced at Stefan, and he nodded quickly. "We have an old carriage house in the back garden. It has a loft apartment upstairs and a large enough space for your own art studio down below. It is yours for as long as you want it."

"I'll pay rent." Chase's male pride quickly asserted itself and Delight felt like smacking him even as she was proud of him at the same time.

"That would be fine, but I would prefer services. A trade, if you will." Lucian had piqued not only Chase's curiosity, but hers as well.

"What do you mean?"

Lucian swept his arm around the room. "We three are vampires, unable to function in the daylight. There is much you could do to help your sister adjust and to assure her safety."

It was absolutely the right thing to say. Delight could see the wheels in her brother's head spinning around, considering Lucian's words from every angle. It surprised her when he turned to Stefan. "That okay with you?"

Stefan nodded once. It was enough for Chase. "I'll go and pack our things and get them moved tomorrow."

Lucian reached into his shirt pocket and drew out a platinum credit card. Chase scowled at it, but Lucian ignored him. "It's not for you. It is for household expenses that you incur on my behalf and that includes moving Delight's belongings to her new home. It is nothing to throw your few boxes and bags in with hers."

She could tell that Chase thought about debating that fact, but reluctantly agreed. Accepting the card, he slipped it into his back pocket. "I'll take care of it."

She hated to see him leave, even if it was for only a few hours. After all he'd been through, she wanted to keep him close to her. But she held her tongue as he took his leave of them.

"May I offer my congratulations as well." Stefan bowed briefly to her. "Welcome to the family, Delight. You will meet Cristofor and Johanna tomorrow night. I took the liberty of calling them earlier this evening." Lucian swore under his breath, but Stefan heard it and smiled. "Our older brother was not pleased that he had not been kept informed about things, but I believe that Johanna has him well in hand."

"Now I must leave you." Before Delight could respond, Stefan slipped through a door to the left of the fireplace, a wrath swallowed up by the dark of the night.

"It is hard for him." Lucian nibbled her neck, distracting her.

"What's hard?" She leaned back into his caress, sighing as his hands slipped up her torso to cup her breasts. Her insides turned soft and she could feel the familiar gush of cream between her thighs. There was no mistaking the fact that she wanted him. Again. Reaching down, she cupped his growing erection that strained at the front of his pants. "Besides that."

"He is alone now that Cristofor and I have found our true loves." Slipping one hand behind her back and the other under her legs, he stood with her cradled in his arms. "And the weight of it lays heavy on him. I worry for him."

"You don't think he'd do anything drastic, do you?" She could sense Lucian's deep fear for his brother. The fact that he was worried scared her. She sensed that she really couldn't understand the depth of Stefan's loneliness, but she knew it was profound.

"No. Not yet at any rate." He carried her easily through the house and up the stairs. "I will confer with Cristofor when he comes. I will not lose him as we have lost others before."

Delight wanted to ask him more, but he kissed her then. His firm lips devoured hers as he thrust his tongue inside her mouth, claiming it as his own. Frantically, she tugged on his hair, pulling him closer to her. He needed this right now and so did she. Eagerly, she gave herself up to the fires of desire that smoldered within her, only waiting for his touch to ignite them.

Chapter Twenty

ɞ

It was better than she'd ever dreamed it would be. Delight stood within the protective circle of her new husband's arms and surveyed the small group of friends and family that had gathered for their wedding. The ceremony had been performed by a member of the clergy, surprising Delight.

Lucian had taken a wicked delight at teasing her about it after the ceremony was over. "Did you expect both of us to burst into flames in the presence of a holy man?" He'd whispered the words in her ear just before kissing her in front of all their witnesses.

She still had a lot to learn, but was discovering more every day thanks to her new sister-in-law. Delight found she'd liked the other woman on sight. With her short, dark brown hair, golden-brown eyes, and a smattering of freckles that she tried to cover with makeup, Johanna was open and friendly with a wonderful sense of humor. Johanna was every bit as practical and grounded as she was, and every bit as normal. Having been human herself until a few months ago, she had helped ease some of Delight's fears.

Children had been a big question on her mind, but she hadn't been able to bring herself to ask Lucian about it. Somehow it was much easier to talk to another woman about these things. She'd had never had another woman friend her age and found that she was enjoying the friendship and camaraderie. It was good to have an ally when it came to dealing with three overbearing, overprotective men. The two of them had bonded instantly, much to the unease of the brothers.

According to Johanna, it was rare for a Dalakis bride to get pregnant, and the children were always male. Always. They aged naturally until they reached their full maturity and then stopped, their bodies muscular and honed to its peak of perfection.

Lucian's mother had been rare in that she'd given birth to three healthy sons all within a one-hundred-year span. Most had only one or two children spread over a span of several hundred years. Johanna suspected it was nature's way of controlling the population given the fact that vampires were basically immortal.

But there had been tragedies. The brothers' parents had died during the seventeenth century when their mother had been caught away from home after sunrise. She'd spent the night nursing a sick child in the nearby town and had taken shelter in the family's root cellar. The members of the child's family had been frightened by her deathlike appearance when they'd discovered her body and had fled to the village priest for help. The priest had declared her a vampire and cut off her head. The moment she died, their father had died as well.

When the brothers awoke that evening, they found their father's lifeless form. Their grief and rage had known no boundaries as they'd scoured the countryside in search of their mother's remains. When they'd discovered what had been done, they'd taken their bloody revenge on the priest and then withdrawn to the castle, shutting out the world around them. The town, which had depended on the Dalakis fortune for survival, had suffered and many moved away, fearing that the land was now cursed. It was something that none of them ever talked about. Johanna had garnered the details from an old journal she'd found in the castle's library.

It was strange to think that Lucian had grown up in a real fifteenth-century castle and that his brother still resided there. "What are you thinking?" Lucian wrapped his arms around her as he nibbled on her neck.

Delight leaned back into his loving embrace and gave a contented sighed. "Can't you tell?"

"I'm trying to respect your privacy by not peeking." Tipping her head back, he kissed her softly. A shiver ran down her spine as her nipples puckered against the bodice of her dress. It was always that way. Whenever he touched her, she was instantly aroused.

"I was just thinking how much I like Johanna and Cris." Snuggling her behind against him, she could feel Lucian's growing arousal.

"Liar," he whispered. "You like Johanna, but Cris intimidates you."

"He's just got that lord-of-the-manor air about him. I feel like I should curtsy or something every time he enters the room." Her panties were getting damper by the minute as Lucian spread his hands across her stomach and pulled her tighter against the bulge in his pants.

His entire body shook with laughter. "He'd love that."

"Don't you dare tell him," she admonished. That certainly wouldn't make a good impression on his family and she did want them to like her.

At first she was worried about Cris reading her thoughts. It was one thing for Lucian to be able to read her thoughts, but quite another for his brother to do it. But, Lucian had assured her that they respected one another's privacy and would only trespass in a dire emergency. She and Lucian slipped in and out of each other's thoughts so easily now that it was beginning to feel normal to her.

In spite of her doubts, both families seemed to be getting along well, considering one was filled with vampires and the other was all human. Cristofor had taken an immediate liking to Chase and the two of them talked art for hours on end. All three Dalakis men, who could be extremely charming when they put their minds to it, had charmed Miss Nadine.

Looking around the drawing room of The Grande, Delight felt a glow of happiness emanate from deep inside her. Classical music played softly in the background and candles burned on the tables and mantel. A small table with refreshments had been set up in the corner and vases of fresh flowers filled the room with their heady scent.

The only outsider, except for the minister who had left immediately after the ceremony, was Sam Cassidy. Delight had been surprised when Lucian asked him to the wedding, but she was pleased that he'd come. He was such a large part of what had happened, it wouldn't have felt right for him not to be there. It seemed that the detective had been adopted into the family whether he liked it or not.

"A toast." Cristofor's strong voice filled the room, drawing every eye his way. "To my brother and his beautiful wife, Delight. It is indeed a delight to welcome you to the family." Cristofor paused until the laughter died away. "I also want to welcome Miss Nadine, Chase and Cassidy to the family."

Cassidy looked startled and opened his mouth to object. But one look at Cristofor's face and he subsided. The older brother's word was law and whether he liked it or not, he was now considered part of their family. Cassidy gazed around the room and when he caught Delight's attention, he gave her a quick wink, raised his wineglass, and saluted her. "To Delight and Lucian."

Delight sipped on her red wine, noting her husband's possessive hold got tighter when Cassidy laid down his glass and approached them. "Thank you for coming." Holding out her hand, she waited for him to take it.

His grip was firm and sure as he bent down and placed a chaste kiss on her cheek. Lucian emitted a low growl from behind her, but the detective wasn't disturbed at all. If anything, the devil looked as if he were enjoying himself. "You're a lucky man, Dalakis. Protect her well." Stepping back from her, he thrust his hand towards Lucian.

"What we have, we hold." Still keeping one arm wrapped tight around her, Lucian offered his other hand to Cassidy. "That is our way."

"Just let me know if you ever need any help." Releasing Lucian's hand, he stepped back and gave her a nod. "I've got to get going. Be happy." Turning on his booted heel, he turned and strode from the room.

Delight watched him leave as Miss Nadine strolled up to her. "You look so beautiful and happy, child."

"I am." The simple three-quarter length dress with its off-white color and simple cut fit her to perfection. The bodice was fitted and beaded, making it fancy enough for a wedding dress without being too fancy. It had frustrated Lucian no end when she'd chosen an off-the-rack dress at a small local boutique, paying for it with her own money. He had wanted to buy her a designer dress, but had finally given in when he'd realized that this was the dress she'd truly wanted.

Leaning over, she kissed the older woman's cheek. "Thank you for letting us have the wedding here."

"As if I'd let you have it somewhere else," she scolded. Turning her shrewd eyes on Lucian, she pinned him with a glare. "You take care of my girl."

"You have my word." Lucian took no offense at her admonishment. Delight knew that he thought the world of Miss Nadine and treated her with a courtly manner at all times.

"I'm heading upstairs now, but you all feel free to stay as late as you want." It was after midnight and Delight knew that Miss Nadine had an early morning as the little inn was filled to capacity. Delight watched, slightly melancholy, as the other woman walk out of the room and disappeared up the stairs.

"You can still see her every day."

"I know, but it's not the same." She shook off her sadness. This was a night for happiness. Looking up at her dark, brooding husband, Delight smiled. "I'm fine, really."

He looked as if he didn't believe her, but didn't speak as Cristofor and Johanna approached. "We will say goodnight." Cristofor kept his arm wrapped around his wife's shoulder. It seemed to be a trait of the men in this family to keep their women close. "We will fly home tomorrow. You will come and visit after the honeymoon." It was more a command than a question and Delight found herself nodding.

Johanna laughed as she swatted her husband's arm. "Ignore him, Delight. You just come for a visit whenever you're ready. You're welcome anytime for as long as you want to stay. Believe me, there's plenty of room in the castle." Giving them both a quick hug, she tugged her husband from the room.

Delight muffled a laugh as she heard Cristofor's voice drifting back. "Woman, that's no way to treat your lord and master." His disgruntled tone was at odds with Johanna's laughter.

"Lord and master." Stefan shook his head in disgust as he approached them. "Johanna has our hard, ruthless brother twisted around her little finger. Oh, how the mighty have fallen."

Stefan looked even more somber than usual in the austere black suit he'd donned for the wedding. Delight had been surprised to see him in something other than jeans, but he certainly cleaned up good. She'd been so wrapped up in Lucian that she had forgotten what a devastatingly handsome man that he really was.

She still had a hard time looking Stefan in the eye without blushing. But not once, by word or action, had he betrayed any hint of what had occurred that memorable night upstairs. It was as if it had never happened.

"It is a disgrace to the family." Cradling her face with his large hands, Stefan brushed a soft, light kiss on her lips. "And now you have done the same to Lucian. Alas, I am the only sensible brother left to uphold the family honor."

Delight sensed the underlying sadness and hurt buried beneath his words. He was alone now that his brothers were mated. Impulsively, she flung her arms around him and hugged him tight. "I'm so glad that you're my brother now."

Stefan swallowed hard and clung to her, his grip almost desperate. Releasing her quickly, he stepped away from her and turned to Lucian. "I am leaving tonight." He ignored her gasp of surprise and continued to address Lucian. "It will be up to you to check out this Zane York and make sure he is no threat to the family. I don't know when I will be back. If you have need of me, you have only to call and I will come."

"I will take care of it," Lucian assured his brother.

Moving so swiftly it looked as if he had vanished into thin air, Stefan was gone. A lone tear slipped down Delight's cheek. With her heightened senses, she could feel the deep despair and pain that filled Stefan.

"I wish I could find a way to ease his pain." Lucian sighed heavily as he pulled her close and tucked her under his shoulder. She nodded, saying nothing. Stefan's pain was beyond words and only time would help him find his equilibrium again. "If he is gone too long, we will find him and bring him home." Delight grasped and held Lucian's promise tight, trusting him to know what was best for his brother right now.

"Well, it's time for me to say goodnight as well." Chase rose from the chair where he'd been sitting and observing everyone for the last hour and strolled towards them. Coming to a halt in front of them, he stared down into her face. "Be happy, Delight." Raising his gaze, he addressed his new brother-in-law. "I'm trusting you to take care of her."

"It is my honor and privilege." Lucian held out his hand to Chase and the men seemed to come to some internal understanding as they shook. Delight watched the two men she loved most in the world, feeling her heart swell with pride.

Then they were alone.

Lucian smiled and her insides melted. The familiar heat surged through her veins as he scooped her up into his arms and walked down the hallway and out through the front door and into the night. "I am taking you home."

Wrapping her arms around his strong neck, she leaned in to nuzzle it. "I'm already there."

The night swallowed them up and then they were gone. Stefan stepped from the shadows where he'd been watching them. He felt more alone at that moment than at any other time in his five hundred years of existence. Forcing himself, he turned away from his family and walked away. The night wrapped its arms around him, embracing him, as he escaped into its inky depths.

Sam Cassidy sat on a barstool and twirled the long-necked bottle between his hands. The whole basis of his belief system had been turned topsy-turvy in the last week. If he weren't so damned sane, he'd figure he was crazy. "Vampires?" He gave a sharp bark of laughter.

"What's so funny?"

He eyed the man who slipped onto the barstool next to him. Zane York was a fellow cop who worked the night shift. He knew him by reputation, but not personally. York had a reputation for being single-minded in pursuit of the truth. Hard, but fair, he was not a man to cross.

"You wouldn't believe me if I told you." Tipping up the bottle, he took a swallow and laid it back on the counter.

"Try me." Zane's dark eyes watched him unwaveringly.

Cassidy had to fight the urge to spill the entire story. He shook his head suddenly feeling as if he'd drunk way too much even though that was his first beer. "Maybe another time." Pushing off the stool, he saluted York and sauntered from the smoky confines of the bar.

"Bet on it," Zane murmured under his breath as he tracked Cassidy's progress across the room, out though the door and into the night.

Why an electronic book?

We live in the Information Age—an exciting time in the history of human civilization, in which technology rules supreme and continues to progress in leaps and bounds every minute of every day. For a multitude of reasons, more and more avid literary fans are opting to purchase e-books instead of paper books. The question from those not yet initiated into the world of electronic reading is simply: *Why?*

1. ***Price.*** An electronic title at Ellora's Cave Publishing and Cerridwen Press runs anywhere from 40% to 75% less than the cover price of the exact same title in paperback format. Why? Basic mathematics and cost. It is less expensive to publish an e-book (no paper and printing, no warehousing and shipping) than it is to publish a paperback, so the savings are passed along to the consumer.

2. ***Space.*** Running out of room in your house for your books? That is one worry you will never have with electronic books. For a low one-time cost, you can purchase a handheld device specifically designed for e-reading. Many e-readers have large, convenient screens for viewing. Better yet, hundreds of titles can be stored within your new library—on a single microchip. There are a variety of e-readers from different manufacturers. You can also read e-books on your PC or laptop computer. (Please note that Ellora's

Cave does not endorse any specific brands. You can check our websites at www.ellorascave.com or www.cerridwenpress.com for information we make available to new consumers.)

3. *Mobility.* Because your new e-library consists of only a microchip within a small, easily transportable e-reader, your entire cache of books can be taken with you wherever you go.

4. ***Personal Viewing Preferences.*** Are the words you are currently reading too small? Too large? Too... ANNOYING? Paperback books cannot be modified according to personal preferences, but e-books can.

5. ***Instant Gratification.*** Is it the middle of the night and all the bookstores near you are closed? Are you tired of waiting days, sometimes weeks, for bookstores to ship the novels you bought? Ellora's Cave Publishing sells instantaneous downloads twenty-four hours a day, seven days a week, every day of the year. Our webstore is never closed. Our e-book delivery system is 100% automated, meaning your order is filled as soon as you pay for it.

Those are a few of the top reasons why electronic books are replacing paperbacks for many avid readers.

As always, Ellora's Cave and Cerridwen Press welcome your questions and comments. We invite you to email us at Comments@ellorascave.com or write to us directly at Ellora's Cave Publishing Inc., 1056 Home Avenue, Akron, OH 44310-3502.

erridwen, the Celtic Goddess of wisdom, was the muse who brought inspiration to storytellers and those in the creative arts. Cerridwen Press encompasses the best and most innovative stories in all genres of today's fiction. Visit our site and discover the newest titles by talented authors who still get inspired - much like the ancient storytellers did, once upon a time.

Cerridwen Press

www.cerridwenpress.com